VIEWPOINTS ON
MODERN WORLD HISTORY

The Armenian Genocide

Other Books of Related Interest

At Issue Series
Casualties of War
How Does Religion Influence Politics?
Immigration Reform
The United Nations

Current Controversies Series
Islamophobia
The Middle Easts
Politics and Religion

Opposing Viewpoints Series
Human Rights
Islam
Refugees
War Crimes

The Armenian Genocide

Paula Johanson, Book Editor

Published in 2018 by Greenhaven Publishing, LLC
353 3rd Avenue, Suite 255, New York, NY 10010

Copyright © 2018 by Greenhaven Publishing, LLC

First Edition

All rights reserved. No part of this book may be reproduced in any form without permission in writing from the publisher, except by a reviewer.

Articles in Greenhaven Publishing anthologies are often edited for length to meet page requirements. In addition, original titles of these works are changed to clearly present the main thesis and to explicitly indicate the author's opinion. Every effort is made to ensure that Greenhaven Publishing accurately reflects the original intent of the authors. Every effort has been made to trace the owners of the copyrighted material.

Cover image: KIRILL KUDRYAVTSEV/AFP/Getty Images

Library of Congress Cataloging-in-Publication Data

Names: Johanson, Paula, editor.
Title: The Armenian Genocide / Paula Johanson, book editor.
Description: First edition. | New York : Greenhaven Publishing, 2018. | Series: Viewpoints on modern world history | Includes bibliographical references and index. | Audience: Grades 9-12.
Identifiers: LCCN 2017032822 | ISBN 9781534501201 (library bound)
Subjects: LCSH: Armenian massacres, 1915-1923. | Genocide--Turkey.
Classification: LCC DS195.5 .A7358 2017 | DDC 956.6/20154--dc23
LC record available at https://lccn.loc.gov/2017032822

Manufactured in the United States of America

Website: http://greenhavenpublishing.com

Contents

Foreword — 9
Introduction — 12

Chapter 1: Historical Background

Chapter Preface — 15

1. Historical Perspective from the Ottoman Empire Onward — 16
   Sara Cohan
   The history of the Armenian people is described, as well as events like the Hamidian and Adana massacres and the 1915 genocide.

2. 1909: The Adana Massacres — 25
   Bedross Der Matossian
   The author studies the Adana massacres and how they are linked to the genocide that came just a few years later.

3. Did the Armenian Genocide Inspire Hitler? — 58
   Hannibal Travis
   This scholarly piece discusses the potential influence of the Armenian genocide upon Adolf Hitler.

4. The Assyrian Genocide Differs from the Armenian Genocide — 72
   The Combat Genocide Association
   The Assyrian genocide and the Armenian genocide may have occurred around the same time, but they are not the same thing.

5. How Kim Kardashian's Ancestors Escaped — 80
   Michael Snyder
   The author describes in simple terms why the Kardashian family emigrated from Armenia.

Chapter 2: Context for the Armenian Genocide

Chapter Preface — 86

1. Government Responsibility in the Armenian Genocide — 87
   United to End Genocide
   This informative piece emphasizes that other nations were aware of the massacres, yet did not intervene.

2. Defining Genocide — 93
   Michael M. Gunter
   The author asks if government incompetence and fear of revolution are to blame for violence rather than genocidal intent.

3. The Armenian Question — 109
   Universidad Iberoamericana
   This guide prepares students to engage in a mock League of Nations debate about the circumstances in Armenia.

4. Human Nature and Ethnic Conflict — 115
   Gregory G. Dimijian
   Acts of war, genocide, and ethnic conflict are explored as an unfortunate part of the human condition.

5. Remembering a Genocide Survivor — 135
   Michael J. Stone
   A moving obituary for centenarian Knar Yemenidjian who survived the Armenian Genocide.

Chapter 3: Lasting Effects of the Armenian Genocide

Chapter Preface — 141

1. Trauma Reverberates Through the Generations — 142
   Anie Kalayjian and Marian Weisberg
   Through a study and workshop, the authors explore how traumatic events of the Armenian Genocide and the Holocaust have effects on subsequent generations.

2. How Ending Genocide Denial Will Help Turkey — 167
   David Tolbert
   This author believes that Turkish denial is not only harming Turkish society but has set a bad precedent internationally.

3. Alternatives for Ending Genocidal Events 177
Alex de Waal and Bridget Conley-Zilkic
This article discusses genocide scholarship and summarizes several genocides during the twentieth century.

4. Students Are Still Fighting for Genocide Recognition 200
Melanie Nakashian
American college students—especially those of Armenian descent—are still battling the poison of genocide denial one hundred years later.

Chronology 206
Bibliography 210
Index 212

Foreword

"The more we know about the past enables us to ask richer and more provocative questions about who we are today. We also must tell the next generation one of the great truths of history: that no past event was preordained. Every battle, every election, and revolution could have turned out differently at any point along the way, just as a person's own life can change unpredictably."

—David McCullough, American historian

History is punctuated by momentous events—turning points for the nations involved, with impacts felt far beyond their borders. Displaying the full range of human capabilities—from violence, greed, and ignorance to heroism, courage, and strength—these events are nearly always complicated and multifaceted. Any student of history faces the challenge of grasping both the broader elements and the nuances of world-changing events, such as wars, social movements, and environmental disasters. Textbooks offer only so much help, burdened as they are by constraints of length and single-perspective narratives. True understanding of history's significant events comes from exposure to a variety of perspectives from the people involved intimately, as well as those observing from a distance of miles or years.

Viewpoints on Modern World History examines global events from the twentieth century onward, presenting analysis and observation from numerous vantage points. The series offers high school, early college level, and general interest readers a thematically arranged anthology of previously published materials that address a major historical event or period. Each volume opens with background information on the event, presents the controversies surrounding the event, and concludes with the implications and legacy of the event. By providing a variety of perspectives, this series can be used to inform debate, help develop critical thinking skills, increase global awareness, and enhance an understanding of international viewpoints on history.

Material in each volume is selected from a diverse range of sources. Articles taken from these sources are carefully edited and introduced to provide context and background.

Each volume in the Viewpoints on Modern World History series also includes:

- An annotated **table of contents** that provides a brief summary of each essay in the volume
- An **introduction** specific to the volume topic
- A **chapter preface** setting up the chapter content and providing historical context
- For each viewpoint, a brief **introduction** that has notes about the author and source of the viewpoint and provides a summary of its main points
- Informational **sidebars** that explore the lives of key individuals, give background on historical events, or explain scientific or technical concepts
- A **chronology** of dates important to the period
- A **bibliography** of additional books, periodicals, and websites for further research
- A **subject index** that offers links to people, places, and events cited in the text

Viewpoints on Modern World History is designed for a broad spectrum of readers who want to learn more about not only history but also current events, political science, government, international relations, and sociology. This includes students doing research for class assignments or debates, teachers and faculty seeking to supplement course materials, and others wanting to improve their understanding of history. The volumes in this series are designed to illuminate a complicated event, to spark debate, and to show the human perspective behind the world's most significant happenings of recent decades.

Introduction

> *"In 1939, a week before the Nazi invasion of Poland, Hitler said, 'Who, after all, speaks today of the annihilation of the Armenians?' We do. We must. We must talk about it until it is recognized by our government, because when we deny our past, we endanger our future."*
>
> *– Kim Kardashian West*

2015 marked the hundred-year anniversary of Ottoman Turks killing and deporting Armenian citizens of the Ottoman Empire. The massacres, which historians estimate killed 1.5 million people, have been recognized as genocide by the United Nations and 28 countries around the world. For its part, the government of Turkey still claims that the number of people killed was inflated, and disputes whether the event could even be called genocide.

Canadian-Armenian filmmaker Atom Egoyan, whose grandparents were orphaned in the genocide was one of many international figures who called on Turkey to acknowledge those deaths as a genocidal event. "It's an open wound and as long as the Turkish State continues to deny this, it continues to bleed," said Egoyan in an interview in 2015. Like many people, he felt the hundred-year anniversary was a significant reminder that the wrongs of a century ago needed to be righted. History can be forgotten when people aren't educated about the past, Egoyan noted when he visited Turkey, and he also drew parallels to Canada coming to terms with its own history and treatment of aboriginal people. There is much to learn about the Armenian Genocide and how it and terrible tragedies like it continue to affect people living today.

Some historians trace the roots of this particular conflict to the disintegration of the Ottoman Empire in the 19th century, as it destabilized due to ethnic uprisings and the fall-out of the 1877-78 Russo-Turkish War. Mass killings like the Hamidian massacres of 1894 and the Adana massacre of 1909, both of which are discussed in this book, only paved the way for further violence. Armenians, who were largely quiet during much of the political turmoil of the 1800s—and referred to as *millet-i sadika* or the 'loyal millet'—hoped simply to find equal recognition under the Empire. But on April 24, 1915, Ottoman authorities rounded up, arrested, and deported more than 200 Armenian community leaders—and most of them were eventually murdered. This led to large-scale murder of more Armenian men, along with forced labor and the deportation of women, children and the elderly.

The Ottoman Empire broke up as the First World War ended and the government of Turkey was reorganized, but the devastating impact of the Armenian Genocide lingers. Though it would seem simple for the current Turkish government to align with the United Nations' stance and acknowledge the genocide and the culpability of a crumbling empire, they remain resolute in minimizing the horrors of a century before. Not only that, but the Turkish government continues to clash with descendants of those who were minority peoples in the Ottoman Empire. During a 2017 visit to Washington DC by Turkish president Recep Tayyip Erdoğan, sixteen of his bodyguards strode into a public demonstration, beating and throttling Kurdish protestors. But the push to acknowledge the Armenian Genocide remains just as strong, and through the following viewpoints, readers will learn what shaped the past, present and future of this ongoing battle for recognition.

CHAPTER 1

| Historical Background

Chapter Preface

The human history of the Caucasus region goes back many thousands of years before today's nations of Armenia or Syria or Turkey, to the Paleolithic times when Neanderthals and Denisovans and early humans roamed the land—and conflict in the area goes back just as far!

The region has been a corridor for human travel since time immemorial—people journeyed through it during the Ice Ages and then later for trade, as the Silk Road saw goods transferred between the Mediterranean and China. People brought their cultural beliefs and religions as well, and there were early Christian believers in the area less than a hundred years after the birth of Christ—paving the way for centuries of ethnic and religious conflict in a volatile region. In what is now modern Turkey, the presence of Islam dates to the 11th century, with the expansion of the Seljuks into Anatolia. Recent polls on religious belief in Turkey show the majority of citizens identify as Muslim.

The viewpoints in this chapter discuss how clashes between cultures and religions—all under the sprawling umbrella of the Ottoman Empire—created an environment ripe for political violence. Experts discuss the Hamidian massacre of the late 1800s, the Assyrian genocide, and other mass killings in tandem with the events surrounding the Armenian Genocide—and even tackle the troubling question of whether Adolf Hitler was inspired by what happened to the Armenians.

Though Turkey and its surrounding countries have a rich history, it's a history littered with tragedy and atrocity—and it is easy to see how past events shaped the Armenian Genocide.

Viewpoint 1

Historical Perspective from the Ottoman Empire Onward

Sara Cohan

In the following viewpoint, writer Sara Cohan details the history of the Armenian people and how changes in the Ottoman Empire affected the lives of many Armenians. As Cohan observes, the Armenian genocide in 1915 was preceded by similar events: the Hamidian massacres from 1894 to 1896, and the Adana massacre in 1909. The author is a former high school teacher and former education director of the Genocide Education Project. She works with USC Shoah Foundation as an Education and Outreach Specialist for iWitness Armenia—Armenian Education Program, designing educational programs and materials for all ages.

> "I am confident that the whole history of the human race contains no such horrible episode as this. The great massacres and persecutions of the past seem almost insignificant when compared with the sufferings of the Armenian race in 1915."
>
> Henry Morgenthau, American ambassador to the Ottoman Empire, 1913–1916. [1]

"A Brief History of the Armenian Genocide," by Sara Cohan, National Council for the Social Studies, August 2014. Reprinted by Permission.

Who Are the Armenians?

The Armenians are an ancient people who have existed since before the first century C.E. Armenia has gained and lost a tremendous amount of territory throughout its long and turbulent history. Boundaries of the past have extended from that of the present-day Republic of Armenia and through most of modern day Turkey. The name "Armenia" was actually given to the country by its neighbors; inhabitants of Armenia refer to it as "Hayastan" derived from the name Haik, a descendent of Noah (from the Bible), and "stan" which means "land" in Persian. The Armenian language is unique from other Indo-European languages, with its own distinct letters and grammar.

Christianity is a deeply rooted aspect of Armenian history and culture. Armenia was the first nation to adopt Christianity as a state religion, in 301 C.E. This early Christian identity has greatly influenced Armenian culture, setting it apart from most of its neighboring peoples. The majority of Armenians belong to the Eastern or Western dioceses of the Armenian Apostolic Church, an orthodox form of Christianity.

Although Armenia was at times a kingdom, in modern times, Armenia has been an independent country for only a few years. It first gained independence in 1918, after the defeat of the Ottoman Empire in World War I, but this ended when Armenia was invaded by the Red Army and became a Soviet state in 1920. With the dissolution of the Soviet Union in 1991, Armenia was the first state to declare its independence, and remains an independent republic today. Armenia is a democracy and its borders only include a very small portion of the land that was historic Armenia.

Early Massacres

The Seljuk Turks began to inhabit Anatolia as early as the eleventh century and by 1453 their descendants, the Ottoman Turks, had captured Constantinople (now Istanbul), firmly establishing the Ottoman Empire. The Ottoman Empire was a multinational state that incorporated several ethnic groups including the Armenians.

The Armenians were second-class citizens of the Ottoman Empire and while they were granted some freedoms, including the ability to practice Christianity, they were faced with extra taxes and discriminatory laws extending to their participation in the justice system, government, and their civil and property rights.

By the mid-1800s, as the idea of constitutionalism swept through Europe, some Armenians began to demand more rights, such as protection from corrupt government officials and biased taxation. While most Armenians saw themselves as members of the Ottoman Empire, organized groups of intellectuals protested the discriminatory laws, seeking reform from the government, though not an independent sovereign state.

During the nineteenth century, the Ottoman Empire experienced a period of decline, during which it lost territories to Russia, Great Britain, and new states created by nationalities that had once been part of the Ottoman Empire, such as Greece, Serbia, Bulgaria and Romania. Early in the century, Russia had gained some of the eastern Armenian provinces, including Tiflis, which became a cultural center for Russian Armenians. Russian Armenians became increasingly interested in supporting Armenians within the Ottoman Empire in their quest for human rights. The newly created Ottoman Armenian political organizations received some support from Russian Armenians and Russia in their quest to gain equal rights under Ottoman law.

The Treaty of Berlin (1878) included a clause that would provide more rights for Ottoman Armenians, including fair taxation practices, protections from tribal attacks, and the right to give evidence in Ottoman courts of law. Unfortunately these rights were never granted as the Sultan was empowered by the treaty to serve as the protector of the Armenians. This was in contrast to the terms of the earlier Treaty of San Stefano, which the Treaty of Berlin replaced, and which had assigned the Russians the responsibility of ensuring that the Armenians in Ottoman territory would gain more rights. The reason for the change was that the presence of Russian troops in the region was of concern to Great

Britain and the other "Great Powers" of Europe who wanted to deter the expansion of Russia.

After the Treaty of Berlin, Ottoman Armenians continued to protest discriminatory laws and eventually the Sultan responded to these protests with massacres. Massacres of the Armenians began in the late nineteenth century under Abdul-Hamid II, the last of the Ottoman Sultans actually to rule the empire. The worst massacres during this time occurred from 1894–1896 after a tax protest by Armenians. They are now known as the Hamidian Massacres and some believe represented a foreshadowing of the genocide to come.

During the Hamidian Massacres, 100,000 to 300,000 Armenians were killed in towns and villages throughout areas of the Ottoman Empire. Thousands of Armenians fled and found refuge in Europe and the United States. Some who stayed converted to Islam in order to save their own lives.

The massacres caught the world's attention because of their unique nature. Armenians were unarmed and adhered to the perimeters set forth by the Ottoman government. The massacres were publicized in newspapers throughout the world. The U.S. media paid particular attention to the events. *The New York Times* as well as other news sources regularly published articles about the brutal killings, coverage that would continue through the Armenian genocide.

Many American missionaries and diplomats who worked throughout the Ottoman Empire witnessed the atrocities firsthand and helped mobilize relief efforts. Aid for Armenian victims became the first international mission of the American Red Cross.

Later during the genocide, a society known as the Near East Relief would raise more than $100 million in assistance to Armenians; the funds collected saved countless Armenian lives in the 1890s and during the genocide, which at the time represented more money than all the aid raised to help tsunami victims this year. While the funds collected saved countless victims' lives, it was the only aid Armenians would see.

Hope to Despair

In 1908, Armenians and other minorities of the Ottoman Empire began to rejoice in what promised to be a new era of tolerance and the establishment of a participatory government in the Ottoman Empire.

Armenians, Arabs, Greeks, Jews, and Kurds had begun working with a group of Turks to challenge the authority of the Sultan. This group was known as the Ottoman Liberals and the Turkish coalition of the group adopted the name "Young Turks." They wanted to create a modern state that represented inhabitants of the Ottoman Empire more equally and render the Sultan politically powerless. In 1908, one of the Young Turk groups, the Committee of Union and Progress (CUP), marched on Constantinople, and overthrew Sultan Abdul-Hamid.

Over the next year, the Ottoman Empire developed a constitutional government providing equal rights for all of its citizens. Ottoman Armenians hoped that the new constitution would protect them from the violence they endured under the Sultan. However, as time passed, advocates of liberalism in the government lost out to a group promoting authoritarian rule and a radical policy of Turkification.

In April 1909, Armenian hopes were dashed as Hamidian supporters in the city of Adana carried out a massacre of Armenians as part of an attempt to reestablish the power of the Sultan. Adana was heavily populated by Armenians and had at one time been part of Armenian territory. Despite attempts at resistance, in the end almost 30,000 Armenians were killed and nearly half the city destroyed.

The Armenian Genocide

The culprits of the Adana Massacre were never punished and after 1909, an extreme nationalist political movement promoting a policy of Pan-Turkism ("Turkey for the Turks") gained backing from Turkish populations throughout the Ottoman Empire. In addition, the Ottoman Empire, now known as the "sick man of

Europe," was weakened by the loss of its lands in south-eastern Europe in the Balkan Wars of 1912-13.

One of the Ottoman Empire's greatest enemies was Russia, as Russia was constantly threatening the security of the Ottoman borders and controlled parts of the eastern edge of the Ottoman Empire that was populated by Armenians. Since the Russians had advocated for Armenian reforms in the past and because the Russian army did have Armenians serving as soldiers, the Ottoman government was concerned that Ottoman Armenians might commit traitorous acts. This fear helped to fuel Turkish public sentiment against Armenians.

The Ottoman Empire entered World War I in 1914, fighting against Russia in campaigns that straddled territory inhabited by Armenians on both sides of the border. The Ottoman Empire was badly defeated by Russia in a campaign in the winter of 1914–15, and the government then made the Armenian community a scapegoat for the military losses that had occurred at the hands of the Russians.

By the spring of 1915, leaders of the ruling party, the CUP, seized the opportunity of a world preoccupied by war to erase the Armenian presence from almost all Ottoman lands. The CUP was a triumvirate led by Mehmet Talaat, Ismail Enver, and Ahmed Jemal. Beginning on April 24, 1915 (now commemorated as the beginning of the Armenian genocide), Armenian civil leaders, intellectuals, doctors, businessmen, and artists were rounded up and killed. Once these leaders of the Armenian communities were killed, the genocide plan was put into motion throughout the empire. Many Armenian men were quickly executed. Using new technologies, such as the telegraph and the railroads, CUP leaders sent orders to province leaders to gather women and children and either load them onto trains headed for the Syrian Desert or lead them on forced marches into the desert. Embarking with little food and few supplies, women and children had little hope of survival.

On these journeys, Turkish gendarmes regularly subjected Armenian women to sexual violence. Special militias were created

Armenia 1915: The Genocide

In 1915, under the cover of the war, the Ottoman government resolved to expel Turkey's Armenian population (at the time about 1.75m) entirely. Their plan included deportation to the deserts of Syria and Mesopotamia (now Iraq). Hundreds of thousands of Armenians were driven out of their homes and either massacred or force-marched into the desert until they died. The German ambassador to Turkey wrote home: "The government is indeed pursuing its goal of exterminating the Armenian race in the Ottoman Empire." Between 1915 and 1923 the western part of historic Armenia was emptied of Armenians. The death toll is reliably estimated to be over a million. Those who did not die fled to the Middle East, Russia or the USA.

The genocide was conducted in a well-organised way, making use of new technology available. Orders to begin the operation were sent to every police station, to be carried out simultaneously at the same time on the same day: April 20, 1915. Once it had begun, the perpetrators kept in touch by telegraph. They also made use of the Istanbul-Baghdad railway: the new line had already been laid as far as the Syrian desert. Tens of thousands of Armenians were packed into railway wagons and sent down the line into the desert, where they were left without shelter, water or food. Many of the workers laying the railway were Armenian, and thought they would escape; their turn for the death trucks came in 1916.

Genocide in wartime is relatively easy to conceal. When Hitler was planning the invasion of Poland in 1939, he gave the order to "kill without mercy men, women and children of the Polish race or language. Only in this way will we get the living space we need. Who after all, speaks today of the annihilation of the Armenians?"

—"The **Genocide**," Peace Pledge Union.

by the government to carry out the deportations and murders; and Turkish and Kurdish convicts who had been set free from jails brutalized and plundered the deportation caravans winding through the severe terrain. Some women and children were abducted and sold, or children were raised as Turks by Turkish families. Some Armenians were rescued by Bedouins and other Arabs who sympathized with the Armenian situation. Sympathetic Turkish families also risked their own lives to help their Armenian neighbors escape.

Within months, the Euphrates and Tigris rivers became clotted with the bodies of Armenian women and children, polluting the water supply for those who had not yet perished. Dysentery and other diseases were rampant and those who managed to survive the march found themselves in concentration camps.

By 1918, most of the Armenians who had resided in this historic land were dead or in the Diaspora. Under the orders of Turkey's new leader, Mustafa Kemal (Ataturk), the remaining Armenians in western Cilicia (the region of the Ottoman Empire originally inhabited by Armenians) were expelled, as were the Greek and Assyrian populations.

By 1923, a 3,000-year-old civilization virtually ceased to exist. One and a half million Armenians, more than half of the Armenian population on its historic homeland, were dead, and the Armenian community and personal properties were lost, appropriated by the government, stolen by others or deliberately destroyed. Only a small number of Armenians remained in the former Ottoman capital of Constantinople.

The Denial

The term "genocide" was not created until 1944. It was devised by a legal scholar, Raphael Lemkin, who had been strongly influenced by his study of the Armenian case and the persecution of Jews under Nazi rule. In 1946, the United Nations adopted the language and two years later the Convention on the Prevention and Punishment of the Crime of Genocide was passed.

Despite the affirmation of the Armenian genocide by the overwhelming majority of historians, academic institutions on Holocaust and Genocide Studies, and governments around the world, the Turkish government still actively denies the Armenian genocide. Among a series of actions enacted to counter Armenian genocide recognition and education, the government even passed a law in 2004 known as Article 305 which makes it a criminal offense, punishable by up to 10 years in prison, to discuss the Armenian genocide.

Most of the survivors of the Armenian genocide have now passed away. Their families still continue to demand recognition for the suffering inflicted upon their beloved ancestors more than 90 years ago.

Notes
1. Henry Morgenthau, *Ambassador Morgenthau's Story* (London: Taderon Press, 2000), 213.

Viewpoint 2

1909: The Adana Massacres
Bedross Der Matossian

This viewpoint focuses on the massacres that took place in 1909 in the Turkish city of Adana. The author believes this event should be studied as part of the process of understanding political and economic changes in the region. It's unfortunately too easy for this event to be overlooked or forgotten when compared to both the Hamidian massacres some 15 years earlier, and the overwhelming genocide six years later. Author Bedross Der Matossian is an associate professor of Modern Middle East History at University of Nebraska-Lincoln, and has taught as well at Massachusetts Institute of Technology and University of Chicago. He is the author of the 2014 book Shattered Dreams of Revolution.

> *On 29 August 1908, one month after the Young Turk Revolution, Mihrdat Noradoungian, an Armenian intellectual from Istanbul, wrote a lengthy opinion piece entitled "The Price of Freedom" in the Armenian daily newspaper* Puzantion. *In this lengthy article, Noradoungian argued that people were looking with hesitation at this freedom that came about without any bloodshed. What Noradoungian was implying in the article is that the Freedom after the revolution should have been received through violence— probably reminiscent of the violence during the French Revolution which was able to get rid of the ancien régime: The change that took place a month ago had the biggest peculiar advantage, to which the entire world views with bewilderment, and that is the lack of blood and uproar. Both of these factors are regular phenomenon in these kinds of situations ... Though during the*

"From Bloodless Revolution to Bloody Counterrevolution: The Adana Massacres of 1909," by Bedross Der Matossian, *Genocide Studies and Prevention: An International Journal*, July 1, 2011. Reprinted by Permission.

The Armenian Genocide

> *[last] 15 years a lot of blood has spilled, there was the fear of greater bloodshed which did not happen. One should know that this [bloodshed] has become a natural law and that natural laws are unavoidable. Whatever did not happen in the beginning could still happen. Whatever the revolution did not do, the counterrevolution will be able to do. There is only one way in order to prevent the occurrence of this contingency (bloodshed) and that is discretion, modesty, wisdom, and patience. New freedom is always fragile. Let us be careful.*[2]

This connection between Revolution, Blood, and the *ancien régime* was endemic and not only to the Armenian press in the Ottoman Empire. During the first days of the constitution, while the revolutionary festivities were at their height, the ethnic presses (Armenian, Arabic, Greek, Ottoman Turkish, and Ladino, among others) warned people to be vigilant about the existing fragile situation and be wary of former officials of the *ancien régime*.[3] However, in comparison to other newspapers, the Armenian press dealt intensively with the concept of the *ancien régime* in its present form, not in its past one.[4] One such editorial sought to enlighten the public about the danger of the situation and the calamities that they should expect.[5] The article is crucial in that it predicts the upcoming calamity of the counterrevolution. It advised Armenians to not create any pretext for the eruption of these agitations. On the contrary, the editorial argued that it is the duty of the Armenians to act with love toward their Turkish brothers and be careful with every act and every word that could make them bitter against Armenians and incite the people of the *ancien régime*. "We repeat that we need to be careful from shouting 'Armenian,' or to talk about an independent Armenia," argued the editorial. "The majority of the nation is in agreement that reforming the condition of the Armenians of Turkey is dependent on the reform of Turkey." The editorial ends by recommending that Armenians cooperate with their Turkish compatriots "who support us and curse the *ancien régime*."[6]

With this connection between revolution and blood in mind, the present article discusses the correlation between the 1908 revolution and the Adana Massacres of 1909. After briefly reviewing the existing historiography of the Adana Massacres, I will introduce a new approach to the understanding of these massacres in the larger context of the revolution, specifically the development of a weak public sphere and the erosion of social and political stability, all of which led to the escalation of violence in Adana. Afterward, I will discuss the impact of the Young Turk Revolution on Adana and demonstrate the ways in which the revolution precipitated the ethnic tensions leading to the massacres.

The Young Turk Revolution of 1908

The Young Turk Revolution of 1908 represents an important historical juncture in Ottoman history and the history of the modern Middle East, not as a new beginning, but rather as a major catalyst in accelerating the dissolution of the empire. Thus, these two contradicting paradigms of a new beginning and dissolution were interconnected and went hand in hand in marking the last phase of Ottoman history, the Second Constitutional Period (1908–1918) that ended with the defeat of the empire in World War I. Within this period two interrelated events took place that shaped the political scene of the era: (1) The counterrevolution of 31 March 1909 which was initiated by the reactionary forces within the empire and (2) the Adana Massacres (April 14–17, April 25–27) which led to the destruction of the physical and the material presence of Armenians in Adana.

The counterrevolution was not a spontaneous outburst by dissatisfied elements in Istanbul; rather, it was organized by oppositional elements mainly represented by conservative religious circles within the empire.[7] On the night of April 12, the troops of the First Army Corps mutinied and marched toward Ayasofya Square, near the parliament, accompanied by a large number of people in religious garb (*softas*) shouting slogans in favor of the sultan and demanding the restoration of the Sher'ia.[8] This resulted in the resignation of Hilmi Pasa's cabinet, which was promptly accepted by the sultan.[9]

By royal order, on April 14, Tevfik Pasa was appointed the Grand Vezir and Ismail Kemal was elected the President of Parliament.[10] This was a huge blow to the Committee of Union and Progress (CUP) whose members either fled or were hiding. On April 17 the CUP began to act. The Action Army (*Haraket Ordusu*) left Salonika and headed to Istanbul to restore public order and discipline among the rebellious troops. It established its headquarters at Aya Stefanos and began negotiations with the new cabinet.[11] After failed negotiations, the Action Army entered Istanbul on April 23 and, after several skirmishes, took control of the city.

The Adana Massacres of 1909, which became a turning point for the Armenians living in the Ottoman Empire, were one of the earliest manifestations of violence during the Second Constitutional Period (1908-1918). Furthermore, the massacres represent a microcosm of the deterioration of ethnic conflict in Anatolia and its culmination in the destruction of the indigenous Armenian population during World War I. Understanding the factors and motives that led to the enactment of violence will shed new light on the future acts of violence perpetrated against the indigenous Armenian population of the Ottoman Empire. The present article contends that the Adana Massacres should be viewed as an integral part of the ongoing power struggle in Anatolia and the Arab provinces after the revolution.[12] An important factor that contributed to the escalation of ethnic tensions was the emergence of a weak public sphere within the empire after thirty years of the Hamidian despotic regime. Hence, to better understand the escalation of ethnic tensions in the empire, it is important to problematize the notion of modern public sphere and understand its implications and challenges within the Ottoman milieu.[13] Doing so will provide us with better ways of understanding communal violence as a by-product of modernity.

The Public Sphere and the Ottoman Empire

The notion of the *public sphere* refers to a social space in which private citizens gather as a public body with the rights of assembly, association, and expression in order to form public opinion.[14] The history of the notion of the public sphere in the Ottoman Empire has yet to be written and the present study does not undertake that task.[15] Of course, the public sphere, both in its pre-modern and modern forms, existed in the Ottoman Empire.[16] However, it had a different background and was affected by different factors from the European milieu.[17] As a result of modern urban development, the public sphere began to enter into its modern form. The modern public sphere(s) in the empire was spurred by the development of peripheral capitalism and through the opening of urban spaces, in the form of public squares, gardens, and wider roads. In addition, the process was accompanied by the proliferation of cafés, associations, theaters, and scientific and literary societies, as a result of which literary public spheres were formed in the empire. However, the main factor that led to the proliferation of these public spheres in the empire during the nineteenth century was the press in general and newspapers in particular.[18] The official Ottoman press began to be published in the nineteenth century and was followed by the emergence of the private press. The transformation of the literary public spheres into political public spheres in the modern sense took place throughout the century, reaching its peak with the promulgation of the Ottoman constitution in 1876.[19] In fact, the creation of the private press and the proliferation of the ethnic press in the second half of the nineteenth century further developed the notion of multiple public spheres as opposed to the public sphere dominated by the Ottoman ruling elite.

In 1878, however, Sultan Abdülhamid dissolved the Ottoman parliament and derailed the constitution, putting an end to the political public sphere. Hence, the institutions that once served as the basis of the developing public sphere(s) were derailed and weakened. He also established one of the most sophisticated spying systems in the history of the Ottoman Empire. As a result, by the

The Armenian Genocide

beginning of the 1880s, the ethnic groups' journalist activities shifted West, from Lebanon, Syria, and Anatolia to European cities and Egypt. Here, an *exilic* public sphere was established in which exiles of different ethnic backgrounds expressed their political views, discussed their projects for the empire, interacted with each other, and attempted to mobilize their host governments by using various means of expression, from exilic media to public gatherings and discussion.[20]

After the Young Turk Revolution of 1908, this exilic public sphere was transformed into a homeland public sphere. The revolution allowed for an immediate boom in the serial publications of different ethnic groups in the empire.[21] In the two years after the revolution, censorship was nonexistent. In the first year alone about 200 periodicals were published in Istanbul.[22] Hence, the media that served the development of multiple/competing public spheres prior to the Hamidian period were reinstated during the post-revolutionary period. However, these contentious and weak public sphere(s) that lacked strong institutional basis would become the medium through which the existing tensions in the empire were going to surface, demonstrating the incompetence of the local administration to deal with contentious situations. The weak public sphere(s) became a medium through which both the satisfied and the dissatisfied elements aired their content or discontent with the new regime and deliberated the political future of the empire by using the tools of modernity. In addition, the weak public sphere(s) also became an important vehicle for the enactment of violence by the dissatisfied groups. Thus, the relationship between public sphere and violence is crucial to understanding the massacres carried out against the indigenous Armenian population. After the revolution, the growth in Adana's public sphere not only fomented political activism within formerly outlawed groups, but it also contributed to an escalation of ethnic tensions. The physical and verbal manifestations of Armenians in the public sphere in the forms of cultural and political processions, the bearing and selling of arms in public,[23] and theatrical presentations as well as the use of print media sent alarming vibes among the dissatisfied elements, which began to use the same medium to air their anxieties about and discontent with the new created order. Thus, the public space in Adana would become not only the place for the re-enactment of identities; it would also become a vehicle through which the existing political, social, and economic anxieties would be manifested in two waves of massacres which took place in conjuncture with the counterrevolution.

Historiography and the Adana Massacres of 1909

The study of ethnic strife, violence, and repression in the Ottoman Empire in general and in Anatolia in particular remains marginalized in the historiography of the Ottoman Empire. Only a handful of scholars have attempted to put these subjects at the core of their inquiries.[24] However, most of these works concentrate on the Armenian Genocide during World War I and do not consider the incidents of violence prior to the war.[25] Other scholars attempt to represent the acts of violence that took place at the end of the nineteenth and the beginning of the twentieth centuries as part of a linear process that culminated in the extermination of the Armenians.[26] A major methodological deficiency of these works stems from the failure to appreciate that violence during the early phase of the Second Constitutional Period was an integral part of the revolutionary process. While some Turkish scholars deny the involvement of local government officials in the massacres by blaming the Armenians who revolted as part of a conspiracy to establish a kingdom in Cilicia,[27] some Armenian scholars, whose work is overshadowed by the Armenian genocide, accuse the CUP of acting behind the scenes to destroy the Armenian economic infrastructure in Adana in order to curb any future political and economic development in the area.[28]

Development of Adana's Public Sphere(s)

It is impossible to understand the development of Adana's public sphere without understanding the impact of the revolution on the

Anatolian provinces and the ways in which it led to the emergence of contentious public sphere(s). The Young Turk Revolution caused major changes in the dynamics of power within the provinces, leading to an erosion of social and political stability. By disturbing a thinly balanced power equilibrium, the revolution produced a great deal of dissatisfaction within some segments of the population. The sudden mushrooming of Young Turk cells and clubs in the provinces caused extreme anxiety among the notables and the *ulema* (religious clerics) in the Anatolian provinces. Although the CUP had branches in all Anatolian and Arab provinces, it was not in full control of the provinces. A major factor in the deterioration of the intra-ethnic relationship among the Muslims in Anatolia was the dismissal of local officials and their replacement with CUP members or people loyal to the CUP. This contributed immensely to the rising tension between the CUP and the people of the *ancien régime*, mainly because a whole stratum of notables who had benefited from the *ancien régime* had lost power. Hence, one cannot understand the changes in Adana after the 1908 revolution without understanding the regional waves of discontent manifested after the revolution, especially in the Anatolian provinces. What distinguished Adana from other provinces was its economic and agricultural centrality to Anatolia—which attracted thousands of migrant workers arriving from Hadjin, Erzerum, Bayburt, and Bitlis—and its complex ethnic composition, which was a main catalyst in the deterioration of this ethnic relationship.[29] Therefore, I argue that the conditions created after the revolution and the emergence of contentious public sphere(s) prepared the ground for a violent backlash.

Adana was also an important spiritual and economic center for Armenians in Anatolia. It housed the Sea of the Catholicosate of Sis (Kozan).[30] In addition, the city had eight churches, two of which were Gregorian, one Protestant, and one Catholic. There were also Greek, Syrian, and Chaldean churches.[31] Armenians had two schools, the Apkarian and the Ashkhenian schools, the French had the Jesuit missionary school for boys and girls, and the Americans had the Girls College. In Tarsus, Americans also had St. Paul's Institute College.[32]

Prior to the massacres of 1909, Adana's population consisted of 62,250 Muslims; 30,000 Armenians; 5,000 Greeks; 8,000 Chaldeans; 1,250 Assyrians; 500 Christian Arabs; and 200 foreign subjects.[33] The Muslim population of Adana included Turks, Kurds, Fellahs, Circassians, Avshars, Cretans, and nomads. In addition, every spring about 30,000–40,000 migratory workers would come to Adana from Aleppo, Harput, Sivas, Diarbekir, Erzerum, Hajin, Bitlis, Bayburt, and Erzerum to work as farmers, tilling, reaping, and cultivating the cotton fields, or to work in factories.[34] The Muslim migrant workers always exceeded the Armenian migrant workers by a ratio of 2:1.

Adana was also the center of the cotton trade on the Cilician Plain.[35] David Fraser who visited Adana prior to the 1908 revolution argued that at the end of the nineteenth century it was customary for 60,000 laborers to visit Cilicia annually for the purpose of assisting with the harvest. However, he argues that this annual migration had ceased at the beginning of the twentieth century because the resident population aided by steam ploughs, steam threshers, and reaping machines was not able to undertake the labor by itself. This point is extremely important because it demonstrates the ways in which the introduction of modern agricultural and production technologies have caused substantial dissatisfaction among the migrant workers who used to benefit from the pre-modern agricultural mediums and has created what Ayhan Aktar calls "accumulated envy" toward the Armenians.[36] This "accumulated envy" would reveal itself in violent backlash by the migrant workers against the Armenians. In addition to this, Adana also housed several large establishments involved with ginning, spinning, and weaving. Among these, the most important factory was owned by the Greek Trypani Brothers who introduced the cotton industry to Cilicia.[37] In addition, the Deutsche Levant Cotton Company, which was financed by German, Swiss, and Austrian financiers, was also active in the region.[38] The Armenian population was very involved in trade and industry. They played a predominant role in exporting materials from Adana.[39] Armenian sources indicate that Armenian prosperity in Adana was lamented by some Turkish notables, such as Abdü lkadir Bagdadizade, one of the most influential notables in Adana.[40]

The Ottoman Public Sphere in Adana: The Climax of Contentious Politics between the CUP and the Notables

As soon as the constitution was enacted, people in Adana and Mersin began rejoicing. Masses were held in honor of the sultan and the Ottoman nation.[41] However, these festivities of the revolution were only euphoric feelings that did not reflect the different social sectors' actual attitudes toward the revolution. The revolution and the reinstatement of the constitution in Adana led to the rise of new figures. Ihsan Fikri, a self-acclaimed Young Turk, suddenly became a public figure. Fikri played an important role in organizing festivities in honor of the revolution. At the end of the festivities, Fikri sent a congratulatory telegram to the CUP branches in Manastir, Salonica, and Istanbul on behalf of the people of Adana. The next day the CUP Central Committee asked Fikri to establish a CUP branch in Adana.[42] To counter the CUP's influence, Abdü lkadir Bagdadizade,[43] one of the most influential notables of Adana, formed a group called the Agricultural Club (*Zirâ at Kulübü*) composed of Adana notables, people from Idlib, and *softas*.[44] They were supported by another anti-CUP committee, the Scientific Committee (*Cemiyet-i Ilmiye*). As with the other CUP branches in the provinces, people from the *ancien régime* entered the ranks and the first task of the new CUP branch was to force the local *vali* (governor) to resign.[45] Bahri Pasa resigned and for some time the CUP branch administered the province. It also succeeded at removing Kâzim Bey, the chief of police (*polisemüdürü*), and police superintendent (*komiser*) Zor Ali from their positions.[46] In addition, the CUP began sending delegates, consisting of one Armenian and one Turk, to villages to preach to the masses about the constitution. In order to better understand the tension that arose between the CUP and the local notables, it is important to give a brief historical background of Ihsan Fikri.

Ihsan Fikri, whose original name was Ahmed Tosun, had been an officer of the Salonica Agriculture Department. He was later exiled to Diyarbekir and then to Payas. After his exile to Payas, he represented himself as a liberal. Bahri Pasa, the *vali*, interceded with the authorities on his behalf to end his exile.[47] After returning to Adana, he married the daughter of a local property owner by the name of Menan Bey. Prior to the revolution, Fikri had been the principal of the Handicraft School (*Sanayi Mektebi*) but was fired by the *vali*, who replaced him with Gergerlizade Ali Effendi. After the revolution and the establishment of the CUP branch in Adana under his leadership, Fikri began to persecute his opponents, particularly Gergerlizade.[48] As a result, two groups emerged in Adana, one supporting Fikri and another supporting Gergerlizade.[49] This tension can be best defined as CUP versus the local notables. In this intra-ethnic struggle the press played an important role. In the post-revolutionary period five newspapers were published in Adana: *Seyhan, Yasasin Ordu, Itidal,* edited by Ihsan Fikri; *Rehberi Itidal,* owned by Ali Ilmi Effendi; and *Çukurova*, a weekly newspaper published by Mahmud Jelaleddin. *Itidal* and *Rehberi Itidal* were in constant conflict. The latter was also supported by *Çukurova*. According to Terzian, Ihsan Fikri wrote erratically, praising the Armenians one day and attacking them the next.

After Bahri Pasa resigned, he was replaced by Mirliva Ali Pasa, who generally kowtowed to the CUP. When Cevad Bey was appointed *vali*, tensions began to escalate dramatically. Ihsan Fikri, seeing Cevad Bey's weakness, tried to manipulate him into removing Gergerlizade from his position as the principal of the school. Gergerlizade, however, gained the *vali*'s favor. In addition, Cevad Bey used to frequently visit the Agricultural Club and the Scientific Committee.[50] This angered Fikri, who began openly attacking the *vali* in *Itidal*, even calling

The Armenian Genocide

for his resignation, but to no avail.[51] Furthermore, he claimed that government was nonexistent in Adana and that it was people like Abdülkadir Bagdadizade who were truly running the affairs of the country. In this tensed atmosphere, Zor Ali, the former police commissary (*komiser*) of Adana who had been dismissed by the CUP, arrived in Adana and declared himself a member of the *Fedakâ rini Millet*, a branch of the Ittihadi Mouhamadi, and called on people of the same mind to join him.[52] In this atmosphere of intra-ethnic tension, news of the counterrevolution reached Adana, further altering the power balance within the provinces.

The Armenian Public Sphere: Testing the Limits of Freedom

The Armenian festivities and demonstrations in honor of the constitution on 24 July 1908 were especially striking. The public sphere created after the 1908 revolution allowed Armenian political parties to be active in Adana. Armenian cultural revival began. Poetry, odes, and dramas about the Armenian national past began to be published and performed, causing anxiety among the local Muslim population. In addition, Armenians, "intoxicated with the new wine of liberty, often gave offense by wild talk or arrogant behavior."[53] In an interview with an Armenian newspaper after the massacres, missionary Christie positioned at Tarsus argued that there is no proof that the Christians as a whole desired separation from the Ottoman people or government. Granted, he argued that there were a very few foolish men (Armenians) who by their boasting and threats exasperated the Turks. However, he adds that "their acts and words ought not to be taken as justifying in the slightest degree the cruelties that make this recent massacre worse than any that have gone before it."[54] Armenian activities in the post-revolutionary period entailed physical and verbal manifestations in the public sphere causing much anxiety among the dissatisfied elements. For example, *Itidal*, the main Young Turk organ in Adana edited by Ihsan Fikri, reported that on Sunday 29 March 1909 a play was performed by Armenians at the Casino of Ziya Pasa in

Mersin.[55] In the words of one contemporary Ottoman official in Adana, "At that night Armenians had opened the first curtains of revolt" (*Iste Ermeniler ilk isyan perdesini o gece açmislardir*).[56] The play was entitled *Temurlane and the Destruction of Sivas*.[57] The local *mutessarif* (subgovernor), as well as other officials, was invited to attend the play. At the beginning of the play, Temurlane gives an order to exterminate all the Armenians. A fierce struggle takes place between Temurlane and an Armenian king. The king, along with his servant and his daughter, becomes Temurlane's prisoner. The king, hands chained and wearing a thorn crown, sits hopelessly in a cell allocated to him by Temurlane. Suddenly, two spirits appear before the king telling him that he will reclaim his kingdom through the unity of his nation. And when the king tells the spirits that all of the Armenians have been massacred, the spirits answer as follows: "These are enough, do not feel sorry, thanks to unity the day will come that you will restore your monarchy [*kraligin tasdik edecekler*]. You are going to preserve your independence, be restful, do not detach yourself from unity, once more in the future you will regain your crown." *Itidal* reported that when the curtain closed all of the Armenians in the audience began shouting and applauding "Long live Armenia," "Long live Armenian kingdom," "Long live Armenians."[58]

On another occasion, a performance of Hamlet by the Armenian students of St. Paul's College of Tarsus made government officials and the local *mufti* (Islamic scholar) uneasy. Helen Davenport (Brown) Gibbons, who taught at the school, described the play and her role in putting on the performance in detail in a letter sent to her mother on 7 April 1909. Gibbons described that when things began to go badly for Hamlet's stepfather, people stopped fanning. The attending dignitaries became uneasy, and hunched their shoulders. They kept their eyes glued to the stage. She continued:

> They are not familiar with our great William, and believe, no doubt, that we invented the play as well as the actors' costumes. Horror of horrors! We had forgotten what they might read into the most realistic scene. An Armenian warning for Abdul Hamid?

> The assassins mastered the struggling king. He lay there with his red hair sticking out from his crown, and the muscles of his neck stiffened as he gasped for breath while his throat was cut with a shiny white letter-opener.[59]

In addition to these, the relationship in Adana between Armenian ecclesiastic leadership and the local government deteriorated after the 1908 revolution, particularly after the removal of the *vali* Bahri Pasa who had a cordial relationship with the Armenians and especially with Bishop Moushegh Seropian.[60] Fearful of what might happen, the Catholicos of Sis, Sahag, sent telegrams to Istanbul warning of imminent massacres in the area. The Ottoman-Turkish newspapers of Istanbul reacted negatively to these telegrams, saying "we do not want to believe in the existence of the threat of massacre."[61] At the time, the prelate of Adana, Bishop Moushegh, was on a mission to Istanbul. When he returned to Adana he found that letters from the villages warning of imminent threats have accumulated. Bishop Moushegh also sent a pastoral letter to the Armenians of Adana emphasizing the need for harmony among the people.[62] However, the uncertain situation and the rising tension led Bishop Moushegh to encourage Armenians to buy arms[63]:

> We advise the people, in order to be able to fulfill their duties towards the country and constitution, every person should be armed more or less according to his ability. That readiness should be at the same time somehow a means for self-defense, against an unfortunate attack, until the constitutional government comes to their aid.[64]

Dr. Christie, the American missionary, criticized Bishop Moushegh's words and deeds and those of the young men who were following him. He argued that it was wrong to bring tin boxes of arms and ammunition to Mersin addressed to Armenians in Adana.[65] However, he explained that even these do not prove that there was an intention to rebel against the government.[66] Thus, Bishop Moushegh in the eyes of the local Muslim population became an agitator and the source of tensions for inciting the

Armenians against the Turks and encouraging them to establish Kingdom Cilicia.[67] As a result, twenty-five days before the massacres Bishop Moushegh was banished from Adana to Cairo by orders from the *vali*.[68]

The Consolidation of Violence: The Breaking Point

In March 1909 ethnic tension began to deteriorate dramatically, as manifested in a couple of sporadic attacks on Armenians.[69] One of these attacks became the catalyst precipitating the first wave of the Adana Massacres/Clashes. On 28 March 1909, an Armenian named Hovhannes was attacked by a group of Turks, led by a man named Isfendiar.[70] During the ensuing fight, Hovhannes killed Isfendiar, wounded some of the other attackers, and fled to the Armenian Quarter in Adana. From there he escaped to Cyprus. Isfendiar's funeral attracted not only those angered by the killing, but also much of the element dissatisfied with the new order, the constitution, and its Armenian "collaborators." The body was dragged through the streets for exhibition and became a catalyst in the manifestation of the existing economic and political anxieties. This immediately led to the mobilization of the masses and prepared the ground for the enactment of violence.[71] Inflammatory remarks were made in the mosques and it was proclaimed that the Armenians of Adana had risen and were "killing true believers and burning their houses."[72] Isfendiar's family demanded that the *vali* capture the murderer.[73] A few days later, one of Hovhannes's other attackers died from the wounds he received, elevating the level of anger and excitement among the Muslim population. As the situation intensified, the *vali* of Adana telegrammed Istanbul warning of an imminent threat in Adana. Adil Bey, on behalf of the Ministry of Internal Affairs responded, "The financial institutions along with foreign buildings should be protected and peace should be preserved" (*Müessesât-i mâliye ile emâkin-i ecnebîyenin muhâfazasi ve iâde-i âsâ yise dikkatolunmasi*).[74] Some Armenian sources understand this telegram as an order to massacre the Armenians.[75] This sentence, however, is too vague to necessarily be understood in that way. With the arrival of news about the counterrevolution from Istanbul, the situation exploded.

The First Waves of Massacres/Clashes (April 14, 15, and 16)

> *"What could I do, if there is Constitution. Whatever the majority wants they will do so."*

In Adana, Tuesdays were market days. Peasants would travel from their villages to Adana in the morning and return in the evening. On Tuesday, 13 April 1909, these peasants did not return to their homes. It is also noteworthy that because of seasonal migration, 30,000-40,000 additional Armenian, Kurdish, and Turkish farm workers inhabited Adana.[77] On April 14, the disturbances began. Armenians opened their shops in the early morning, but soon saw groups of Turks, Kurds, Circassians, Basibozuks,[78] Cretans, and Muslim refugees along with the seasonal workers carrying hatchets, blunt instruments, axes, and swords in their hands and wearing white bandages (*saruks*) around their fezzes[79] in various quarters of the city.[80] This made the Armenians extremely anxious, and they quickly closed their shops.[81] When the Muslims saw that Armenians were closing their shops early they too became anxious, and a rumor spread that the Armenians were going to attack them. The mob, consisting of Turks, Kurds, Fellahs, Circassians, Gypsies, and Cretan refugees along with the migrant workers, began looting and attacking the center of the town.[82] Zor Ali, the police superintendent, rallied his troops and besieged the Armenian Quarter of Sabaniye. Meanwhile, Armenians took a defensive position in the Armenian Quarter and fortified themselves in houses.[83]

The first day of the massacres/clashes saw sporadic and unorganized attacks. On the first night, the mob began burning the Armenian Quarter.[84] The attacks and the clashes intensified the next day.[85] The majority of the Armenian population found shelter in Armenian churches and schools and some in foreign missions. By the third day, the mob grew as Turks arrived from Aleppo and Sivas to take part in the pillage. Since the Armenians were running short on ammunition, they asked the government for protection.[86] In response, the *vali* organized a reconciliation meeting between Turkish and Armenian notables.[87] By the fourth day the situation had calmed. It is impossible to accurately assess the number of casualties. Hundreds of wounded Armenians were taken to the Apkarian Armenian school which was turned into a hospital. Many Armenians escaped to Mersin.[88] The carnage, looting, and killing lasted for three days (April 14, 15, and 16). Many Armenians were killed as well as many Muslims, some of whom were killed while attacking the Armenian Quarter. It seems that the first wave of massacres/ clashes was minor compared to the second wave that will be discussed next. Nevertheless, Armenian shops, businesses, and institutions suffered immense damage.[89]

Public Sphere and the Transition from Verbal to Physical Violence

Most Armenian and European sources indicate that Ihsan Fikri, the leader of the CUP in Adana, and his newspaper *Itidal* played an important role in inciting the masses before the initiation of the second wave of massacres.[90] However, these sources do not tell us exactly what kind of discourse was being propagated by *Itidal*. This raises important questions about the transition from violent political discourse to physical violence. In cases of extreme escalation of ethnic tensions, during which the existing political and civil institutions are unable to contain the lawlessness and disorder of a region, the public sphere becomes the medium through which violence manifests itself. Furthermore, it contributes to the precipitation of ethnic tensions and accelerates the motives for the perpetration of violence against the vulnerable group. In the case of Adana, instead of declaring a state of siege, the local government chose to reconcile both parties who were involved in the violence by making superficial statements about coexistence and harmony. The public sphere was not restrained nor did the local government take the necessary steps to suppress provocative statements by reactionary groups. On the contrary, the printed form of communication, one of the most important components of a public sphere, was used to instigate the public against the vulnerable population. Hence, Ihsan Fikri was able to verbally attack the Armenians, using extraordinarily violent language, and to convince the masses that the Armenians had attempted a coup d'etat to establish the Kingdom of Cilicia.[91] According to the British vice consul in Adana, Doughty-Wylie, every Turk in Adana was fully persuaded at the time that the Armenians had set fire to their own houses with the idea of bringing about foreign intervention. Stories about Armenian atrocities on Muslim men and women were also widely spread.[92] According to Doughty-Wylie, the Turks put all of the blame on the Armenians because they armed themselves and because certain delegates of the Hunchak Party, and preachers like Bishop Moushegh, had urged the Armenians to openly fight the Turks and set up a principality; the Turks also believed that they had fixed a day on which to rise and rebel against the Turks.[93] Although Doughty-Wylie believed that the Hunchak Party was planning something, he nevertheless argued that they represented a fraction of the people. On the contrary, he argued that such widespread destruction could not have taken place without some "secret preparation on the Turkish side,"[94] demonstrating the premeditated nature of the event.[95]

On 20 April 1909, thousands of free copies of *Itidal* were distributed in the streets of Adana. In this issue, Fikri along with his colleagues Ismail Sefa[96] and Burhan Nuri vehemently attacked the Armenians.[97] In an article entitled "An Awful Uprising" (*Müdhis bir Isyân*), Sefa stated that a wave of boiling rage and independence was destroying the country.[98] He argued that Armenians, like the Turks, had been oppressed for thirty-three years by the despotic regime. Then they united with the Turks and applauded their "holy revolution." However, Sefa argued that Armenians soon began preparing themselves for the ensuing uprising by stockpiling weapons. According to Sefa, once the Armenians possessed weapons, their rhetoric changed. The phenomenon of Armenian *fedayees* (fighters) with Mauser rifles roaming the streets alarmed the Turks. According to Sefa, the first signs of agitation occurred on Friday when two Muslim youths were killed in the Sabaniye neighborhood. He was referring to the murder of Isfendiar. Sefa argued that although the *vali* had assured the Turkish population that he would capture the murderer, thus restoring order, the Armenians refused to turn over the murderer. For Sefa this was nothing less than an uprising (*isyân*). Sefa concluded that when the Armenians, "after all this barbarism and crime," saw the profusion of soldiers and people pouring in from the villages and understood that they would not succeed, they stopped their attacks.

In the same issue, an article by Burhan Nuri posed the rhetorical question "can the Armenians establish a state?" Burhan answered that only the foolish would believe that Armenians, numbering less than two million scattered throughout the empire, could defeat the Ottoman Empire and be able to establish an independent country.[99] Burhan attacked the European powers in his article saying that any European power cannot impose on the Ottoman Empire the establishment of an Armenian state in Cilicia. Burhan concluded as follows:

> *If the Armenians intend to form a state, the land for that state should not be in the Ottoman Empire, rather they should look for it in the poles, in the desert lands of Africa and immigrate there. They cannot reach their goal scattered in Istanbul, Adana, Aleppo, Diyarbekir, Bitlis, and Van.*

In the section of *Itidal* on news from the provinces, an editorial lamented that Adana would be "the victim of this horrible barbarism." The editorial argued that while the Turks were striving to live with the Armenians in happiness, the Armenians caused a "huge calamity on the head of the country through the organization of an agitation."[100]

Armenians, according to the editorial, had arrived in Adana from Marash, Hadjin, Harput, Diyarbekir, and from the Armenian populated provinces of Anatolia. The article argued that by forming a majority in the area, Armenians hoped to create agitation and demand autonomy.[101] They were encouraged in this by the success of Austria-Hungary in annexing Bosnia and Herzegovina and by the *de jure* independence of Bulgaria from the Ottoman Empire on 5 October 1908. For this purpose, they hoped to provoke the intervention of the European powers. The article concluded by saying that "looking at the painful situation, there is no doubt that they [the Armenians] were the reason of their own destruction, the Turks, and of the country."[102]

The editorial board of *Itidal* provided its own version of the causes and reasons for the deterioration of the ethnic relations and their culmination in the massacres. Whether or not the claims made by *Itidal* were true, they were vital in shaping public opinion in Adana, particularly the claims regarding an Armenian conspiracy. These articles in *Itidal* fumed public opinion in Adana after the first wave of massacres/clashes.

The Second Wave of the Massacres (April 25—27)

When Armenians heard the news that additional troops were going to come to Adana from Mersin to help preserve order, they were elated.[103] On April 25, 850 soldiers from the second and the third regiments arrived from Dede Agaç. After the regiments set up a camp in Adana, shots were fired at their tents. A rumor immediately spread that the Armenians had opened fire on the troops from a church tower in town.[104] The military commander of Adana, Mustafa Remzi Pasa, made no attempt to validate these rumors, but nevertheless ordered his soldiers to strike back at the Armenians. On Sunday, April 25 at 1:00 p.m. a battalion attacked the Armenian school that housed the injured from the first wave of the massacres. Soldiers poured kerosene on the school and set it on fire with people inside.[105] Regular soldiers, reserve soldiers, and mobs along with the Basibozuks attacked the Armenian Quarter. They burned down churches and schools. The conflagration in the city of Adana continued until Tuesday morning, April 27, and destroyed the entire Armenian residential quarter and most of the houses in the outlying districts inhabited by Christians.[106]

Another factor which precipitated the massacres was the unwillingness of Turkish troops to maintain order. Armenian sources indicate that weapons were distributed freely by the government to local civilians who took part in the massacres, looting, and carnage. The second wave of the massacres was larger in scale and more violent than the first. While the massacres in the city of Adana were taking place, rumors spread throughout the province that Armenians had revolted in Adana, killed all the Muslims, and were going to destroy the villages. This caused extreme anxiety and provoked retaliatory attacks by the Muslims on Armenian villages.

Conclusion

More than 100 years have passed since the massacres of Adana and historians continue to debate what the main causes of the massacres were. Indeed, the revolution should be regarded as the major catalyst in the deterioration of the situation. However, the massacres would not have taken place without the host of other factors mentioned in this article. The violence inflicted on the indigenous Armenian population should be understood as a manifestation of the anxieties caused by the major change within the political framework brought by the revolution. The weak institutions of the public sphere(s) in Adana played a dominant role in intensifying these anxieties and causing much distress among the local population and the notables of the *ancien régime*. This anxiety was not only political; rather it had serious economic ramifications at a time when modern agricultural technologies had replaced the old ones, causing much dissatisfaction among the poor migrant workers who were benefiting from pre-modern modes of production. Thus, the dominant role played by the migrant population in the massacres could also be interpreted as an attack on modernization, represented by drastic changes in the mediums of production.

The bloodshed that Mihrdat Noradoungian was so much worried about did materialize during the counterrevolution. What followed was two waves of clashes, massacres, pillaging, and looting. The complicity of local government officials, such as the *vali* Cevad Bey and the commander of the army Mustafa Remzi Pasa, is undeniable as the Military Tribunals and the investigation commissions sent from Istanbul attested.[107] Worse yet was the role that one of the most important notables of Adana, Abdü lkadir Bagdadizade, and his faction played in the massacres.[108] The CUP representative in Adana, Ihsan Fikri, along with Ismail Sefa, played a dominant role in shaping public opinion and transforming verbal into physical violence.[109] The reaction of the central government and the CUP against the real culprits of the massacre was lenient, as the court martial's decision attested.[110] Most of the key architects of the massacres mentioned above received light sentences. About fifty Muslims (some of them innocent)[111] and six Armenians were sentenced to death and many were sentenced to imprisonment with hard labor.[112] It seems that the CUP, having just recovered from a huge blow as a result of the counterrevolution, was afraid to take drastic action against the real culprits of the massacres because it was afraid that this would have wider effects in the region and would endanger its existence. The Adana massacres not only resulted in huge Armenian loss of life, but also led to the destruction of one of the most important Armenian economic centers in Anatolia.

Notes

1. I would like to thank Arpi Siyahian and Michael Bobelian for reading and commenting on earlier drafts of this article. Of course, I alone am responsible for this article.

2. Mihrdat Noradoungian, "Azatut'ian ginĕ" (The Price of Freedom), *Puzantion* 3617, 1 September 1908, 1. Unless otherwise noted, all translations are my own.

3. "Ba'd al-dustūr" (After the Constitution), *Al-Muqattam* 5903, 27 August 1908, 1; "Hame'ora' ot be-mamlakhtenu" (*The Incidents in Our Empire*), Hashkafa-Hazvi 30, 31 July 1908, 1–2; "Los Aḵont*isimiyent**os en la Asya Minor" (The Incidents in Asia Minor), *El-Tiempo* 10, 28 October 1908, 92.

4. "Hin rejimĕ wana mēch" (The *ancien régime* in Van), *Arevelk* 6918, 12 October 1908, 3; Yervant Sermakeshkhanlian, "Hin Derut'ian Sharunakut'iwnĕ" (The Continuation of the Old Regime), *Arevelk* 6924, 27 October 1908, 1; "Gavar,nerun irawijagĕ" (The

Condition of the Provinces), *Arevelk* 6896, 23 September 1908, 3; "Katsut'iwně Mushi měch" (The Situation in Mush), Puzantion 3629, 2 September 1908, 3; "Pědk ē Vakhnal Esbar,nalik'nerēn" (We Have to Fear from Threats), *Jamanag* 6, 3 October 1908, 1; Yervant Sermakeshkhanlian, "Sahmanadrut'iwně chi Gordzaderwirkor" The Constitution is Not Being Implemented), *Arevelk* 6919, 21 October 1908, 1.

5. "Gatsut'ian wedank'nern ew p'ortsak'arerě" (The Dangers and the Calamities of the Situation), *Puzantion* 3592, 31 July 1908, 2.

6. Ibid.

7. Erik J. Zürcher, "The Ides of April: A Fundamentalist Uprising in Istanbul in 1909," in *State and Islam*, ed. Cees van Dijk and Alexander H. de Groot (Leiden: CNWS, 1996), 64–76; David Farhi, "The Şeriat as a Political Slogan–or the 'Incident of the 31st of Mart,'" *Middle Eastern Studies* 7, no. 3 (1971): 275–99. On the counterrevolution, see Sina Akşin, 31 [*Otuz bir*] Mart Olayı (The Incident of March 31) (Ankara: Sevinç Matbaası, 1970); Talat Fuat, 31 [*i.e., Otuz bir*] *Mart İrtica* (March 31st Reaction) (Istanbul: Türk Matbaası, 1911 [1327]); Cemal Kutay, 31 [*i.e., Otuz bir*] *Mart ihtilâlinde Abdülhamit* (Abdulhamid during the Rising of March 31) (Istanbul: Cemal Kutay Kitaplığı ve Tarih Sevenler Kulübü, 1977); Ecvet Güresin, 31 [i.e., Otuz bir] Mart Isyanı (The Revolt of March 31) (Istanbul: Habora Kitabevi, 1969); Mustafa Baydar, 31 [i.e., otuz bir] Mart Vak'ası (March 31st Incident) (Istanbul: Amil Matbaası, 1955); Sadık Albayrak, 31 Mart gerici bir hareket mi? (Is the 31st of March a Reactionary Movement?) (Cağaloğlu, Istanbul: Bilim-Araştırma Yayınları, [1987]); Süleyman Kâni İrtem, 31 Mart isyani ve hareket ordusu: Abdülhamid'in Selânik Sürgünü (The Revolt of the 31st of March and the Action Army: The Banishment of Abdulhamid to Salonica) (Istanbul: Temel, 2003); Mustafa Eski, 31 Mart olayının Kastamonu'daki yankıları (The Repercussion of the 31st of March Incidents in Kastamonu) (Ankara: Ayyıldız Matbaası A.S, 1991).

8. Yunus Nadi, İhtilâl ve İnkilâb-i Osmanî: 31 Mart-14 Nisan 1325; hadisat, ihtisasat, hakayik (Ottoman Insurrection and Coup d'etat) (Dersaadet, Istanbul: Matbaayi Cihan, 1909), 35. For the other interpretation of the event on the same day, see Lütfi, "Dunki Hâl" (Yesterday's Situation), Volkan 104, 14 April 1909 (1 Nisan 1325), 1–2.

9. Nadi, İhtilâl ve İnkilâb-i Osmanî, 44.

10. Ibid., 45.

11. For a detailed contemporary description of the action army's entrance into Istanbul, see the ten-volume journal Azatarar Sharzhumn Banakin Haght'akan Mutk'n i K. Polis (The Victorious Entrance of the Freedom Action Army to Istanbul) (K. Polis: Tparan ew Gratun H.G. P'alagashean, 1909), vols. 1–10.

12. See Elie Kedourie, "The Impact of the Young Turk Revolution in the Arabic-Speaking Provinces of the Ottoman Empire," in Arabic Political Memoirs and Other Studies (London: Frank Cass, 1974), 124–61; Hasan Kayalı, Arabs and Young Turks: Ottomanism, Arabism, and Islamism in the Ottoman Empire, 1908–1918 (Berkeley: University of California Press, 1997); and Bedross Der Matossian, "Ethnic Politics in Post-Revolutionary Ottoman Empire: Armenians, Arabs, and Jews in the Second Constitutional Period (1908–1909)" (unpublished doctoral dissertation, Columbia University, 2008), 203–83.

13. For a discussion on the emergence of public spheres after the Young Turk Revolution, see Der Matossian, "Ethnic Politics in Post-Revolutionary Ottoman Empire," 55–65.

14. The concept of the public sphere, which is very much associated with the experience of Europe and North America, was introduced by Jürgen Habermas in his work The Structural Transformation of the Public Sphere. Scholars have criticized and modified the theory in different ways. Habermas himself has even revisited his approach and admitted that his notion of bourgeois public sphere is a "eurocentrically limited view." Jürgen Habermas, "A Philosophico-Political Profile," interview by Perry Andersen and Peter Dews, New Left Review 151 (1985 May–June): 104. For example, in his recent writings, Habermas has shown that there is no inherent reason that the notion of public sphere must be confined to an idealized European bourgeoisie. Jürgen Habermas, "Faktizität und Geltung" (Frankfurt: Suhrkamp, 1992), 62–77, quoted in Dale F. Eickelman and Armando Salvatore, "The Public Sphere and Muslim Identities," Archives européennes de sociologie / European Journal of Sociology 43, no. 1 (2002): 92–115. Some have argued that the notion of public sphere applies to periods well before the late eighteenth century, while others challenged the distinction and relationship that Habermas envisions between "public" and "particular" realism. See, for example, Harold Mah, "Phantasies of the Public Sphere: Rethinking the Habermas of Historians," The Journal of Modern History 72, no. 1 (2000): 153–82, 158. Some have criticized Habermas's idealization of the liberal public sphere while others point out that he failed to examine other, non-liberal and non-bourgeois, competing public spheres. See Nancy Fraser, "Rethinking the Public Sphere: A Contribution to the Critique of Actually Existing Democracy," in Habermas and the Public Sphere, ed. Craig Calhoun (Cambridge, MA: MIT Press, 1992), 115. The criticism of Habermas' public sphere created new approaches to our understanding of the public sphere. See Calhoun, Habermas and the Public Sphere; Nick Crossley and John Michael Roberts, eds., After Habermas: New Perspectives on the Public Sphere (Oxford: Blackwell Publishing/ Sociological Review, 2004). First, criticism revealed the exclusionary nature of the Habermasan public sphere in its classical liberal form. Second, it argued for the multiplicity of public spheres or publics as opposed to the existence of one dominant public sphere. Third, it introduced the notion of counter-public or subordinate public sphere. Nancy Fraser proposes calling them subaltern counter-publics "in order to signal that they are parallel discursive arenas where members of subordinated social groups invent and circulate counterdiscourses to formulate oppositional interpretations of their identities, interests and needs" (123). This is important, because in the Ottoman case we see not only the emergence of one dominant public sphere, but also the development of competing/contending non-dominant public sphere(s). The interaction between these competing/contending public spheres would become an important catalyst in the deterioration of ethnic relations in Anatolia.

15. One of the best studies that exist on the public sphere in Muslim societies is Miriam Hoexter, Shmuel N. Eisenstadt, and Nehemia Levtzion, eds., The Public Sphere in Muslim Societies (Albany: State University of New York Press; Jerusalem: Van Leer Jerusalem Institution, 2002). See also Eickelman and Salvatore, "The Public Sphere and Muslim Identities"; Srirupa Roy, "Seeing a State: National Commemorations and the Public Sphere in India and Turkey," Comparative Studies in Society and History 48, no. 1 (2006): 200–232.

16. Harold Mah argues that what distinguishes modern from pre-modern forms of the public is the particular mode of form of the public subject. Harold Mah, "Phantasies of the Public Sphere," 165.

17. Haim Gerber, "The Public Sphere and Civil Society in the Ottoman Empire," in Hoexter, Eisenstadt, and Levtzion, Public Sphere in Muslims Societies, 75.

18. See Ami Ayalon, The Press in the Arab Middle East (New York: Oxford University Press, 1995).

19. Notably, for different ethnic groups the emergence of the political public sphere took place in different decades of the nineteenth century.

20. The Pro-Armenia, Meşveret, Şuray-i ümmet, and al-Muqattam could be regarded as the best example of such a tool.

21. The best study on the post-revolutionary press is Palmira Brummett, Image and Imperialism in the Ottoman Revolutionary Press, 1908–1911 (Albany: State University of New York Press, 2000). Although it concentrates primarily on the satirical press during the post-revolutionary period— mainly on the Ottoman press—it provides important information on political discourse on the Ottoman press from the Turkish perspective. The same kind of work needs to be undertaken on the ethnic press.

22. Ibid., 25. For example, during the first two years after the revolution, about seventy-nine new Armenian newspapers were published in the Ottoman Empire: forty-nine in Istanbul, eight in Van, six in Izmir, and the rest in Diyarbekir, Erzincan, Trebizond, Erzerum, and Sivas. See Amalya Kirakosian, Hay Barperagan Mamuli Madenakruitiun (1794–1967) (The Literature of the Armenian Periodical Press) (Yerevan: Haykakan SSH Kulturayi Ministrut'yun, 1970), 488–89.

23. Armenians along with the Muslims began selling arms after the revolution as one of the fruits of the revolution. Famous merchants like Haigazun Bezdigian, Mihran Yolciyan, and Revin Dikran Jeridian began selling arms in Adana. Later, when the incidents began, they were accused of preparing a revolt. Karebet Çalyan, Adana Vak'ası Hakkında Rapor (Report Pertaining to the Adana Incident) (Istanbul, 1911 [1327]), 19–21.

24. David Gaunt, Massacres, Resistance, Protectors: Muslim-Christian Relations in Eastern Anatolia during World War I (Piscataway, NJ: Georgias Press, 2006); Fatma Müge Göçek, "The Decline of the Ottoman Empire and the Emergence of Greek, Armenian, Turkish, and Arab Nationalisms," in Social Constructions of Nationalism in the Middle East, ed. Fatma Müge Göçek (Albany: State University of New York Press, 2002), 15– 83; Fatma Müge Göçek, "Silences in the Turkish Republican Past: An Analysis of Contemporary Turkish-Armenian Literature" (paper presented at a workshop at the Hagop Kevorkian Center for Near Eastern Studies, New York University, 27 October 2003); Fatma Müge Göçek, "Reconstructing the Turkish Historiography on the Armenian Deaths and Massacres of 1915," in Looking Backward, Moving Forward: Confronting the Armenian Genocide, ed. Richard G. Hovannisian (New Brunswick, NS: Transaction Publishers, 2003), 209–30; Taner Akçam, Insan hakları ve Ermeni sorunu (Human Rights and the Armenian Question) (Istanbul: Image Press, 1999); Fatma Müge Göçek, Turk ulusal kimliği ve Ermeni Sorunu (Turkish National Identity and the Armenian Question) (Istanbul: İletişim Publications, 1994); Fatma Müge Göçek, Ermeni Tabsusu Aralanırken: Diyalogdan Başka Bir Çözum Var Mı? (While the Armenian Taboo is Being Cracked: Is There Any Solution Other than a Dialogue?) (Istanbul: Su Publications, 2000); Fatma Müge Göçek, From Empire to Republic: Turkish Nationalism and the Armenian Genocide (New York: Zed Books, 2004); Fatma Müge Göçek, A Shameful Act: The Armenian Genocide and the Question of Turkish Responsibility (New York: Metropolitan Books, 2006); Fatma Müge Göçek, Ermeni Meselesi Hallolunmustur' Osmanli Belgelerine Göre Savas Yillarinda Ermenilere Yönelik Politikalar (The Armenian Issue is Resolved: Policies Toward Armenians During the War Years, Based on Ottoman Documents) (Istanbul: Iletişim Press, 2008); Taner Timur,

Türkler ve Ermeniler: 1915 ve Sonrası (Turks and Armenians: 1915 and Its Aftermath) (Ankara: Image Press, 2001); Fuat Dündar, Ittihat ve Terakki'nin Müslümanları iskan politikası (1913–1918) (The Muslim Settlement Policy of the Union and Progress Party) (Istanbul: Iletişim Press, 2001); Fuat Dündar, Modern Türkiye'nin Şifresi: İttihat Ve Terakki'nin Etnisite Mühendisliği (1913–1918) (The Cipher of Modern Turkey: The Ethnic Engineering of the Union and Progress [1913–1918]) (Istanbul: Iletişim Press, 2008); Fuat Dündar, Crime of Numbers: The Role of Statistics in the Armenian Question (1878–1918) (New Brunswick, NJ: Transaction Publishers, 2010); Selim Deringil, "The Study of the Armenian Crisis of the Late Ottoman Empire, or, 'Seizing the Document by the Throat,' " New Perspectives on Turkey 27 (2002): 35–59; Üngör Uğur Ümit, "When Persecution Bleeds into Mass Murder: The Processive Nature of Genocide," Genocide Studies and Prevention 1, no. 2 (2006): 173–96; Üngör Uğur Ümit, "Seeing like a Nation-State: Young Turk Social Engineering in Eastern Turkey, 1913–1950," Journal of Genocide Research 10, no. 1 (2008): 15–39; Üngör Uğur Ümit, "Geographies of Nationalism and Violence: Towards a New Understanding of Young Turk Social Engineering," in "Demographic Engineering – Part 1," ed. Nikos Sigalas and Alexandre Toumarkine, special issue, European Journal of Turkish Studies 7 (2008), http://www.ejts.org/document2583. html (accessed 24 March 2010). See also the collected essays in Tarih ve Toplum Yeni Yaklaşımlar 5 (Spring 2007). For a review of Turkish liberal historiography, see Bedross Der Matossian, "Venturing in the Minefield: Turkish Liberal Historiography and the Armenian Genocide," in The Armenian Genocide: Cultural and Ethical Legacies, ed. Richard Hovannisian (New Brunswick, NS: Transaction Publishers, 2007), 369–88.

25. Rarely do we see scholars working on the pre-1915 era. See Selim Deringil " 'The Armenian Question is Finally Closed': Mass Conversions of Armenians in Anatolia during the Hamidian Massacres of 1895–1897," Comparative Studies in Society and History 51, no. 2 (2009): 344–71; Meltem Toksöz, "Adana Ermenileri ve 1909 'iğtişâşı' " (Armenians of Adana and the 1909 Revolt), Tarih ve Toplum Yeni Yaklaşımlar 5 (2007): 147–57; and Matthias Bjørnlund, "Adana and Beyond: Revolution and Massacre in the Ottoman Empire Seen through Danish Eyes, 1908/9," Haigazian Armenological Review 30 (2010): 125–56. 26. See, for example, Vahakn N. Dadrian, The History of the Armenian Genocide: Ethnic Conflict from the Balkans to Anatolia to the Caucasus (Providence, RI, and Oxford: Berghahn Books, 1995); Raymond H. Kévorkian, Le génocide des Arméniens (Paris: Jacob, 2006). 27. Esat Uras, Tarihte Ermeniler ve Ermeni Meselesi (Armenians in History and the Armenian Question) (Ankara: Yeni Press, 1950); Salahi Sonyel, İngiliz Gizli Belgelerine Göre Adana'da Vuku Bulan TürkErmeni Olayları (Temmuz 1908-Aralık 1909) (The Turco- Armenian "Adana Incidents" in the Light of Secret British Documents [July 1908– December 1909]) (Ankara: Türk Tarih Kurmum Baismevi, 1988). Even in their memoirs, the Ottoman officials involved in the events at the time argue that Armenians were preparing to establish their Cilician Kingdom. These are Mehmed Asaf (the mutessarif of Cebel-i Bereket), Ali Münif Bey (Adana's deputy in the parliament at the time), and Cemal Paşa (Adana's vali after the massacres). See Mehmet Asaf, 1909 Adana Ermeni Olaylari ve Anılarım (Armenian Incidents of Adana and My Memoirs), yay. haz., Ismet Parmaksizoglu (Ankara: Türk Tarih Kurumu, 1982). Asaf wrote his memoirs in order to exonerate himself from the accusations against him by Bishop Moushegh; Ali Münif Bey, Ali Münif Bey'in hâtıraları (hazırlayan), Taha Toros (Istanbul: İsis Yayımcılık, 1996); and Cemal Paşa, Hatıralar, Ittihat-Terakki ve Birinci Dünya Harbi (Memoirs, the Union and Progress and the First World War), haz. Behçet Cemal (Istanbul: Selek Yayınları, 1959).

28. Vahakn N. Dadrian, "The Circumstances Surrounding the 1909 Adana Holocaust," Armenian Review 41, no. 4 (1988): 1–16; Raymond H. Kévorkian with the collaboration of Paul B. Paboudjian, "Les massacres de Cilicie d'avril 1909," in La Cilicie (1909 1921) de massacres d'Adana au mandat français, ed. Raymond H. Kévorkian, Revue d'histoire Arménienne contemporaine (Tome III, 1999), 7–248; Raymond H. Kévorkian, Le génocide des Arméniens (Paris: Jacob, 2006), 97–150; Raymond H. Kévorkian, "The Cilician Massacres, April 1909," in Armenian Cilicia, ed. Richard G. Hovannisian and Simon Payaslian, UCLA Armenian History and Culture Series: Historic Armenian Cities and Provinces 7 (Costa Mesa, CA: Mazda Publishers, 2008), 339–69.

29. On economic and agricultural centrality, see Meltem Toksöz, "The Çukurova: From Nomadic Life to Commercial Agriculture, 1800–1908" (unpublished doctoral dissertation, SUNY Binghamton University, Binghamton, 2001).

30. The deputy of Adana, Ali Münif Bey, highlights this fact in his memoirs in order to demonstrate the strategic location of Adana for Armenians and the ways in which the Church became a center of revolutionary activities for the Armenian committees. In addition, he argues that during a congress of Orthodox Armenians, who had gathered in Paris in 1905, a decision was taken to establish Cilicia as an independent entity. See Ali Münif Bey, Ali Münif Bey'in hâtıraları, 46–48.

31. Hampartsoom H. Ashjian, Atanayi Yegeherně ew Goniyayi Husher (The Massacres of Adana and the Memoirs of Konya) (New York: Gochnag Press, 1950), 15.

32. Ibid.

33. Hagop Terzian, Atanayi Kiank'ě (The Life of Adana) (Istanbul: Zareh Berberian Press, 1909), 7. For detailed information about the population, see Yeghyayan, Atanayi Hayots' Patmut'iwn, 148–51.

34. Terzian, Atanayi Kiank'ě, 6; David Fraser, The Short Cut to India: The Record of the Journey along the Route of the Baghdad Railway (Edinburgh and London: William Blackwood and Sons, 1909), 80–81; Çalyan, Adana Vak'ası Hakkında Rapor, 6.

35. According to David Fraser, about 70,000 bales of cotton are produced annually in Cilicia. Fraser, The Short Cut to India, 76.

36. Ayhan Aktar, "On Ottoman Public Bureaucracy and the CUP: 1915–1918" (paper presented at The State of the Art of Armenian Genocide Research: Historiography, Sources and Future Directions, Strassler Center for Holocaust and Genocide Studies, Clark University, 8–10 April 2010).

37. Fraser, The Short Cut to India, 77–78.

38. Henry Charles Woods, The Danger Zone of Europe: Changes and Problems in the Near East (Boston: Little, Brown, 1911), 128.

39. Garabed Ashekian, a merchant from Adana, provides detailed information about the Armenian families that were involved in local trade as well as in the fields of import and export. See Yeghyayan, Atanayi Hayots' Patmut'iwn, 157–64. See also Çalyan, Adana Vak'ası Hakkında Rapor, 2–3. The book that Çalyan wrote after the Adana Massacres provides ample information on the ways in which the interethnic relations deteriorated. It also in a sense protests the ways in which justice was served after the massacres by the different military tribunals. Çalyan was a prominent Dashnak leader in Adana and was accused by the mutessarif of Cebel-i Bereket of agitating the masses. See Asaf, 1909 Adana Ermeni Olaylari ve Anılarım, 9.

The Armenian Genocide

40. Çalyan, Adana Vak'ası Hakkında Rapor, 3. Ferriman Duckett, The Young Turks and the Truth about the Holocaust at Adana in Asia Minor, during April, 1909 (London, 1913), 12.

41. "Mukātabāt: Mersin" (Correspondence: Mersin), Lisan al-Hal 5793, 19 August 1908, 3. For detailed information about the event see "Azatut'yan Dōnĕ Gawar. in Mēch: Mersin 28 Hulis" (The Feast of Freedom in the Province), Puzantion 3608, 20 August 1908, 1; "Mukatabāt: Mersin" (Correspondence: Mersin), Lisan al-Hal 5793, 19 August 1908, 3; "Les Province: Lettre d'Adana," The Levant Herald and Eastern Express, 13 August 1908, 2. On the manifestations of the constitution in Adana, see Kudret Emiroğlu, Anadolu'da Devrim Günleri: II. Meşrutiyet'in İlanı, Temmuz-Ağustos 1908 (Revolutionary Days in Anatolia: the Proclamation of the Second Constitution, July August 1908) (Ankara: İmge Kitabevi, 1999), 188–93.

42. Terzian, Atanayi Kiank'ĕ, 35.

43. On Abdülkadir Bağdadizade and his anti-Armenian sentiments, see Çalyan, Adana Vak'ası Hakkında Rapor, 40–41.

44. Moushegh Seropian, Atanayi Jardĕ ew Pataskhanatunerĕ: nakhent'ats' paraganer (The Massacres of Adana and the Accountable People: Precedent Circumstances) (Gahire: Tparan Ararat-S. Darbinean, 1909), 19.

45. Çalyan, Adana Vak'ası Hakkında Rapor, 17.

46. Ibid.

47. During the reign of Bahri Paşa all three (Ihsan Fikri, Abdülkadir Bağdadizade, and Gergerlizade) were exiled. Some returned with Bahri Paşa's aid. See L. Papazian, "Shahekan Tesaktsut'iwn mĕ Atanayi Nakhkin Vali Pahri Bashayi Hed" (An Interesting Meeting with the Previous Vali of Adana Bahri Pasha), Jamanag 191, 15 June 1909, 1–2.

48. Ali Münif Bey, the deputy of Adana, describes the tension between Ali Gergerlizade and Ihsan Fikri and mentions that Bishop Moushegh sat on the committee that replaced Fikri with Gergerlizade. Ali Münif Bey, Ali Münif Bey'in hâtıraları, 49.

49. Terzian, Atanayi Kiank'ĕ, 36. Ali Münif Bey argues that Armenians benefited from this tension between the two groups. Ali Münif Bey, Ali Münif Bey'in hâtıraları, 50.

50. Çalyan, Adana Vak'ası Hakkında Rapor, 22.

51. Ibid., 41.

52. Ibid., 43.

53. F. D. Shepard, "Personal Experience in Turkish Massacres and Relief Work," The Journal of Race Development 1 (1910–1911): 327.

54. Interview with Dr. Christie of Tarsus (from an Armenian newspaper), 13 August 1909, American Board of Commissioners for Foreign Missions (ABCFM) Archives, 2.

55. "Mulhakat: Mersinden Bir Mektup" (A Letter from Mersin), İtidal 39, 12 May 1909 (29 Nisan 1325), 2–3. This report also appeared in Arabic. See "Riwayat Istiqlāl al-Arman" (The Story of the Independence of Armenians), al-Ittihad al-'Uthmani 29, 31 May 1909, 3. Mehmet Asaf also discusses the play arguing that it was the first sign of the uprising. See Asaf, 1909 Adana Ermeni Olayları ve Anılarım, 7–8, 27–28.

56. Asaf, 1909 Adana Ermeni Olayları ve Anılarım, 27.

57. İtidal's information about the play and its content is totally misleading. The real title of the play was Sev Hogher kam Hetin Gisher Araratyan (Black Soil and the Nights of Ararat). The play is a tragedy written by Armenian poet and playwright Bedros Turian (1851–1872). The original play is found in the Armenian Patriarchate of Jerusalem. It was performed for the first time in the Osmaniye Theater in Gedig Paşa on 6 March 1871. The ad was first published on the front page of the Menzume-i Efkâr on 5 March 1871. The play was first published after the Young Turk Revolution of 1908. The subject and plot totally differ in the original from the subject that was reported in İtidal. For the whole play, see Petros Duryan, Erkeri zhoghovatsu (Collection of Works) (Yerevan: Haykakan SSH GA Hratarakch'ut'yun, 1971), 1: 67–131.

58. "Mulhakat: Mersinden Bir Mektup," 3.

59. Helen Davenport (Brown) Gibbons, The Red Rugs of Tarsus: A Women's Record of the Armenian Massacre of 1909 (New York: The Century, 1917), 98.

60. Çalyan, Adana Vak'ası Hakkında Rapor, 3.

61. Ikdam dismissed these reports from the provinces as total fabrication for political aims. See Ikdam, 21 October 1908, 3. Asaf also said that Bishop Moushegh was complaining to the central government against local officials and spreading false rumors about threats against Armenians. Asaf, 1909 Adana Ermeni Olaylari ve Anılarım, 32, 34.

62. Moushegh Seropian, Atanayi Jardě ew Pataskhanatuneṛě, 26.

63. Thomas D. Christie to Mr. Peet, Tarsus, 6 May 1909, ABCFM Archives, 1. As a matter of fact, Christie provides one of the most excised accounts of the deterioration of the ethnic tensions after the revolution.

64. Moushegh Seropian, Atanayi Jardě ew Pataskhanatuneṛě, 32.

65. According to the mutessarif of Cebel-i Bereket, the weapons were brought from Cyprus to be distributed to the Armenians of Adana by convincing them that the Turks were going to kill them. Asaf, 1909 Adana Ermeni Olaylari ve Anılarım, 7.

66. Interview with Christie of Tarsus, ABCFM Archives, 2.

67. The deputy of Adana accused him of agitating the revolutionary activities of the Armenians in Adana. See Ali Münif Bey, Ali Münif Bey'in hâtıraları, 49; Asaf, 1909 Adana Ermeni Olaylari ve Anılarım, 5–7. Asaf accused him of being a member of the Dashnak party and planning for the establishment of the Kingdom of Cilicia. In his booklet composed of two letters sent to the First Military Tribunal, Artin Arslanian exonerates Bishop Moushegh of all charges saying that on the contrary he appealed for the unity of elements (ittihad-i al-anasır). The booklet furthermore criticizes the ways in which justice was performed. Arslanian himself was imprisoned by the First Military Court and, under torture, had confessed that the aim of the Armenian agitation was to establish the Kingdom of Cilicia. Artin Arslanian, Adana'da Adalet Nasıl Mahkûm Oldu (Comment la justice a été condamnée á Adana) (Le Caire – El-Kâhire, 1909 [1325]), 11.

68. Çalyan, Adana Vak'ası Hakkında Rapor, 3. Another account says that two days before the events Hovhannes escaped to Cyprus and from there to Cairo. See Asaf, 1909 Adana Ermeni Olaylari ve Anılarım, 10.

69. Çalyan, Adana Vak'ası Hakkında Rapor, 13–14.

70. Hagop Terzian, Kilikioy Aghetě: akanatesi nkaragrut'iwnner, vawerat'ught'er, pashtonakan teghekagirner, t'ght'akts'ut'iwnner, vichakagrut'iwnner, amenen karewor patkernerov (The Catastrophe of Cilicia: Eyewitness Accounts, Documents, Official

Reports, Correspondence, Census, with theMost Important Pictures) (Istanbul, 1912), 18–19; Çalyan, *Adana Vakʾası Hakkında Rapor*, 14–16; Asaf, *1909 Adana Ermeni Olaylari ve Anılarım*, 10–11.

71. Stephen R. Trowbridge to William Peet, 20 April 1909, ABCFM Archives, 1; Çalyan, *Adana Vakʾası Hakkında Rapor*, 25.

72. Thomas D. Christie to William Peet, Tarsus, 6 May 1909, ABCFM Archives, 2.

73. Terzian, *Kilikioy Aghetĕ*, 20.

74. Çalyan, *Adana Vakʾası Hakkında Rapor*, 47.

75. Kévorkian, *La Cilicie (1909–1921) de Massacres d'Adana au mandat français*, 139. Çalyan, *Adana Vakʾası Hakkında Rapor*, 47–49. Even during the parliamentary debates in the post-massacre period, Armenian deputies in the Ottoman parliament understood the telegram that was sent by Adil Bey as an order to massacre the Armenians. For example, Armenian deputy Krikor Zohrab discussed the issue saying, "I saw the telegram from the Ministry of the Interior of which complaint has been made, and its purport was in keeping with the traditions of the old regime. It did not say 'Kill the Armenians,' but 'restore order.' The hon. Members know that that was the formula used under the despotic regime; formulas depend upon their interpretations and it is certain that the phrase, 'Keep order and protect the foreigners and banks in particular,' would be misunderstood there." Summary of the Debate in the Chamber of Deputies on the Adana Massacres, in Sir G. Lowther to Sir Edward Grey (received 11 May 1909), Constantinople, 4 May 1909, inclosure, no. 84.

76. Ben ne yapabilirim. Mâdemki Meşrû tiyet vardır. Ekseriyet-i âhâli ne isterse öyle yapar. The quote is attributed to the vali of Adana, Cevad Bey. See Çalyan, *Adana Vakʾası Hakkında Rapor*, 30.

77. On the seasonal migration see Toksöz, "Adana Ermenileri ve 1909 'iğtişâşı,' " 148–49.

78. Başıbozuks were literary known as "damaged head" meaning "disorderly" and were irregular soldiers of the Ottoman army. They were armed and maintained by the government but did not receive pay. They did not wear uniforms or distinctive badges. They were notorious for being brutal and undisciplined, thus giving the term its second, colloquial meaning of "undisciplined bandit" in many languages.

79. All Muslims who participated in the massacres were wearing the white hatbands round the fez. See Doughty-Wylie to Sir G. Lowther, Adana, 3 May 1909, inclosure 4, no. 96; Çalyan, *Adana Vakʾası Hakkında Rapor*, 29.

80. Lawson P. Chambers to William Peet, 4 May 1909, ABCFM Archives, 1. Lawson Chambers was the nephew of Nisbet Chambers, a Canadian-British subject, head of the American Mission in Adana.

81. Herbert Adam Gibbons to Doughty-Wylie, Mersina, 2 May 1909, ABCFM Archives, 1. Gibbons provides in the letter a lengthy account of the incidents that occurred during the first waves of massacres.

82. The Fellahs are "Turkified" Arabs who are the descendants of the Egyptian Fellahin and brought to work in the cotton fields of Cilicia.

83. P. Rigal, "Adana. Les massacres d'Adana," *Lettres d'Ore, relations d'Orient* (revue confidentielle des missions jésuites éditée par le siege de Lyon et publiée a` Bruxelles, Novembre 1909), 143; Shepard, "Personal Experience in Turkish Massacres," 328.

Historical Background

84. Duckett, The Young Turks and the Truth about the Holocaust at Adana, 24.

85. See F. W. Macallum to Dr. J. L. Barton, Adana, 19 April 1909, ABCFM Archives, 2. Macallum provides a detailed report based on the various notes made by Rev. W. N. Chambers.

86. Lawson P. Chambers to William Peet, 4 May 1909, ABCFM Archives, 8.

87. See F. W. Macallum to Dr. J. L. Barton, 5; Terzian, Kilikioy Aghetĕ, 54.

88. For a detailed list of the casualties and deaths, see Stephen R. Trowbridge to William Peet, 21 April 1909, ABCFM Archives.

89. For a detailed account of the damaged places, see Çalyan, Adana Vak'ası Hakkında Rapor, 31.

90. Hag-Ter, "Atanayi Yergrord Jartĕ" (The Second Massacre of Adana), Jamanag 179, 1 June 1909, 1–2. See also the lengthy article of Suren Bartevian, "Hayots Dēm Zrpartut'iwnk' ew 'İtidal'i Stut'iwnnerĕ " (False Accusations against Armenians and the Falsifications of İtidal), Puzantion 3831, 19 May 1909, 1; Doughty-Wylie to Sir G. Lowther, Adana, 2 May 1909, inclosure 2, no. 96.

91. Fikri was tried by the Military Tribunal [Dîvân-i Harb-i Örfî] and sentenced to two years in exile for agitating the public during the massacres. From his exile in Alexandria he wrote to the Ministry of Internal Affairs complaining about the unjust accusations against him and the unfair trial. See Fikri to the High Commissioner of Egypt, 21 October 1909 (Teşrîn-i Evvel 1325), DH.MUİ.23–2/21_4 and DH.MUİ.23–2/21_5 (archives).

92. See Doughty-Wyllie to Sir G. Lowther, Adana, 2 May 1909. See also Çalyan, Adana Vak'ası Hakkında Rapor, 10–13.

93. Asaf, 1909 Adana Ermeni Olayları ve Anılarım, 21–25.

94. See Doughty-Wylie to Sir G. Lowther, Adana, 21 April 1909, inclosure 1, no. 83.

95. On the premeditated nature of the massacres see DH.MKT, 2854/6. The document includes a copy of the telegram submitted by the governmental and parliamentary investigation commission which was sent to Adana and which indicates clearly that the incidents were part of a premeditated plan (evvelce tertib ve ittihâz edilmiş bir plan). The report was submitted to the Sublime Porte on 16 June 1909 (3 Haziran 1325). For Mustafa Remzi Pasha, see Grand Vezir Hüseyn Hilmi, telegram to the Council of Ministers, 1456, 14 July 1909. See also Ministry of Internal Affairs, telegram to the Administration of Adana, 14 July 1909 (Temmuz 1325), DH.MKT, 2875/81. Doughty-Wylie argued that the fact that the massacres were perpetrated on the same day in distant places shows that the authorities knew of the intended massacre beforehand. Doughty-Wylie to Sir G. Lowther, Adana, 21 April 1909.

96. Ismail Sefa was an officer in the provincial administration.

97. The arguments made by Ihsan Fikri and his friends can be found in Çalyan, Adana Vak'ası Hakkında Rapor, 32–34.

98. Ismail Sefa, "Müdhiş bir Isyân" (An Awful Uprising), İtidal 33, 7 April 1909 (25 Mart 1325), 1–2.

99. Burhan Nuri, "Ermeniler Hükümet Teşkil Edebilirler mı" (Can Armenians Form a Government), İtidal 33, 7 April 1909 (25 Mart 1325), 1–2. Even after the second wave of massacres, Fikri continued to claim that the main reason for the disturbances was the Armenians' quest to establish their kingdom. See Ihsan Fikri, "Ermeni Hemşerilerimize:

The Armenian Genocide

İtilafa Doğru" (To Our Compatriot Armenians: Toward Entente), İtidal 37, 4 May 1909 (18 Nisan 1325), 1–2.

100. "Vilayat Havadisi" (Incidents in the Province), İtidal 33, 7 April 1909 (25 Mart 1325), 2.

101. Arslanian, who lived among Armenians for four years, had not found any desires by the local population for separation because such a thing would have been impossible. Arslanian, Adana'da Adalet Nasıl Mahkûm Oldu, 17. The same argument was made by Çalyan, who claimed that after the revolution the Armenian committees did not have any desire to promote separatist tendencies and that it would have been impossible to separate because they did not form a majority in any of the provinces. On the contrary, he argues that their first task became to preach brotherhood among all the elements of the empire. Çalyan, Adana Vak'ası Hakkında Rapor, 14, 18–19. On the other hand, Mehmed Asaf argues that Moushegh brought Armenians from Maraş, Zeytun, Van, Harput, Diyarbekir, Bitlis and had been seeking to settle them in Adana in order to alter the demographic composition. Asaf, 1909 Adana Ermeni Olayları ve Anılarım, 24.

102. "Vilayat Havadisi," 2.

103. Terzian, Kilikioy Aghetě, 94.

104. See Doughty-Wylie to Sir G. Lowther, Adana, 7 May 1909, inclosure 3, no. 103. The vice-consul argues that some of the Roumeliot soldiers indicated that the shots that were fired at them and started the whole affair had been fired by Turks either with the wish to bring about a quarrel between the different sorts of soldiers or to raise more hope to rush the hated Armenian Quarter. See also Woods, The Danger Zone of Europe, 135.

105. Hampartsoum H Ashjian, Atanayi Yegehernĕ ew Goniyayi Husher (The Massacres of Adana and the Memoirs of Konya) (New York: Gochnag Press, 1950), 55. See also Lawson P. Chambers to William Peet, 4 May 1909, ABCFM Archives, 10.

106. Woods, The Danger Zone of Europe, 137.

107. See note 95 above.

108. See Ministry of Internal Affairs, telegram to the Vilayet of Adana, 11 July 1909 (28 Haziran 1325), DH.MKT, 2872/68.

109. See Ministry of Internal Affairs, telegram to the Prime Minister, 12 July 1909 (29 Haziran 1325), DH.MKT, 2873/58.

110. Çalyan is extremely cynical in terms of the way that justice was achieved in Adana. See Çalyan, Adana Vak'ası Hakkında Rapor, 36–55. The phase of the court martials, the Military Tribunals, and the government/parliamentary investigation commissions is the subject of a separate study. The trials were conducted in a manner unsatisfactory to the Armenians, who were extremely angry when the court's decision was announced. Nine Muslims and six Armenians were subjected to capital punishment in the autumn of 1909. In addition, twenty-five Muslims were hung in December 1909. These included the mufti of Bahçe. Armenians condemned the court for hanging six innocent Armenians. Articles and booklets were written denouncing the court's decision. Kassab Missak, one of the Armenians who were hung became the symbol of injustice for Armenians. Some even represented him as the Armenian Dreyfus. See Arslanian, Adana'da Adalet Nasıl Mahkûm Oldu, 13. Armenian sources also indicated that some of the Turkish peasants who were hung were innocent. The real culprits of the Adana Massacres escaped justice. Besides the Military Tribunals, two other official bodies were sent to Adana on May 12 to investigate

the massacres. Faiz Bey and Harutiwn Mosdichian were sent on behalf of the government by the Ministry of Justice, and Hagop Babigian and Yusuf Kemal Bey were sent by the parliament. Babigian and Kemal Bay were accompanied by the mutessarif of Mersin. Both bodies conducted their investigations in Adana and were supposed to send their official reports to their respective bodies. On Babigian's report, see Hagop Babigian, Atanayi Egherně (The Massacres of Adana) (Istanbul: Ardzagang Press, 1919); Yusuf Kemal Tengirşenk, Vatan Hizmetinde (Istanbul: Bahar Matbaası, 1967), 110–24.

111. Arslanian, Adana'da Adalet Nasıl Mahkûm Oldu, 12. Other sources provide the number 41 for the Muslims who were hung. See 1909 Adana Olaylari, http://www.adanayorum.com/haber_detay. asp?haber=14896 (accessed 29 April 2009).

112. See, for example, War Ministry, telegram to the Ministry of Internal Affairs, 23 November 1909 (10 Teşrîn-i Sânî 1325), DH.MUİ, 43–1/32_2. The same orders were sent to Adana on 25 November 1909 (11 Teşrîn-i Sânî, 1325). See DH.MUİ, 43–1/32_1; War Ministry, telegram to the Ministry of Internal Affairs, 22 November 1909 (9 Teşrîn-i Sânî, 1325), DH.MUİ, 43–1/23_2. The same orders were sent to Adana on 23 November 1909 (10 Teşrîn-i Sânî, 1325). See DH.MUİ, 43–1/23_1.

Viewpoint 3

Did the Armenian Genocide Inspire Hitler?
Hannibal Travis

In this viewpoint, the author discusses the influence of the Armenian genocide upon Hitler. The Nazi invasion of Poland and the Holocaust are described in historical context. In particular, the author explores differences of opinion among scholars about whether Hitler's beliefs, writing, and speeches include overt references to the extermination of the Armenians. Hannibal Travis is a professor at Florida International University College of Law, where he has taught Intellectual Property, Copyright Law, Computer and Internet Law, and more, and does research in cyberlaw, intellectual property, antitrust, telecommunications, and human rights law. He is also author of the 2010 book Genocide in the Middle East: The Ottoman Empire, Iraq and Sudan.

It is well known by genocide scholars that in 1939 Adolf Hitler urged his generals to exterminate members of the Polish race.[1] "Who speaks today of the extermination of the Armenians?" Hitler asked, just a week before the September 1, 1939 invasion of Poland.[2] However, while it is generally agreed that Hitler was well aware of the Armenian genocide,[3] some genocide scholars and historians of the Ottoman Empire have questioned whether he actually made the above statement or even intended to exterminate portions of the "Polish race."[4]

Still, there is evidence that the massacre of the Ottoman Armenians helped persuade the Nazis that national minorities

"Did the Armenian Genocide Inspire Hitler? Turkey, Past and Future," by Hannibal Travis, The Middle East Forum, 2013. Reprinted by Permission.

posed a threat to empires dominated by an ethnic group such as the Germans or the Turks. Furthermore, these minorities could be exterminated to the benefit of the perpetrator with little risk. Indeed, it was German officials who had smuggled out of the Ottoman Empire the leaders of the Young Turk regime, culpable for the deaths of over a million Armenians and a million or more other Christian minorities such as the Assyrians and Greeks.[5] Diverse historical evidence suggests that Hitler viewed the Armenians and Poles as analogous; in several ways, his statement about the Armenians was consistent with his other beliefs and writings.

The Assassin's Leak

The historical context of Hitler's statement and the manner in which it came to Western attention has long been problematic. On November 24, 1945, *The Times* of London published an article stating that Hitler referred to the extermination of the Armenians during an address to his commanders-in-chief on August 22, 1939, a statement that was read at a hearing of the Nuremberg trial. Hitler's speech asserted that the

> *aim of the war is not to attain certain lines, but consists in the physical destruction of the opponent. Thus, for the time being, I have sent to the East only my "Death's Head units" with the order to kill without pity or mercy all men, women, and children of Polish race or language. Only in such a way, will we win the vital living space that we need. Who still talks nowadays of the extermination of the Armenians?*[6]

The anti-Nazi writer Louis Lochner, a former bureau chief of the Associated Press in Berlin, quoted Hitler's statement from an original Nazi document before the Nuremberg trials had even convened.[7] Lochner had a variety of sources within the Nazi government and had been interned from December 1941 to May 1942 before being exchanged for German diplomats interned in the United States. After his release, he published *What about Germany?* containing the quote mentioning the Armenians.[8] The quote was

The Armenian Genocide

used in the November 1945 *The Times* article, which cited the ongoing proceedings of the Nuremberg trials.

Two additional copies of the memorandum describing Hitler's speech were found immediately after the war in the files of the Oberkommando der Wehrmacht (German High Command, OKW), but neither contained the Armenian quote. Nor was either military document signed as would be expected for an official record of a meeting. These incongruities led Nuremberg prosecutors to conclude that there had been two Hitler speeches on August 22 and that the Lochner version containing the quote was a merger of notes from both. As a result of the disparities, objections were made by lawyers for two Nuremberg defendants, Hermann Göring and Erich Raeder, to the authenticity of the OKW versions and to the inclusion of the Lochner document in evidence. The key issue for the defense was not the Armenian quote per se but rather the term "brutal measures," which they claimed was never used by Hitler although they conceded that he had used "severe" expressions.[9]

Since the prosecution had other records of the meetings, as well as one introduced by defendant Raeder, the Lochner document was included in the trial record but was not introduced as evidence. In the context of the Nuremberg trials, the overriding issue was not the Armenian quote but Hitler's call for a brutal war of aggression against Poland. But defenders of the Ottoman Empire regard the court's decision as key: The military versions of Hitler's speech without the quote are viewed as more reliable, and the Lochner version as suspect or tainted.[10]

The question of Lochner's source for the document, and hence the quote, has therefore been the crux of intense historical interest. Lochner himself indicated only that he had obtained it from "Mr. Maass" without saying who the original source was at the August 22, 1939 meeting. But subsequent research had shown that the Lochner and *The Times* versions have a clear chain of transmission.[11] The original source of Hitler's speech on the Poles and the Armenians and of its transmission to *The Times* was Wilhelm Canaris,[12] head of the Abwehr, a German military intelligence organization, and a leading figure in the military opposition to Hitler. Canaris became involved with several conspiracies against the dictator, including a July 20, 1944 assassination plot. Another member of the German resistance, Hans Bernd Gisevius, confirmed that Canaris took notes of the speech even though it was "forbidden to do so."[13]

Canaris's notes were passed to three men, all of whom were executed before the Nuremberg trials convened and thus could not be questioned: Hans Oster, Ludwig Beck, and Hermann Maass. Historian Kevork Bardakjian concluded that Canaris likely passed the notes to his deputy, Oster, who then transmitted them to Beck, a conservative general and former chief of the General Staff, who had long opposed Nazi influence on the German military and foreign policy. Beck probably instructed Maass, formerly general manager of the Reich Committee of German Youth Associations, to give the document to Lochner due to Beck's role as a "leader of the German resistance." Like Canaris, Beck was involved in a number of conspiracies and was executed after the failure of the July 20, 1944 plot to assassinate Hitler, in which he had a leading role.[14] Finally, historian Winfried Baumgart has argued that Canaris's notes also appear to have been the source of the two unsigned documents in the German high command files.[15]

Gisevius and Oster believed that the invasion of Poland gave them a unique chance to get rid of Hitler and ensure peace with Poland.[16] Canaris's opposition to Hitler was wide-ranging. An official with British intelligence boasted of having "buil[t] … up" Canaris as a potential assassin of Hitler.[17] In 1944, the Gestapo found documents revealing Canaris to be conspiring with Catholics and the West against Hitler. The admiral was executed in a concentration camp on April 9, 1945, for plotting a coup against Hitler, along with Oster.[18]

Turkish Historians on the "Armenian Quote"

Hitler's citation of the Armenians in his August 22, 1939 meeting has been an important concern for Turkish historians and pro-

The Armenian Genocide

Ottoman analysts. Türkkaya Ataöv of Ankara University, with the apparent endorsement of the Turkish government, has contended that the Armenian quote does not appear in Nuremberg documents and is a forgery. He goes further to assert that no Armenian genocide took place, that Armenians had collaborated with the Nazis, and that Turks had welcomed Jews.[19]

Similarly, Princeton University professor Heath Lowry suggested in 1985 that the lack of clear evidence that Hitler's alleged statement about the Armenians was "authentic" should have put an end to attempts to recognize the Armenian genocide in exhibits of the U.S. Holocaust Memorial Museum, resolutions of the U.S. Congress, or in the curricula on the Holocaust established by state boards of education. The logical outcome, Lowry argued, was that the Armenian genocide was simply a type of "propaganda" and "vilification against the Republic of Turkey."[20] Finally, Guenter Lewy, professor emeritus of the University of Massachusetts at Amherst, has contended that any attempt to link the anti-Armenian massacres and the Holocaust rests "on a shaky factual foundation." But Lewy has conceded that the document containing Hitler's statement about the Armenians might "represent an embellishment of points made in the speech" by Hitler to his generals in August 1939.[21]

In contrast, in a notable 1995 article in *Holocaust and Genocide Studies*, Roger W. Smith, Eric Markusen, and Robert Lifton argued that Lowry was being professionally irresponsible in claiming that the Armenian genocide was simply a "ludicrous" Armenian claim. In their view, it was the more recent claim that Hitler did not refer to the Armenian genocide that lacked an evidentiary basis.[22] Moreover, they demonstrate that Lowry, like historian Justin McCarthy, had engaged in a pattern of protesting academic characterizations of the Armenian genocide that was welcomed by the Turkish government.[23] According to *Inside Higher Education*, McCarthy once called the Armenian genocide a "meaningless" idea and served on the board of a grant-making organization in Washington, D.C., the Institute for Turkish Studies, which has ties to the Turkish government. McCarthy argues that the Armenian case is dissimilar to the Holocaust and resembles the U.S. Civil War.[24]

One of Lewy's preferred sources for Hitler's speech were the copies from the OKW, used by Nuremberg prosecutors to demonstrate command responsibility for numerous crimes in Poland. Lewy has argued that Hitler's statement about the Armenians was not "accepted as evidence by the Nuremberg Tribunal," citing Lowry to this effect.[25] Ankara University's Ataöv similarly asserted: "Hundreds of thousands of captured Nazi documents were assembled as evidence in the trial of the major Nazi war criminals. One cannot find the oft-repeated Hitler 'statement' among these documents."[26] The idea that the Hitler quote is a forgery and that it does not appear in the Nuremberg trial documents is frequently repeated on websites dedicated to denial of the Armenian genocide.

While the Lochner document was not used at Nuremberg, even Lowry admits that volume VII of the compilation of evidence against the Nazis, entitled *Nazi Conspiracy and Aggression*, reproduced the statement.[27] That compilation contained in its introduction a description of the document series as the tribunal's "documentary evidence demonstrating the criminality of the former leaders of the German Reich."[28] This means that the document was introduced as evidence before the International Military Tribunal at Nuremberg even if it was not used on a specific day of the trials. The Lochner document with the Armenia quote was also included in the 1961 publication of foreign policy documents by the German Foreign Office.[29]

The Armenian Genocide as Nazi Precedent

As part of a larger effort to deny or downplay the Armenian genocide, some historians have claimed that Hitler did not cite the Armenians as an example of the impunity of perpetrators. They have also denied that the Armenian genocide provided the inspiration or any form of precedent for the design and conduct of Nazi aggression and genocide.

The Armenian Genocide

One method has been to suggest that the Nazi program of extermination was a late creation. Thus, for example, Lewy suggested that Hitler did not order exterminations in Poland—or mention the extermination of the Armenians—because "by August 1939, Hitler had not yet decided upon the destruction of the Jews."[30]

This argument is unpersuasive for several reasons. First, as has been shown, there are compelling reasons to believe that Hitler's statements about extermination in 1939 indeed cited the Armenians and were aimed at the Poles. Hitler's intentions toward the Jews had been spelled out across many statements, including in the notorious January 1939 speech in which Hitler "prophesied" that another world war would result in the "annihilation of the Jewish race in Europe." Second, Hitler had repeatedly engaged in virulent anti-Polish and anti-Slavic rhetoric prior to August 1939.[31] Third, Hitler's decision to destroy Poland as a nation, while allowing some Poles to survive, was entirely consistent with his political philosophy that nations played out a chaotic struggle for life in an unforgiving world, as shown by history. Finally, there was the tacit acquiescence of the major powers in the Turkish model of ethnic cleansing and genocide. These may have provided Hitler with reasons to adopt it for Poland and the East.

To what extent was the Armenian genocide understood as a model by Hitler? In a 1931 interview, he told a German newspaper editor that when deciding Germany's future, one should "[t]hink of the biblical deportations and the massacres of the Middle Ages (Rosenberg refers to them) and remember the extermination of the Armenians."[32] Hitler and other contemporary European leaders admired Mustafa Kemal Atatürk as a national leader who won for the Turkish people the living space it needed from the Slavs and the British. Speaking in 1925, Hitler "dwelt at length on patriotism and national pride and quoted approvingly the role of Kemal Atatürk of Turkey and the example of Mussolini, who had marched on Rome" a few weeks prior.[33]

The parallels between Hitler and Atatürk were also noted at the time. The influential *Foreign Affairs* journal published an article in the 1930s stating, "Just as in Italy since 1922, and as in Germany since early in the present year, the conduct of political affairs in Turkey rests today on the personality of a leader. ... By means of a clever scheme ... the President, while constitutionally without undue influence, becomes the real autocrat.'" It argued that with the end of foreign "influence," Turkey "had become an almost homogeneous state" in "national and religious" terms, so that its "Christian minorities hardly existed any longer."[34] In early 1939, the German socialists had also pointed out the similarity between the Nazis and past leaders of Turkey.[35] Three days after the speech reported by Canaris, Hitler wrote to Mussolini that he hoped that the Turks could be persuaded to join Italy, Japan, and Russia in an anti-British coalition.[36] He planned to hand over parts of the southern Soviet Union to Turkey in due time.[37]

The fate of the Armenians was also understood within Nazi ideology. A key influence on Hitler was the Prussian-educated British writer Houston Stewart Chamberlain. His work *Foundations of the Nineteenth Century* sold 250,000 copies by 1938 and secured his fame in Germany.[38] Volume 1 of this work offered a model for Germany, arguing that Turkey was "the last little corner of Europe in which a whole people lives in undisturbed prosperity and happiness," and blaming non-German world powers (Britain and France) for encouraging an Armenian rebellion, in response to which "the otherwise humane Moslem rises and destroys the disturber of the peace."[39]

In 1927, leading Nazi theorist Alfred Rosenberg had published a booklet calling Chamberlain the "apostle and founder of a German future."[40] In 1938, Rosenberg published a collection of speeches in which he commented that in 1921, after the Turkish minister Talat Pasha was murdered in Berlin by an Armenian, a campaign was waged in the "international press" to release the killer due to the history of struggle between Armenians and Turks.[41] Rosenberg endorsed the Turks' resistance to Armenian claims for autonomy ("*den armenischen Staat im Staat*"), comparing the Armenians to the Jews, because he claimed the Armenians engaged in espionage

The Armenian Genocide

against Turkey as the Jews did against Germany.[42] He "praised Talat Pasha … [and] minimized the [Ottoman Christian] genocide."[43]

Rosenberg also introduced Max Erwin von Scheubner-Richter to Hitler. Scheubner-Richter had been the German vice-consul in Erzerum and documented the planning and implementation of the murder of Armenians by the Young Turks in the name of Islam and pan-Turkic ideology. Scheubner-Richter's relationship to Hitler was so close that he was killed standing next to Hitler and Rosenberg during the failed Munich "Beer Hall" putsch of 1923. Hitler then dedicated the first part of *Mein Kampf* to his "irreplaceable" fallen comrade.[44] Armenian-American historian Vahkan Dadrian has argued that Scheubner-Richter had a "direct" influence on Hitler that may have included introducing him to the example of how the Ottoman Armenians (then called the "Jews of the Orient") were deported from their villages, worked to death, starved, and frozen to death during exposure to harsh winter conditions.[45] Mike Joseph has called Scheubner-Richter the "personal link from [the Armenian] genocide to Hitler."[46] Scheubner-Richter's reports regarding the genocidal solution to the Armenian question foreshadow and may have inspired Hitler's later ideas and rhetoric regarding the Jews as did his descriptions of Turkish methods, including provocations and allegations of terrorism and revolution. Prior to his death, Scheubner-Richter urged that Germany be "cleansed" of alien peoples by "ruthless" measures.[47]

Other high-ranking Nazis were also well-placed to learn how the Armenian genocide occurred and to inform Hitler. Franz von Papen became Hitler's vice chancellor after serving as chief of staff of the Fourth Turkish Army during World War I and was responsible for managing German-Austrian and German-Turkish relations under the Nazis. Rudolf Hess, deputy inspector of concentration camps under Himmler, had served in the Ottoman-German forces fighting the Russians during World War I. Hans von Seeckt was chief of the Ottoman General Staff in 1917 and 1918 and "laid the groundwork for the later emergence of the Third Reich's Wehrmacht" and "embraced Hitler and his ideology."[48]

The similarity of the genocidal methods employed by the Nazis and the Ottomans is also inescapable. Parallels between Ottoman and Nazi theory and practice include the central place of race in the self-conception of the fascist elites and the notion of relocating ethnic minorities to reservations. Hitler often expressed his belief that race was the dominant independent variable in history and that it had to be dealt with directly by any ethnonationalist leader who wanted to be successful.[49] "When the race is in danger of being oppressed," he wrote, "the question of legality plays only a secondary role."[50]

Both the Ottomans and the Nazis also used the concept of ethnic "cleaning" or "cleansing." While the Young Turks implemented a "clean sweep of internal enemies—the indigenous Christians," according to the then-German ambassador in Constantinople,[51] the Nazis implemented a "housecleaning of Jews, intelligentsia, clergy, and the nobility."[52] The official who announced the ethnic cleansing plan for Poland may have been aware of similar policies of the internal security officials of the Ottoman Empire, which resulted in "hundreds of thousands of the Ottoman Empire's Muslims, Christian Armenians, and Orthodox Greeks [being] expelled or murdered."[53] Hitler himself used "cleaning" or "cleansing" as a euphemism for extermination[54] and described his rule as being characterized by an "unheard of cleansing process."[55] On December 12, 1941, Joseph Goebbels wrote in his diary that "with respect of the Jewish question, the Führer has decided to make a clean sweep."[56] Finally, the impunity with which the Armenians had been slaughtered—the essence of Hitler's August 22, 1939 remark—was reinforced by the international community's failure to prevent the massacre of other peoples, including later massacres by the Italians using poison-gas and machine-guns in Ethiopia.[57]

Conclusion

Numerous ideological and political influences led from the Armenian genocide to the rape of Poland and the Holocaust. Chamberlain, Hess, Rosenberg, Seeckt, Scheubner-Richter, and von

The Armenian Genocide

Papen all likely played a role in prompting Hitler to use Turkey's example as a model for Poland. Hitler compared the two cases in his 1939 speech, which, like most evidence that the Holocaust took place, was not relied upon in the tribunal's judgment.[58] Subsequent efforts to discredit the speech by defenders of the Ottoman Empire should not, however, blind us to the manifold connections between the Armenian genocide and that perpetrated by the Nazis.

Notes

1. Adam Jones, *Genocide: A Comprehensive Introduction*, 2nd ed. (London: Routledge, 2010), p. 149.

2. *Akten zur deutschen auswärtigen Politik 1918-1945*, Federal Republic of Germany, Federal Foreign Office, ser. D, vol. 7, 1961, p. 193, fn. 1; Louis P. Lochner, *What about Germany?* (London: Hodder and Stoughton, 1943), p. 12.

3. Jones, *Genocide*, p. 173.

4. Heath W. Lowry, "The U.S. Congress and Adolf Hitler on the Armenians," *Political Communication and Persuasion*, 3, 1985, pp. 111-39.

5. Vahakn Dadrian, "The Armenian Genocide in German and Austrian Sources," in Israel Charny, ed., *The Widening Circle of Genocide*, vol. 3 (New Brunswick: Transaction, 1994), pp. 122-4.

6. *Nazi Conspiracy and Aggression*, vol. 7, U.S. Chief Counsel for the Prosecution of Axis Criminality (Washington, D.C.: Govt. Printing Office, 1946), p. 753.

7. Lowry, "The U.S. Congress and Adolf Hitler on the Armenians," pp. 113-4, 121.

8. Lochner, *What About Germany?* pp. 11-2.

9. Kevork B. Bardakjian, *Hitler and the Armenian Genocide* (Toronto: Zoryan Institute, 1985), pp. 14-5, 18.

10. Lowry, "The U.S. Congress and Adolf Hitler on the Armenians," p. 116.

11. Bardakjian, *Hitler and the Armenian Genocide*, pp. 20-3; idem, "Hitler's 'Armenian Extermination' Remark, True or False?" *The New York Times*, July 6, 1985.

12. Vahakn Dadrian, "The Historical and Legal Interconnections between the Armenian Genocide and the Jewish Holocaust: From Impunity to Retributive Justice," *The Yale Journal of International Law*, 23 (1998): 539-40; Allan Bullock, *Walter Schellenberg, The Labyrinth: Memoirs of Walter Schellenberg, Hitler's Chief of Counterintelligence* (New York: Harper and Bros., 2000), pp. x-xi, 353, 359-60; Joachim Fest, *Plotting Hitler's Death: The Story of German Resistance*, Bruce Little, trans. (New York: Metropolitan Books, Henry Holt, 1997), p. 5.

13. Bardakjian, *Hitler and the Armenian Genocide*, pp. 20-1.

14. Ibid., pp. 20-3; Bardakjian, "Hitler's 'Armenian Extermination' Remark, True or False?"; Helen Fein, "Political Functions of Genocide Comparisons," in Yehuda Bauer, Alice Eckardt, and Franklin H. Littell, eds., *Remembering for the Future: Working Papers and Addenda*, vol. 3 (Oxford: Pergamon Press, 1989), p. 2432.

Historical Background

15. Winfried Baumgart, "Zur Ansprache Hitler's vor den Führern der Wehrmacht am 22. August 1939. Eine quellenkritische Untersuchung," *Vierteljahrshefte für Zeitgeschichte*, Apr. 1968, pp. 120-49.

16. Fest, *Plotting Hitler's Death*, p. 110.

17. John H. Waller, *The Unseen War in Europe: Espionage and Conspiracy in the Second World War* (London: I.B. Tauris, 1996), pp. 237, 357.

18. Bardakjian, *Hitler and the Armenian Genocide*, p. 22; Michael Mueller and Geoffrey Brooks, *Canaris: The Life and Death of Hitler's Spymaster* (Annapolis: Naval Institute Press, 2007), pp. 208, 245-57.

19. Türkkaya Ataöv, "The 'Armenian Question': Conflict, Trauma and Objectivity," Ministry of Foreign Affairs, Center for Strategic Research, Republic of Turkey, *SAM Papers*, no. 3 / 97 (1999), accessed Jan. 5, 2012.

20. Lowry, "The U.S. Congress and Adolf Hitler on the Armenians," pp. 123-4.

21. Guenter Lewy, *The Armenian Massacres in Ottoman Turkey: A Disputed Genocide* (Salt Lake City: University of Utah Press, 2005), p. 265.

22. Roger W. Smith, Eric Markusen, and Robert Jay Lifton, "Professional Ethics and the Denial of Armenian Genocide," *Holocaust and Genocide Studies*, Spring 1995, pp. 9, 12.

23. Ibid., pp. 9-10.

24. Scott Jaschik, "Genocide Deniers," *Inside Higher Education*, Oct. 16, 2007.

25. Lewy, *The Armenian Massacres in Ottoman Turkey*, p. 265; Lowry, "The U.S. Congress and Adolf Hitler on the Armenians," p. 120.

26. Ataöv, "The 'Armenian Question,'" accessed Jan. 5, 2012.

27. Lowry, "The U.S. Congress and Adolf Hitler on the Armenians," Appendix II.

28. Roger W. Barrett and William E. Jackson, "Preface," in *Nazi Conspiracy and Aggression*, vol. 1, Nuremberg Commission, Jan. 20, 1946.

29. *Akten zur deutschen auswärtigen Politik*, p. 193, fn. 1.

30. Lewy, *The Armenian Massacres in Ottoman Turkey*, p. 265.

31. Richard Veatch, "Minorities and the League of Nations," in United Nations Library, ed., *The League of Nations in Retrospect* (Boston-New York: Walter de Gruyter, 1983), p. 380; Otto Tolischus, "German Army Attacks Poland," in Douglas Brinkley, ed., *The New York Times Living History: World War II, 1939-1942: The Axis Assault* (New York: Macmillan, 2003), p. 82; Henrik Eberle and Matthias Uhl, eds., *The Hitler Book: The Secret Dossier Prepared for Stalin from the Interrogations of Hitler's Personal Aides* (Jackson, Tenn.: Public Affairs, 2006), pp. 47-8; William Shirer, *The Rise and Fall of the Third Reich* (New York: Simon and Schuster, 1960), pp. 872, 875.

32. Richard Breiting, *Secret Conversations with Hitler: The Two Newly-discovered 1931 Interviews*, Édouard Calic, ed. (New York: John Day, 1971), p. 81; Édouard Calic, *Unmasked: Two Confidential Interviews with Hitler in 1931*, Richard Barry, trans. (London: John Day, 1971), p. 81; Dadrian, "The Historical and Legal Interconnections between the Armenian Genocide and the Jewish Holocaust," p. 540.

33. Martyn Housden, *Hitler: Study of a Revolutionary* (New York: Psychology Press, 2000), p. 47.

34. Hans Kohn, "Ten Years of the Turkish Republic," *Foreign Affairs*, Oct. 1933, pp. 143, 145.

35. Robert Gellately, *Backing Hitler: Consent and Coercion in Nazi Germany* (New York: Oxford University Press, 2002), p. 129.

36. Hitler to Mussolini, Aug. 25, 1939, in Max Domarus, ed., *Hitler: Speeches and Proclamations 1932-1945: The Chronicle of a Dictatorship*, vol. 3 (London: I.B. Tauris, 1996), p. 1689.

37. Robert Gellately, *Lenin, Stalin, and Hitler: The Age of Social Catastrophe* (New York: Random House, 2009), p. 422.

38. Shirer, *The Rise and Fall of the Third Reich*, pp. 152, 156.

39. Houston Stewart Chamberlain, *The Foundations of the Nineteenth Century*, vol. 1, John Lees, trans. (London: J. Lane, 1911), pp. 6-7.

40. Fritz Nova, *Alfred Rosenberg: Nazi Theorist of the Holocaust* (New York: Hippocrene Books, 1986), p. 12.

41. Alfred Rosenberg, *Kampf um die Macht: Aufsätze von 1921-1932*, Thilo von Trotha, ed. (Munich: F. Eher nachf., 1943), p. 435.

42. Ibid., p. 436.

43. Tessa Hofmann, "An Eye for an Eye: The Assassination of Talaat Pasha on the Hardenbergstrasse in Berlin," in Huberta von Voss, ed., *Portraits of Hope: Armenians in the Contemporary World*, Alasdair Lean, trans. (New York: Berghahn Books, 2007), p. 295.

44. Jay W. Baird, *To Die for Germany: Heroes in the Nazi Pantheon* (Bloomington: Indiana University Press, 1992), p. 46.

45. Dadrian, "The Historical and Legal Interconnections between the Armenian Genocide and the Jewish Holocaust," pp. 534-7.

46. Mike Joseph, "Max Erwin von Scheubner-Richter: The Personal Link from Genocide to Hitler," in Hans-Lukas Kieser and Elmar Plozza, eds., *Der Völkermord an Den Armeniern, Die Türkei und Europa* (Zurich: Chronos, 2006), pp. 147, 198.

47. Dadrian, "The Historical and Legal Interconnections between the Armenian Genocide and the Jewish Holocaust," pp. 535-6.

48. Dadrian, "Documentation of the Armenian Genocide," p. 107; idem, "The Historical and Legal Interconnections between the Armenian Genocide and the Jewish Holocaust," pp. 533-6.

49. Domarus, *Hitler: Speeches and Proclamations 1932-1945*, vol. 3, pp. 2618, 2748-9, 2593, 2717-8, 2764, 2774, 3130, 3260; Adolf Hitler, *My Struggle* (London: Hurst and Blackett, 1938), pp. 152-85.

50. Albert Camus, "State Terrorism and Irrational Terror," in Roger Griffin and Matthew Feldman, eds., *Fascism: Critical Concepts in Political Science* (London: Routledge, 2004), p. 16.

51. German Ambassador in Constantinople, Wangenheim, to the German Imperial Chancellor, Bethmann Hollweg, DE/PA-AA/R14086, DuA Dok. 081 (gk.), June 16, 1915, in Wolfgang and Sigrid Gust, eds., *A Documentation of the Armenian Genocide in World War I* (n.p., 1995-2012); Richard Hovannisian, "Introduction: History, Politics, Ethics," in

Richard Hovannisian, ed., *The Armenian Genocide: History, Politics, Ethics* (New York: St. Martin's Press, 1992), pp. xi-xii.

52. Shirer, *The Rise and Fall of the Third Reich*, p. 874.

53. Robert Gerwarth, *Hitler's Hangman: The Life of Heydrich* (New Haven: Yale University Press, 2011), p. 151.

54. M. Cherif Bassiouni, "From Versailles to Rwanda in Seventy-Five Years: The Need to Establish a Permanent International Criminal Court," *Harvard Human Rights Journal*, Spring 1997, p. 21.

55. Norman Hepburn Baynes, ed., *The Speeches of Adolf Hitler, April 1922-August 1939*, vol. 1 (New York: H. Fertig, 1969), pp. 1115-6.

56. *Die Zeit* (Hamburg), Jan. 9, 1998; Richard Weikart, *Hitler's Ethic: The Nazi Pursuit of Evolutionary Progress* (New York: Palgrave Macmillan, 2009), p. 193.

57. George Baer, *Test Case: Italy, Ethiopia, and the League of Nations* (Stanford: Hoover Institution Press, 1976), pp. 66, 92-3, 170, 183, 199-214, 274, 281, 290-6; A.J. Barker, *The Rape of Ethiopia*, 2nd ed. (New York: Ballantine Books, 1971), pp. 106-29; Angelo Del Boca, *The Ethiopian War, 1935-1941*, P.D. Cummins, trans. (Chicago: University of Chicago Press, 1969), pp. 78-84, 109, 120; John W. Turner, "Mussolini's Invasion and the Italian Occupation," in *A Country Study: Ethiopia* (Washington, D.C.: Library of Congress, 1991), call no. DT373 .E83 1993.

58. Lewy, *The Armenian Massacres in Ottoman Turkey*, p. 265.

Viewpoint 4

The Assyrian Genocide Differs from the Armenian Genocide
The Combat Genocide Association

The Assyrian peoples in Turkey suffered a genocide during the same time as the Armenians. For many people, the two events have been considered as a single genocidal action. The writer of the following viewpoint discusses how the Assyrian genocide was a distinct element of that troubled time in history. The Combat Genocide Association was formed by the Dror Israel Movement to fight against all forms of genocide. They struggle against the indifference and silencing of the existence of genocide which allowed the world to stand idly by so many times in the past, and they assist genocide survivors around the world. Their goal is to stop and prevent all acts of violence against any distinct group, minority, ethnicity, or nationality.

The Assyrian nation is one of the world's most ancient. As an ethnic and religious minority in the Middle East, the Assyrians have long suffered from riots and persecution. During World War I, the Turks murdered hundreds of thousands of Assyrians; between one half and two third of all Assyrians living in the Ottoman Empire. The Turkish government continues to deny the Assyrian Genocide.

Background

The Assyrians are an ancient, Semitic people whose roots are in ancient Mesopotamia—in the region of the Fertile Crescent—and who speak in an Eastern Aramaic dialect. The roots of the Assyrian

---

"Assyrian Genocide," The Combat Genocide Association. Reprinted by Permission.

Historical Background

people can be traced to the Sumerian-Akkadian Empire founded around 2,350 BCE. The Assyrian Empire emerged after the fall of the Akkadian Empire; at its height it controlled most of the territories in the ancient Near East. It was eventually overrun and occupied by the Babylonians.

The ancient Assyrian people traditionally prayed to multiple gods; in the early Middle Ages they converted to Christianity. Today the Assyrians are Christian and belong to various churches under the umbrella of Eastern Christianity, among others the Assyrian Church of the East and the Chaldean Catholic Church. Following the spread of Islam, in the period in which it controlled the Middle East, the Assyrians were subjected to many pogroms and massacres; with time they became a persecuted and oppressed minority in their historical homeland.

The Assyrians in the Ottoman Empire

In the 16th century the Ottoman Empire conquered Eastern Anatolia and the Middle East. The Assyrians lived in the area of Upper Mesopotamia (present-day southeast Turkey and northwest Iran). The population of the Ottoman Empire was ethnically, religiously and culturally diverse, and its ruling religion was Islam. Jews and Christians living in the Empire were considered second-class citizens and termed "millets." The millets were granted political and religious autonomy on the condition that they did not challenge Islamic rule. Community leaders governed their members according to their religious laws insofar as those did not clash with the laws and interests of the country. In return the communities pledged their loyalty to the Empire and accepted the limitations that were placed on them as legally protected minority groups: the imposition of special taxes, the prohibition of carrying a weapon, the mandate to carry visible markers of identity, and in some areas the prohibition of speaking their native language. Over a million Assyrians lived around Iran's Lake Urmia, in the area of Turkey's Lake Van, in the Hakkari Mountains, in Damascus, in Mesopotamia, and likewise in the eastern Ottoman districts of

Diyarbakir, Erzurum, and Bitlis. Despite their protected status, the Assyrians were frequently persecuted, forcibly converted by their Muslim rulers and Kurdish neighbors, and even slaughtered.

The dominance of the Empire began to wane toward the end of the 19th century, due to internal corruption and threats posed by external European powers, particularly Russia. The rise of regional nation states took place concurrently, followed by a surge in Turkish nationalism and Islamic envy, and the faltering of the various millets' standing. Ethnic minorities—in particular the large Kurdish minority—leveraged the weakening of the Empire to their advantage and began working to increase their power. Amid the Assyrians there lived a Kurdish majority, and when the Ottoman rulers turned to crack down on Kurds, the Kurds in turn unleashed their wrath on the Assyrians. Thus manifested the violent upheavals against the Assyrians.

From 1842–1845, during the Massacres of Badr Khan, the Kurds butchered the Assyrians on the Hakkari Mountains and in the vicinity of Tiyari. 10,000 Assyrians were murdered in the massacre and thousands more were imprisoned. An unknown number of Assyrian women and children were enslaved; many Assyrian leaders, priests and tribal heads were murdered. Violence against the Assyrians ensued throughout the latter half of the 19th century and included the desecration of holy sites, the kidnapping of women and children for slavery, and massacres. Approximately 23,000 Assyrians were murdered in the year 1860 alone.

The Hamidean Massacre

In August 1894 an Armenian revolt erupted in the Sason district. The Ottomans responded to the revolt with great cruelty, murdering scores of Armenians. Armenian protests led to further massacres of Armenians, committed by Turks and Kurds over a three-year period. The killing initially directed at the Armenian population quickly spread to and afflicted all Christian minorities in the Empire. In the years 1895–1896 the Turks and Kurds butchered Assyrians in Diyarbakir and Urhoy. Some 25,000 Assyrians were murdered in this massacre, which became known as the "Hamidean Massacre," named after Sultan Abdul Hamid II.

Rise of the Young Turks

In 1908, a military revolution shook the Ottoman Empire. The Young Turks, a political party whose members were educated in Europe and sought to establish a parliamentarian regime that would unite the various streams, seized control. Their slogan was "unity and progress." As more nations began asserting their right to self-determination, and the Empire weakened as a consequence of defeats in battle—which resulted in the Empire losing territories in Europe and north Africa—the idea of "Pan-Turkism" took hold of the Young Turks. At the 1911 Young Turks' conference on unity and change the movement announced it aim to initiate a process of "Ottomanizaton"—in essence a process of "Turkificiation" and "Islamization"—throughout the Empire. The direct result of this decision was the dawn of a dark era that entailed the ethnic cleansing of the Ottoman Empire's Christian minorities—among them the Assyrians, the Armenians, and the Greeks.

The Extermination

The Assyrian genocide was part of a policy of "Pan-Islamism" and "holy war" (Jihad) that the Ottoman regime enacted against the Christian minorities within the Empire: Armenians, Greeks, and Assyrians. The Ottoman Empire's Turkish military forces—in conjunction with armed Islamic militias (among them Kurds, Circassians, and Chechens)—carried out the genocide. The genocide took place mostly in 1915, nicknamed "Year of the Sword."

Western Iran

The genocide was launched in northwest Iran, which the Turks infiltrated in August 1914. Toward the end of 1914, Turkish and Kurdish forces successfully entered the villages surrounding Urmia and began evacuating Assyrians from their homes on the Ottoman-Iranian border. Upwards of 8,000 Assyrians were evacuated by

The Armenian Genocide

January 1915. In January 1915, Djevdet Bey, the governor of Van, invaded Iran from the north and destroyed the Assyrian population in each city he conquered. He also burned the Assyrian villages he encountered and butchered the masses of refugees who attempted to flee. In February 1915, he stated: "We cleansed the Armenians and the Syrians (the Christians) from Iran and we'll do so in Van as well." On February 22, 1915 the Turkish army beheaded 41 Assyrian leaders. During February and March the Ottomans conquered more than 100 defenseless Assyrian villages, butchering all men, women and children and burning the villages to the ground. Approximately 20,000 Assyrians were murdered in this spree of slaughter. When the Ottomans reached Urmia they butchered 10,000 more Assyrians while an additional 4,000 died of hunger and disease after their forced evacuation from their homes. There are known cases of Turkish soldiers passing through the homes of Persians in order to look for Assyrians and Armenians in hiding and executing those found.

Southeast Turkey

More than half of the residents of Siirt province in the Diyarbakir district (southeast Turkey) were Assyrians, and among them lived many Armenians. The Chaldean archbishop resided there. In the summer of 1915, a brigade of 8,000 soldiers, known as "The Brigade of Butchers," entered Siirt. The Turks murdered the archbishop along with 4,000 Christians in the city of Siirt alone, in addition to 20,000 or so Assyrians in some 30 surrounding villages.

The 300,000 Armenians and 90,000 Assyrians living in the districts of Diyarbakir, Van and Aleppo were annihilated under the command of Rashid Bey beginning in June 1915; thousands were murdered on-site, others were led in convoys to the desert.

Failure of Self-Defense in the Hakkari Mountains and Urmia

The Assyrians were successful in fending off the Turks for a few months on the Hakkari Mountains in southeast Turkey. Finally in July 1915, the Turks broke the Assyrian line of defense and burned the remaining villages and with it destroyed every trace of Assyrian presence.

Following the Russian invasion of Urmia, Agha Petros commanded an Assyrian army of volunteers that fought alongside the Entente Powers. Following the Russian retreat from the military campaign the Assyrians were cut off, few in number, and surrounded. After they were defeated the entire Assyrian population of Urmia was wiped out, 200 villages were destroyed and 65,000 Assyrian refugees died in episodes of mass murder, "convoys of death," and as a result of hunger and disease. Several thousand refugees who managed to make it to Turkey were massacred on arrival.

On the eve of the First World War, estimates of between 500,000 and 1,000,000 Assyrians lived in the Ottoman Empire and Iran; between 275,000 and 400,000 of them were murdered in the genocide.

The Persecution of Assyrians Following the Genocide

In mid-1918 the British army convinced the Ottomans to grant them access to 30,000 or so Assyrians across Iran. The British decided to transport the Assyrians from Iran to Baquba, Iraq. The transfer lasted a mere 25 days, yet 7,000 Assyrians died on the way. Some died of hunger, exhaustion and disease, while others fell victim to attacks by Islamic and Kurdish militias. In Iraq, too, the Assyrians suffered from similar incursions.

In 1920 the British decided to close down the camps in Baquba. The majority of Assyrians who lived in the camps preferred to return to the Hakkari Mountains; the rest dispersed across Iraq, where a 5,000-year-old Assyrian community lives.

The Simele Massacre and Continued Assyrian Persecution in Iraq

On August 7, 1933, with the help of Kurdish forces, the Iraqi military butchered Assyrians in Simele and other parts of Iraq.

The Armenian Genocide

Approximately 3,000 Assyrians died that day. Since then the day is commemorated as "Assyrian Martyrs' Day" during which Assyrian communities around the world remember the oppression suffered by their people throughout the decades.

In the years since the genocide and in light of their continued persecution in Iraq, many Assyrians left their homeland. Today some 550,000 Assyrians live in Europe. Particularly large Assyrian communities have formed in Sweden, Germany, the United States and Australia.

During the 1988 Al-Anfal Campaign—in which 180,000 Kurds were murdered by the Iraqi army under Saddam Hussein—hundreds of Assyrians who lived among them were also targeted, including tens of children. When the United States and NATO invaded Iraq in 2003, estimates of 1.5 million Assyrians lived in the country, constituting a total of 8% of the total population. In June 2014, as NATO forces departed Iraq, ISIS fighters seized control of the Nineveh Valley, where the majority of Assyrians live. Approximately one million refugees fled from their homes, of whom 40% were Assyrian. Many Assyrians have since died at the hands of ISIS, and their sacred sites have been destroyed.

Genocide Denial

Modern Turkey was founded in the wake of the First World War. The nation has failed to acknowledge the Assyrian Genocide, and has even worked to deny it and conceal it along with the Armenian Genocide. Following the economic depression of the 1930's, and then the Second World War, the Assyrian Genocide failed to warrant recognition and received little attention. With the exception of a few publications, it was not until the 1980's that scholars began researching and writing about the Assyrian Genocide. At first, it was seen as part of the Armenian Genocide; only later were the two distinguished from each other.

Denial of the Assyrian Genocide is inherently linked to the denial of Assyrian nationhood—one with ancient ethnic and cultural roots. The Assyrians are termed Aramaics, Nestorians,

Chaldeans, Kurdish Turks and Arab Christians. This is to undermine their envied right to cultural, spiritual and material treasures—all of which are thousands of years old—and on the basis of their being one of the oldest cultures to have survived as an ethnic group. In addition, it is to validate the denial of the systematic annihilation of the Assyrians, and to portray the genocidal campaign as a response to the disobedience of various Christian groups throughout the Ottoman Empire.

The European and Australian parliaments recently recognized the Assyrian Genocide, and in the wake of these actions memorials were erected in Europe and Australia in memory of the victims.

Viewpoint 5

How Kim Kardashian's Ancestors Escaped
Michael Snyder

Kim Kardashian is arguably the most recognizable person of Armenian descent in modern pop culture. In this viewpoint, the author uses her and her celebrity family to connect the past events of the Armenian Genocide with recent news stories the readers already know from television and the internet. Religious viewpoints are featured in this piece written by Michael Snyder, who frequently opines on his politically conservative values, his Christianity, and his beliefs against abortion. In August 2017 he was running for Congress on a pro-Trump ticket to represent Idaho's first congressional district.

Between 1915 and 1917, 1.5 million Armenians (most of them Christians) were slaughtered by the Turks. Armenians were systematically abducted, tortured and marched to their deaths just because of who they were and what they believed. At one point, 60,000 corpses were found in a single mass grave. It was one of the greatest genocides in history, but it didn't end in 1917. Between 1920 and 1923, Turkey either deported or wiped out almost all of the Armenians that had survived the first wave of persecution. This genocide was one of the most horrifying examples of how evil humanity can be, and yet to this day the U.S. government continues to refuse to call it a "genocide". Because of the sensitive nature of our relationship with the Turkish government, Barack Obama absolutely will not use the "g word" when speaking of what

---

"The Incredible Story Of How Kim Kardashian's Ancestors Escaped The Armenian Genocide," by Michael Snyder, End of the American Dream, April 24, 2015. Reprinted by Permission.

happened to the Armenians. And as I wrote about the other day, Obama also seems to care very little about the Christian genocide that is going on in parts of the Middle East controlled by ISIS today. But whether Obama ever recognizes the Armenian genocide or not, it is vitally important that the world remembers what happened to those precious people. One very prominent celebrity that is leading the call to remember the Armenian genocide is Kim Kardashian. In this article, I am going to share the story of how her ancestors were able to escape the genocide. I promise you, it is a story that you are not likely to ever forget.

If you are not familiar with the Armenian genocide, the following is a pretty good summary of what happened from the *Washington Post*…

> *One hundred years ago, in April 1915 as World War I raged across Europe, the government of the Ottoman Empire attacked its Armenian citizens. Over the next several years, it is estimated that as many as 1.5 million Armenians died. Able-bodied men were murdered or enslaved as forced labor in the army, and hundreds of thousands of women, children, the infirm and the elderly were marched into the Syrian desert to face death.*
>
> *Supported by the Young Turks, an ultranationalist party that approved systematic deportation, abduction, torture, massacre and the expropriation of Armenian wealth, the German-allied Ottoman government used the excuse of war to initiate the forcible removal of Armenians from Armenia and Anatolia where they had lived for centuries.*

But there is one fact in that article which is wrong.

The Armenians had not just been living there for centuries. They had been living there for thousands of years.

In fact, Armenia was the very first Christian nation on the entire planet. Shortly after the time of Christ, the early apostles visited Armenia and the gospel was eagerly accepted. Many of the Armenian people actually had roots in ancient Israel, and many of them were still familiar with what the Hebrew Scriptures said about

The Armenian Genocide

the coming of a Messiah. Very quickly, Armenia was transformed into one of the early hubs of the Christian faith.

And Armenia remained strongly Christian for the most part up until the time of the Armenian genocide. The Turks hated the Armenians (and still do) and were determined to wipe them out. This included the elderly, women and children…

> *"Rape and beating were commonplace," wrote acclaimed historian David Fromkin in his Pulitzer Prize-winning book on the Ottoman Empire's downfall, A Peace to End All Peace. "Those who were not killed at once were driven through mountains and deserts without food, drink or shelter. Hundreds of thousands of Armenians eventually succumbed or were killed."*
>
> *An Armenian man in Istanbul, who as a schoolboy discovered his family was Armenian, told The WorldPost one story passed down to him by his parents: His grandfather, too exhausted to walk any farther in the death march toward the Syrian desert, refused to go on. He would rather drown than walk another mile to his death, he told the Turkish Ottoman guards. And so, the man says, they held his grandfather under the water until he was dead.*

Sadly, much of the world continues to refuse to recognize this genocide.

This includes the United States government.

Could you imagine a president refusing to acknowledge the Holocaust?

Well, that is essentially what Obama is doing when he refuses to recognize the genocide that took place in Armenia. The reason why Obama will not acknowledge the Armenian genocide is because he doesn't want to offend the Turks…

> *If President Obama decided to label the 1915 killings as genocide, already strained relations would likely only worsen with Turkey, where the United States has an important air base in the south, close to Syria. Turkey and the U.S. government have butted heads over the Syrian crisis, with a U.S.-led coalition targeting solely Islamic State extremists, while Turkey insists military efforts must also focus on bringing down Syria's Bashar Assad.*

Historical Background

There are not words to describe what a disgrace this is.

Fortunately, there were some Armenians that were able to flee before the genocide. Among them were the Armenian ancestors of Kim Kardashian. The following comes from the *Daily Mail…*

> *Known at the time as the Kardaschoffs, in Russian style, the family made their way from their home village of Karakale in the late 19th Century to German ports. From there, they travelled to a new life in America on the passenger vessels SS Brandenberg and SS Koln.*
>
> *By doing so, they escaped the triple horror of the First World War from 1914-18, the 'Armenian Genocide' starting in 1915—exactly a century ago this year—and the Russian Revolution in 1917.*

So how did they know to leave?

Well, if you can believe this, Kim Kardashian's ancestors actually belonged to a group of Christians known as the Molokans, and they fled Armenia and came to America due to a warning from an Armenian Christian prophet named Efim Klubnikin…

> *In the first years of the 20th century, Efim renewed the warning that he made to stunned believers in Karakale as a child, saying his premonition was now coming to pass.*
>
> *'Efim called a meeting, he invited the elders from all the Molokan villages including the two elders of the Armenian Molokan church. He prophesied this was the time for them to leave Russia as there were terrible times coming, especially for the Armenians,' said Ms Keosababian-Bivin.*

Thanks to this warning, large numbers of Armenians left their ancestral homes and were able to escape the horrors that were coming. Here is more from the *Daily Mail…*

> *America was, he said, 'a land of the living' while mass slaughter would engulf their homeland.*
>
> *Presciently, he urged them to go quickly—as he himself would do—and cautioned: 'The doors will close, and leaving Russia will be impossible.'*
>
> *Many families sold up their homes and land at knockdown prices, or simply fled, to escape the coming horrors.*

It is substantially due to the prophecy that many of Kim's forebears came to Los Angeles, a city where the clan thrived and made their name.

But many were jeered as they left Karakale, now known as Merkez Karakale, and mocked for their belief in the prophesy of coming doom.

And don't we see a similar thing happening today?

Those that are trying to warn Americans about what is coming are often jeered and ridiculed.

But if Kim Kardashian's ancestors had not listened to the warning that they received, they probably would have been slaughtered with the rest of the Armenians and Kim Kardashian would not be alive right now.

So the next time that you see something on the Internet about Kim Kardashian, you will know that there is a whole lot more to her story than just fashion, television shows and money. Her family history is deeply rooted in one of the most persecuted groups of people in the history of the planet, and the story of how her ancestors escaped the Armenian genocide is quite incredible.

Context for the Armenian Genocide

Chapter Preface

Ethnic conflict is a part of human nature, according to one expert in this chapter—and because of that unfortunate reality, countless conflicts arose in what's now Turkey, under the rule of the Ottoman Empire. European wars and colonialism also factored in during the latter part of the 19th century, leading up to World War I. The Armenian Genocide was certainly not unprecedented.

As observed in several of the following viewpoints, the so-called "Great War" changed the organization of both warfare and western government, making it all too easy for events like the Armenian Genocide to occur. As Charles Darwin said upon visiting Australia, "Death pursues the native in every place where the European sets foot."

Indeed, when Australia was colonized with British criminals, the aboriginal peoples were crowded out; between 1800 and 1860, the Tasmanian aboriginals in one area were exterminated. Millions of Bengalis died in famines during India's British Raj. Belgium's King Leopold II extracted a fortune from the Congo from 1885 to 1908; under his regime of forced labor and mutilations some ten million people were killed. It is as hard for colonizing nations to acknowledge their responsibility for genocides of aboriginal peoples as it is for the Turks to acknowledge responsibility for the Armenian Genocide.

These viewpoints discuss the responsibilities of governments concerning ethnic conflicts, within nations and regions, as explored by the League of Nations. While one viewpoint asks if government incompetence rather than intent was to blame for the Armenian Genocide, another observes that intent is not necessary when results are so final. One such finality comes in the form of a survivor's obituary, which closes out this in-depth and informative chapter.

VIEWPOINT 1

Government Responsibility in the Armenian Genocide

United to End Genocide

The description of the genocide in the following viewpoint sheds light on a few important elements not always discussed—such as how the possessions of dead and departed Armenians were confiscated by the government, not passed on to heirs. The writer also discusses how western countries were well aware that massacres were occurring, but no nation came to the aid of the Armenians or the other minorities being killed. With over half a million members after merging with other groups, United to End Genocide is building the largest activist organization in America dedicated to preventing and ending genocide and mass atrocities around the world. Their group maintains a powerful, sustainable, and global network of genocide survivors, students, activists, faith leaders, artists, and human rights champions.

> Hitler did not fear retribution for the Holocaust. Why? He didn't think the world would care, asking as he prepared to invade Poland "Who today still speaks of the massacre of the Armenians?" In 1915, there were 2 million Armenians living in the declining Ottoman Empire. But under the cover of World War I, the Turkish government systematically destroyed 1.5 million people in attempts to unify all of the Turkish people by creating a new empire with one language and one religion.
>
> This ethnic cleaning of Armenians, and other minorities, including Assyrians, Pontian and Anatolian Greeks, is today known as the Armenian Genocide.

"The Armenian Genocide," United to End Genocide. Reprinted by Permission.

> *Despite pressure from Armenians and activists worldwide, Turkey still refuses to acknowledge the genocide, claiming that there was no premeditation on the deaths of the Armenians.*

Precursors to Genocide

History of the Region

The Armenians have lived in the southern Caucasus since the 7th century BC and have fought to maintain control against other groups such as the Mongolian, Russian, Turkish, and Persian empires. In the 4th century, the reigning king of Armenia became a Christian. He mandated that the official religion of the empire be Christianity, although in the 7th century AD all countries surrounding Armenia were Muslim. Armenians continued to be practicing Christians, despite the fact that they were many times conquered and forced to live under harsh rule.

The roots of the genocide lie in the collapse of the Ottoman Empire. At the turn of the 20th Century, the once widespread Ottoman Empire was crumbling at the edges. The Ottoman Empire lost all of its territory in Europe during the Balkan Wars of 1912–1913, creating instability among nationalist ethnic groups.

The First Massacres

There was growing tension between Armenians and Turkish authorities at the turn of the century. Sultan Abdel Hamid II, known as the "bloody sultan", told a reporter in 1890, "I will give them a box on the ear that will make them relinquish their revolutionary ambitions."

In 1894, the "box on the ear" massacre was first of the Armenian massacres. Ottoman forces, military and civilians alike attacked Armenian villages in Eastern Anatolia, killing 8,000 Armenians, including children. One year later, 2,500 Armenian women were burned to death in Urfa Cathedral. Around the same time, a group of 5,000 were killed after demonstrations begging for international intervention to prevent massacres upset officials in Constantinople. By 1896, historians estimate that over 80,000 Armenians had been killed.

Context for the Armenian Genocide

The Rise of the Young Turks
In 1909, the Ottoman Sultan was overthrown by a new political group—the "Young Turks", a group eager for a modern, westernized style of government. At first, Armenians were hopeful that they would have a place in the new state, but they soon realized that the new government was xenophobic and exclusionary to the multi-ethnic Turkish society. To consolidate Turkish rule in the remaining territories of the Ottoman Empire, the Young Turks devised a secret program to exterminate the Armenian population.

WWI
In 1914, the Turks entered World War I on the side of Germany and the Austro-Hungarian Empire. The outbreak of war would provide the perfect opportunity to solve the "Armenian question" once and for all.

Military leaders accused Armenians of supporting the Allies under the assumption that the people were naturally sympathetic toward Christian Russia. Consequently, Turks disarmed the entire Armenian population. Turkish suspicion of the Armenian people led the government to push for the "removal" of the Armenians from the war zones along the Eastern Front.

Genocide Begins
Transmitted in coded telegrams, the mandate to annihilate Armenians came directly from the Young Turks. Armed roundups began on the evening of April 24, 1915, as 300 Armenian intellectuals—political leaders, educators, writers, and religious leaders in Constantinople—were forcibly taken from their homes, tortured, then hanged or shot.

The death marches killed roughly 1.5 million Armenians, covered hundreds of miles and lasted multiple months. Indirect routes through wilderness areas were deliberately chosen in order to prolong marches and keep the caravans away from Turkish villages.

In the wake of the disappearance of the Armenian population, Muslim Turks quickly assumed ownership of everything left

The Armenian Genocide

behind. The Turks demolished any remnants of Armenian cultural heritage including masterpieces of ancient architecture, old libraries and archives. The Turks leveled entire cities including the once thriving Kharpert, Van and the ancient capital at Ani, to remove all traces of the three thousand year old civilization.

No Allied power came to the aid of the Armenian Republic and it collapsed. The only tiny portion of historic Armenia to survive was the easternmost area because it became part of the Soviet Union. The University of Minnesota's Center for Holocaust and Genocide Studies compiled figures by province and district that show there were 2,133,190 Armenians in the empire in 1914 and only about 387,800 by 1922.

An Unsuccessful Call to Arms in the West

At the time, international informants and national diplomats recognized the atrocities being committed as an atrocity against humanity.

Leslie Davis, U.S. consul in Harput noted, "these women and children were driven over the desert in midsummer and robbed and pillaged of whatever they had ... after which all who had not perished in the meantime were massacred just outside the city."

In a 1915 letter home, Swedish Ambassador Per Gustaf August Cosswa Anckarsvärd noted, "The persecutions of the Armenians have reached hair-raising proportions and all points to the fact that the Young Turks want to seize the opportunity ... [to] put an end to the Armenian question. The means for this are quite simple and consist of the extermination of the Armenian nation."

Even Henry Morgenthau, the U.S. Ambassador to Armenia, noted "When the Turkish authorities gave the orders for these deportations, they were merely giving the death warrant to a whole race."

The New York Times also covered the issue extensively—145 articles in 1915 alone—with headlines like "Appeal to Turkey to Stop Massacres." The newspaper described the actions against the Armenians as "systematic," "authorized," and "organized by the government."

The Allied Powers (Great Britain, France, and Russia) responded to news of the massacres by issuing a warning to Turkey, "the Allied governments announce publicly that they will hold all the members of the Ottoman Government, as well as such of their agents as are implicated, personally responsible for such matters." The warning had no effect.

Because Ottoman Law prohibited taking pictures of Armenian deportees, photo evidence that documented the severity of the ethnic cleansing is rare. In an act of defiance, officers from the German Military Mission documented atrocities occurring in concentration camps. While many pictures were intercepted by Ottoman intelligence, lost in Germany during WWII, or forgotten in dusty drawers, the Armenian Genocide Museum of America has captured some of these photos in an online exhibit.

Recognizing Genocide

Today Armenians commemorate those who lost their lives during the genocide on April 24, the day in 1915 when several hundred Armenian intellectuals and professionals were arrested and executed as the start of the genocide.

In 1985, the United States named this day "National Day of Remembrance of Man's Inhumanity to Man", in "honor of all of the victims of genocide, especially the one and one-half million people of Armenian ancestry who were the victims of the genocide perpetrated in Turkey."

Today, recognizing the Armenian Genocide is a hot-button issue as Turkey criticizes scholars for both inflating the death toll and for blaming Turks for deaths that the government says occurred because of starvation and the cruelty of war. In fact, speaking about the Armenian genocide in Turkey is punishable by law. As of 2014, 21 countries total have publicly or legally recognized this ethnic cleansing in Armenia as genocide.

In 2014, on the eve of the 99th anniversary of the genocide, Turkish Prime Minister, Recep Tayyip Erdogan, offered condolences to the Armenian people, saying, "The incidents of the first world war are our shared pain."

However, many feel that offerings are useless until Turkey recognizes the loss of 1.5 million people as genocide. In response to Erdogan's offering, Armenian President Serzh Sarkisian said, "The denial of a crime constitutes the direct continuation of that very crime. Only recognition and condemnation can prevent the repetition of such crimes in the future."

Ultimately, the recognition of this genocide is not only important to redress the affected ethnic groups, it is essential for the development of Turkey as a democratic state. If the past is denied, genocide is still occurring. A Swedish Parliament Resolution asserted in 2010 that, "the denial of genocide is widely recognized as the final stage of genocide, enshrining impunity for the perpetrators of genocide, and demonstrably paving the way for future genocides."

Viewpoint 2

Defining Genocide

Michael Gunter

In the following viewpoint, author Michael Gunter gives his opinion that genocide can only be defined as something intentional. The massacres of Armenians are compared to the deaths of Turkish nationals and also to more recent international events. Gunter suggests that incompetence and fear of revolutionary resistance are more to blame for mass violence than intentional genocide. Michael M. Gunter is a board member of the Center for Eurasian Studies. He has taught at Kent State University, and for universities in Turkey, China, and Austria; additionally, he has written several books as an authority on Kurds in Turkey.

Shortly after World War II, genocide was legally defined by the U.N. Genocide Convention as "any... acts committed with intent to destroy, in whole or in part, a national, ethnical, racial or religious group, as such."[1] The key word from the perspective of this article is "intent." For while nobody can deny the disaster wrought on the Armenians by the 1915 deportations and massacres, the question is whether or not it can be defined as genocide—arguably the most heinous crime imaginable.

The Ambiguity of Genocide

The strict international law definition of genocide has not prevented its application to virtually every conflict involving a large number of civilian deaths from the Athenian massacre of the inhabitants of

"What Is Genocide? The Armenian Case: Turkey, Past and Future," by Michael M. Gunter, The Middle East Forum, 2013. Reprinted by Permission.

Milos in 416 B.C.E., to the Mongol sacking of Baghdad in 1258, to the fate of the native North American Indians, to Stalin's induced famine in the Ukraine in the early 1930s, to the recent conflicts in Bosnia, Burundi, Chechnya, Colombia, Guatemala, Iraq, Sudan, and Rwanda, which is not to deny that some of these cases do indeed qualify as genocide.

The liberal use of the term has naturally stirred numerous controversies and debates. Israel Charny offers little help by arguing that any massacre constitutes genocide, even the 1986 Chernobyl nuclear meltdown.[2] At the other end of the spectrum, Stephen Katz views the Holocaust as the only true genocide in history.[3] In between these two polar definitions, Ton Zwaan has attempted to distinguish between "total" and "complete" genocide and "partial" genocides.[4]

Even the U.N. definition suffers from some ambiguities owing to being a compromise among all signatories. Thus, the convention legally protects only "national, racial, ethnic, and religious groups," not those defined politically, economically, or culturally, giving rise to varying interpretations of its intentions. For example, while the International Criminal Tribunal for the Former Yugoslavia convicted seven Bosnian Serbs of genocide for their role in the July 1995 Srebrenica massacre of some 8,000 Bosnian Muslims,[5] the International Court of Justice, in its judgment in *Bosnia vs. Serbia*, focused on Serbia's "intent" rather than "outcome" regarding the murder of Bosnian Muslims, absolving it of the charge of genocide.[6] Clearly, these contradictory decisions have added to the confusion of what genocide legally constitutes.

Likewise, the debate whether the Darfur events constituted genocide continues apace. U.S. secretary of state Colin Powell characterized Darfur as a case of genocide based on a U.S. government-funded study, which had surveyed 1,136 Darfur refugees in neighboring Chad.[7] By contrast, a study commissioned by U.N. secretary-general Kofi Annan concluded that, while the Darfur events should be referred to the International Criminal Court (ICC) for crimes against humanity, they did not amount to genocide.[8] Amnesty International and Human Rights Watch also declined to characterize the violence in Darfur as genocide while the Arab League and the African Union took a similar position, emphasizing instead the civil war aspect of the conflict. For their part EU, British, Canadian, and Chinese officials, among others, have shied away from calling it genocide. Samantha Power, the author of a Pulitzer Prize winning study on genocide, favored the term ethnic cleansing to describe what was occurring.[9]

When in July 2008, ICC chief prosecutor Luis Moreno-Ocampo accused Sudanese president Omar Bashir of genocide and asked the court to issue an arrest warrant, many in the Arab League and the African Union criticized the genocide charge as biased against their region.[10] It remains to be seen how wise the ICC has been in bringing genocide charges in this case. Clearly, there was a lack of agreement on what did or did not constitute genocide in Darfur. Such a situation illustrates the ambiguity surrounding the concept of genocide.

In an attempt to alleviate these problems, scholars have offered such additional detailed concepts as "politicide" to refer to mass murders of a political nature, "democide" to describe government-perpetrated mass murders of at least one million people, ethnocide, Judeocide, ecocide, feminicide, libricide (for the destruction of libraries), urbicide, elitocide, linguicide, and culturicide, among others.[11] In addition we now have such concepts as crimes against humanity, war crimes, and ethnic cleansing.

Why this semantic disarray? Henry Huttenbach has argued, "Too often has the accusation of genocide been made simply for the emotional effect or to make a political point, with the result that more and more events have been claimed to be genocide to the point that the term has lost its original meaning."[12] Jacques Semelin has similarly explained: "Whether use of the word 'genocide' is justified or not, the term aims to strike our imagination, awaken our moral conscience and mobilise public opinion on behalf of the victims." He adds: "Under these circumstances, anyone daring to

The Armenian Genocide

suggest that what is going on is not 'really' genocide is immediately accused of weakness or sympathizing with the aggressors." Thus,

> The term genocide can be used as a propaganda tool by becoming the hinge for a venomous rhetoric against a sworn enemy. Given the powerful emotional charge the word genocide generates, it can be used and re-used in all sorts of hate talk to heap international opprobrium on whoever is accused of genocidal intent. ... The obvious conclusion: The word is used as much as a symbolic shield to claim victim status for one's people, as a sword raised against one's deadly enemy.[13]

Intent or premeditation is all important in defining genocide "because it removes from consideration not only natural disasters but also those man-made disasters that took place without explicit planning. Many of the epidemics of communicable diseases that reached genocidal proportions, for example were caused by unwitting human actions."[14] Although some would disagree, the fate of the North American indigenous people is a case in point as they died largely from disease, not intent. Therefore, a large loss of life is not in itself proof of genocide. Ignoring intent creates a distorted scenario and may lead to incorrect conclusions as to what really occurred.

The Armenians

What then of the Armenian case? Unfortunately, as the well-known journalist and scholar Gwynne Dyer concluded more than thirty-five years ago, most Turkish and Armenian scholars are unable to be objective on this issue resulting in a situation of "Turkish falsifiers and Armenian deceivers."[15]

The main purpose of this discussion, therefore, is not to deny that Turks killed and expelled Armenians on a large scale; indeed what happened might in today's vocabulary be called war crimes, ethnic cleansing, or even crimes against humanity. To prove genocide, however, intent or premeditation must be demonstrated, and in the Armenian case it has not. It must also be borne in mind that what occurred was not a unilateral Turkish action but part of a long-term process in which some Armenians were guilty of killing as many Turks as they could in their attempt to rebel. Christopher de Ballaigue argues that "what is needed is a vaguer designation for the events of 1915, avoiding the G-word but clearly connoting criminal acts of slaughter, to which reasonable scholars can subscribe."[16]

Arnold Toynbee, the renowned historian who coedited the Blue Book compilation of Turkish atrocities during World War I,[17] later wrote: "In the redistribution of Near and Middle Eastern Territories, the atrocities which have accompanied it from the beginning have been revealed in their true light, as crimes incidental to an abnormal process, which all parties have committed in turn, and not as the peculiar practice of one denomination or nationality."[18] Indeed, in his final statement on the subject, Toynbee declared: "Armenian political aspirations had not been legitimate. ... Their aspirations did not merely threaten to break up the Turkish Empire; they could not be fulfilled without doing grave injustice to the Turkish people itself."[19] In addition, Adm. Mark Bristol, U.S. high commissioner and then-ambassador to Turkey after World War I, wrote in a long cable to the State Department in 1920: "While the Turks were all that people said they were, the other side of the coin was obscured by the flood of Greek and Armenian propaganda painting the Turks as completely inhuman and undeserving of any consideration while suppressing all facts in favor of the Turks and against the minorities."[20]

More recently, Edward J. Erickson, a military historian, concluded after a careful examination: "Nothing can justify the massacres of the Armenians nor can a case be made that the entire Armenian population of the six Anatolian provinces was an active and hostile threat to Ottoman national security." This said, Erickson added: "However, a case can be made that the Ottomans judged the Armenians to be a great threat to the 3rd and 4th [Ottoman] Armies and that genuine intelligence and security concerns drove that decision. It may also be stated that the Ottoman reaction was escalatory and responsive rather than premeditated and preplanned."[21]

The Armenian Genocide

On the other hand, Taner Akçam, a Turkish sociologist who has prominently broken with his country's official narrative, concluded after compiling weighty evidence that the "Ottoman authorities' genocidal intent becomes clear."[22] This conclusion was challenged by Turkish researcher Erman Sahin who accused Akçam of "dishonesty—which manifests itself in the form of numerous deliberate alterations and distortions, misleading quotations and doctoring of data—casts doubt on the accuracy of his claims as well as his conclusions."[23] In a later critique of Akçam's subsequent work, Sahin concluded: "These are substantive matters that raise serious concerns as to the author's theses, which appear to be based on a selective and distorted presentation of Ottoman archival materials and other sources. ... Such errors seriously undermine the author's and the book's credibility."[24]

More recently, Akçam claimed that despite Turkish attempts to "hide the evidence" through systematic "loss" and destruction of documents, his new work in the Ottoman archives "clearly points in the direction of a deliberate Ottoman government policy to annihilate its Armenian population."[25] Maybe, but maybe not. Equally likely is that any destruction of documents at the end of World War I was simply designed to protect military secrets from falling into enemy hands, something any government would want to do. More to the point, Akçam also states that "the clearest statement that the aim of the [Ottoman] government's policies toward the Armenians was annihilation is found in a cable of 29 August 1915 from interior minister Talat Pasha" in which he asserted that the "Armenian question in the eastern provinces has been resolved. ... There's no need to sully the nation and the government['s honor] with further atrocities."[26] This document, however, does not prove genocidal intent except to those determined to find it. Rather, Talat's statement might simply mean precisely what it states: The Armenian deportations, although resulting in many atrocities and deaths, have solved the issue.

In a carefully nuanced study, historian Donald Bloxham concluded that what happened was premeditated and therefore genocide.[27] Though stating in an earlier article "that there was no a priori blueprint for genocide, and that it emerged from a series of more limited regional measures in a process of cumulative policy radicalization,"[28] he, nevertheless, used the term genocide because of the magnitude of what happened and because "nowhere else during the First World War was revolutionary nationalism answered with total murder. That is the crux of the issue."[29] At the same time, he wondered "whether recognition [of genocide] is really going to open the door to healing wounds and reconciliation, as we are often told, or whether it is a means of redressing nationalist grievances. Is it an issue of historical truth, morality and responsibility, or of unresolved political and material claims?"[30]

Finally, it should be noted that the Armenian claims of genocide are encumbered by intrinsic legal and philosophical problems. This is due to the fact that any finding under international law of genocide in the Armenian case at this late date would constitute a legally untenable ex-post-facto proclamation, namely: Make a crime of an action which, when originally committed, was not a crime. The concept of genocide did not even exist until it was formulated during World War II by Raphael Lemkin, while the genocide convention only entered into force in 1951.

The Manifesto of Hovhannes Katchaznouni

Hovhannes Katchaznouni was the first prime minister (1918–19) of the short-lived Armenian state following World War I. It is useful to turn to his April 1923 address to the Armenian revolutionary and nationalist Dashnak party congress, held in the Romanian capital of Bucharest. While not gainsaying "this unspeakable crime … the deportations and mass exiles and massacres which took place during the Summer and Autumn of 1915,"[31] Katchaznouni's speech constitutes a remarkable self-criticism by a top Armenian leader. No wonder that many Armenians have done their best to remove this telling document from libraries around the world. It is, therefore, useful to cite what Katchaznouni had to say at some length:

The Armenian Genocide

In the Fall of 1914, Armenian volunteer bands organized themselves and fought against the Turks because they could not refrain themselves from fighting. This was an inevitable result of psychology on which the Armenian people had nourished itself during an entire generation. ... It is important to register only the evidence that we did participate in that volunteer movement to the largest extent. ...

We had embraced Russia wholeheartedly without any compunction. Without any positive basis of fact, we believed that the Tsarist government would grant us a more or less broad self-government in the Caucasus and in the Armenian vilayets liberated from Turkey as a reward for our loyalty, our efforts, and assistance.

We overestimated the ability of the Armenian people, its political and military power, and overestimated the extent and importance of the services our people rendered to the Russians. And by overestimating our very modest worth and merit was where we naturally exaggerated our hopes and expectations. ...

The proof is, however—and this is essential—that the struggle began decades ago against the Turkish government [which] brought about the deportation or extermination of the Armenian people in Turkey and the desolation of Turkish Armenia. This was the terrible fact![32]

K.S. Papazian's *Patriotism Perverted?*

A decade after the publication of Katchaznouni's speech, but still much closer to the events of World War I than now, Kapriel Serope Papazian produced a most revealing critique of the Dashnaks' perfidy, terrorism, and disastrous policies that had helped lead to the events in question. Written by an Armenian who bore no love for the Turks, but hushed up, ignored, and virtually forgotten by many because its self-critical revelations do not mesh with the received Armenian thesis of innocent victimization, Papazian's analysis[33] calls for close scrutiny.

Authored just after the notorious Dashnak murder of Armenian archbishop Leon Tourian in New York City on

Context for the Armenian Genocide

Christmas Eve 1933,[34] Papazian began by expressing disdain for the group's "predatory inclinations" before examining the "terrorism in the Dashnaks' early [1892] program," which sought "to fight, and to subject to terrorism the government officials, the traitors, the betrayers, the usurers, and the exploiters of all description." Having analyzed the movement's ideological and operational history, Papazian explored what actually transpired during World War I:

> *The fact remains, however, that the leaders of the Turkish-Armenian section of the Dashnagtzoutune did not carry out their promise of loyalty to the Turkish cause when the Turks entered the war. ... Prudence was thrown to the winds ... and a call was sent for Armenian volunteers to fight the Turks on the Caucasian front.*
>
> *Thousands of Armenians from all over the world flocked to the standards of such famous fighters as Antranik, Kery, Dro, etc. The Armenian volunteer regiments rendered valuable services to the Russian Army in the years of 1914-15-16.*
>
> *On the other hand, the methods used by the Dashnagtzoutune in recruiting these regiments were so open and flagrant that it could not escape the attention of the Turkish authorities ... Many Armenians believe that the fate of two million of their co-nationals in Turkey might not have proved so disastrous if more prudence had been used by the Dashnag leaders during the war. In one instance, one Dashnag leader, Armen Garo, who was also a member of the Turkish parliament, had fled to the Caucasus and had taken active part in the organization of volunteer regiments to fight the Turks. His picture, in uniform, was widely circulated in the Dashnag papers, and it was used by Talat Paha, the arch assassin of the Armenians, as an excuse for his policy of extermination.*[35]

What then should be made of Papazian's *Patriotism Perverted*? Without denying that the Turks played a murderous role in the events analyzed, his long-ignored and even suppressed revelations indicate that the Armenians were far from innocent victims in what ensued. Indeed, Papazian's text makes it clear that incompetent but treacherous Armenians themselves were also to blame for

The Armenian Genocide

what had befallen their cause. It is unfair to fix unique blame upon the Turks.

Guenter Lewy's Critic

A major contribution to the debate over the Armenian atrocities, Guenter Lewy's *The Armenian Massacres in Ottoman Turkey*,[36] rejects the claim of a premeditated genocide as well as the apologist narrative of an unfortunate wartime excess, concluding that "both sides have used heavy-handed tactics to advance their cause and silence a full and impartial discussion of the issues in dispute." In his view, "the key issue in this quarrel is not the extent of Armenian suffering, but rather the question of premeditation: that is, whether the Young Turk regime during the First World War intentionally organized the massacres that took place."

Lewy questions the authenticity of certain documents alleged to contain proof of a premeditated genocide as well as the methods of Vakhakn N. Dadrian,[37] one of the foremost current Armenian scholar-advocates of the genocide thesis, whom he accuses of "selective use of sources … [which] do not always say what Dadrian alleges" and "manipulating the statements of contemporary observers."

As for the argument that "the large number of Armenian deaths … [offers] proof that the massacres that took place must have been part of an overall plan to destroy the Armenian people," Lewy counters that it "rests on a logical fallacy and ignores the huge loss of life among Turkish civilians, soldiers, and prisoners-of-war due to sheer incompetence, neglect, starvation, and disease. All of these groups also experienced a huge death toll that surely cannot be explained in terms of a Young Turk plan of annihilation."

So how does Lewy explain what happened to the Armenians? "The momentous task of relocating several hundred thousand people in a short span of time and over a highly primitive system of transportation was simply beyond the ability of the Ottoman bureaucracy. … Under conditions of Ottoman misrule, it was possible for the country to suffer an incredibly high death toll without a premeditated plan of annihilation."[38]

Lewy's book was reviewed prominently and positively in two leading U.S. journals of Middle East studies. Edward J. Erickson noted the finding that "both camps have created a flawed supporting historiography by using sources selectively, quoting them out of context, and/or ignoring 'inconvenient facts,'" concluding that "simply having a large number of advocates affirming that the genocide is a historical fact does not make it so."[39] Robert Betts, while claiming that "for the Turkish government to deny Ottoman responsibility for the Armenian suffering makes no sense," also stated that "what emerges from Lewy's study is the dire state of the empire and its population in 1915 and its inability to protect and feed its own Muslim citizenry, let alone the Armenians."[40] Moreover, such distinguished scholars of Ottoman history as Bernard Lewis,[41] Roderic Davison,[42] J. C. Hurewitz,[43] and Andrew Mango,[44] among others, have all rejected the appropriateness of the genocide label for what occurred. On May 19, 1985, sixty-nine prominent academics in Turkish Ottoman and Middle Eastern studies (including Lewis) published a large advertisement in the *New York Times* and the *Washington Post* criticizing the U.S. Congress for considering the passage of a resolution that would have singled out for special recognition "the one and one half million people of Armenian ancestry who were victims of genocide perpetrated in Turkey between 1915 and 1923." Instead, they argued that such questions should be left for the scholarly community to decide.

Indeed, the Armenian massacres of 1915 did not come out of the blue but followed decades of Armenian violence and revolutionary activity that elicited Turkish counter violence. There is a plethora of Turkish writings documenting these unfortunate events, just as there are numerous Armenian accounts.[45] The Armenians, of course, present themselves as freedom fighters in these earlier events, but it is possible to understand how the Ottomans saw them as treasonous subjects.

Moreover, throughout all these events, the Armenians were never more than a large minority even in their historic provinces.[46] Yet they exaggerated their numbers before World War I and their losses during the war. Had the Armenian fatality figures been correct, very few would have survived the war. Instead, the Armenians managed to fight another war against the nascent Turkish republic in the wake of World War I for mastery in eastern Anatolia. Having lost, many Armenians claimed that what transpired after World War I was a renewed genocide. As Christians, the Armenians found a sympathetic audience in the West whereas the Muslim Turks were the West's historic enemy. Add to this the greater Armenian adroitness in foreign languages—hence their greater ability to present their case to the world—to understand why the Turks consider the genocide charge to be grossly unfair, especially since the Armenians have adamantly rejected any culpability on their part in this tragic event.

Conclusion

Without denying the tragic massacres and countless deaths the Armenians suffered during World War I, it is important to place them in their proper context. When this is done, the application of the term "genocide" to these events is inappropriate because the Turkish actions were neither unilateral nor premeditated. Rather, what transpired was part of a long-continuing process that in part started with the Russo-Turkish war of 1877-78, which triggered an influx of Balkan Muslims into Anatolia with the attendant deterioration of relations with the indigenous Christian Armenians.[47]

To make matters worse, Patriarch Nerses, an Ottoman subject and one of the leaders of the Armenian community, entered into negotiations with the victorious Russians with an eye to achieving Armenian autonomy or even independence. This was followed in coming decades by continued Armenian nationalist agitation, accompanied by the use of terror, aimed at provoking retaliation, which they hoped would be followed by European intervention.

When World War I broke out, some Armenians supported the Russian enemy. Kurdish/Muslim-Armenian animosities also played a role in this process.[48]

As for the necessary attribute of premeditation to demonstrate genocide, there are no authentic documents to such effect. Although there are countless descriptions of the depravations suffered by the Armenians, they do not prove intent or premeditation. The so-called Andonian documents that purport to demonstrate premeditation are almost certainly a fabrication.[49] And in response to the Armenian contention that the huge loss of Armenian lives illustrates premeditation, what then should be said about the enormous loss of Turkish lives among civilians, soldiers, and prisoners-of-war? Were these Turkish deaths also genocide or rather due to sheer incompetence, neglect, starvation, and disease? And if the latter were true of the ethnic Turkish population, they were all the more so in respect to an ethnic group that had incurred upon itself suspicion of acting as a fifth column in a time of war.

Even so, Armenian communities in such large Western cities as Istanbul and Smyrna were largely spared deportation probably because they were not in a position to aid the invading Russians. Is it possible to imagine Hitler sparing any Jews in Berlin, Munich, or Cologne from his genocidal rampage for similar reasons? If, as the Armenians allege, the Turkish intent was to subject their Armenian victims to a premeditated forced march until they died of exhaustion, why was this tactic not imposed on all Armenians? Therefore, without denying outright murders and massacres that today might qualify as war crimes, it seems reasonable to question the validity of referring to the Armenian tragedy as genocide.

Notes

1. *Convention on the Prevention and Punishment of the Crime of Genocide*, 78 U.N. Treaty Series (UNTS) 277, adopted by the General Assembly, Dec. 9, 1948, entered into force, Jan. 12, 1951.

2. Israel W. Charny, "Towards a Generic Definition of Genocide," in George J. Andreopoulos, ed., *Genocide: Conceptual and Historical Dimensions* (Philadelphia: University of Pennsylvania Press, 1994), pp. 64-94.

3. Stephen Katz, *The Holocaust in Historical Context*, vol. 1 (New York: Oxford University Press, 1994).

4. Ton Zwaan, "On the Aetiology and Genesis of Genocides and Other Mass Crimes Targeting Specific Groups," Office of the Prosecutor of the International Criminal Tribunal for the Former Yugoslavia, Center for Holocaust and Genocide Studies, University of Amsterdam/Royal Netherlands Academy of Arts and Sciences, Nov. 2003, p. 12.

5. David Rhode, *Endgame: The Betrayal and Fall of Srebrenica, Europe's Worst Massacre since World War II* (New York: Farrar, Straus and Giroux, 1997), p. 167; Jacques Semelin, *Purify and Destroy: The Political Uses of Massacre and Genocide* (New York: Columbia University Press, 2007), pp. 34-5, 65-6, 138-9, 195-8, 213-20, 245-6; "Report of the Secretary General Pursuant to General Assembly Resolution 53/35: The Fall of Srebrenica," U.N. doc. no. A/54/549, Nov. 15, 1999.

6. *The Application of the Convention on the Prevention and Punishment of the Crime of Genocide (Bosnia and Herzegovina vs. Serbia and Montenegro)*, case 91, International Court of Justice, The Hague, Feb. 26, 2007.

7. "Documenting the Atrocities in Darfur," Bureau of Democracy, Human Rights, and Labor, and Bureau of Intelligence and Research, U.S. Department of State, Washington, D.C., Sept. 2004.

8. *The Guardian* (London), Feb. 1, 2005.

9. Scott Straus, "Darfur and the Genocide Debate," *Foreign Affairs*, Jan.-Feb. 2005, pp. 128, 130.

10. Public Radio International, July 28, 2008; Voice of America, July 22, 2010.

11. Semelin, *Purify and Destroy*, pp. 319-20.

12. Henry R. Huttenbach "Locating the Holocaust under the Genocide Spectrum: Toward a Methodology of Definition and Categorization," *Holocaust and Genocide Studies*, 3 (1988): 297.

13. Semelin, *Purify and Destroy*, pp. 312-3.

14. Kurt Jonassohn, "What Is Genocide?" in Helen Fein, ed., *Genocide Watch* (New Haven: Yale University Press, 1992), p. 21.

15. Gwynne Dyer, "Turkish 'Falsifiers' and Armenian 'Deceivers': Historiography and the Armenian Massacres," *Middle Eastern Studies*, Jan. 1976, pp. 99-107.

16. Christopher de Ballaigue, *Rebel Land: Among Turkey's Forgotten Peoples* (London: Bloomsbury, 2009), p. 104; M. Hakan Yavuz, "Contours of Scholarship on Armenian-Turkish Relations," *Middle East Critique*, Nov. 2011, pp. 231-51.

17. James Bryce, compiler, "The Treatment of Armenians in the Ottoman Empire, 1915-16," *Parliamentary Papers Miscellaneous*, Great Britain, no. 31 (London: Joseph Cavston, 1916).

18. Arnold J. Toynbee, *The Western Question in Greece and Turkey: A Study in the Contact of Civilizations* (Boston and New York: Houghton Mifflin, 1922), pp. vii-viii.

19. Arnold J. Toynbee, *Acquaintances* (London: Oxford University Press, 1967), p. 241.

20. Laurence Evans, *United States Policy and the Partition of Turkey, 1914-1924* (Baltimore: Johns Hopkins Press, 1965), p. 272.

21. Edward J. Erickson, "The Armenians and Ottoman Military Policy, 1915," *War in History*, no. 2, 2008, p. 167.

22. Taner Akçam, *A Shameful Act: The Armenian Genocide and the Question of Turkish Responsibility* (New York: Henry Holt and Co., 2006), p. 187.

23. Erman Sahin, "Review Essay: A Scrutiny of Akçam's Version of History and the Armenian Genocide," *Journal of Muslim Minority Affairs*, Aug. 2008, p. 316.

24. Erman Sahin, "Review Essay: The Armenian Question," *Middle East Policy*, Spring 2010, p. 157.

25. Taner Akçam, *The Young Turks' Crime against Humanity: The Armenian Genocide and Ethnic Cleansing in the Ottoman Empire* (Princeton: Princeton University Press, 2012), pp. 19, 27.

26. Ibid., p. 203.

27. Donald Bloxham, *The Great Game of Genocide: Imperialism, Nationalism, and the Destruction of the Ottoman Armenians* (New York: Oxford University Press, 2005); Ronald Grigor Suny, "Truth in Telling: Reconciling Realities in the Genocide of the Ottoman Armenians," *American Historical Review*, Oct. 2009, pp. 930-46.

28. Donald Bloxham, "The Armenian Genocide of 1915-1916: Cumulative Radicalization and the Development of a Destruction Policy," *Past & Present*, Nov. 2003, p. 143.

29. Ibid., pp. 143, 186.

30. Ibid., p. 232.

31. Hovhannes Katchaznouni, "The Armenian Revolutionary Federation (Dashnagtzoutiun) Has Nothing To Do Anymore," Arthur A. Derounian, ed., Matthew A. Callender, trans. (New York: Armenian Information Service, 1955), p. 2.

32. Ibid., pp. 2-3.

33. Kapriel Serope Papazian, *Patriotism Perverted: A Discussion of the Deeds and the Misdeeds of the Armenian Revolutionary Federation, the So-Called Dashnagtzoutune* (Boston: Baikar Press, 1934).

34. See Christopher Walker, *Armenia: The Survival of a Nation* (New York: St. Martin's Press, 1989), p. 354; Maggie Lewis, "Armenian-Americans," *The Christian Science Monitor* (Boston), Nov. 18, 1980.

35. Papazian, *Patriotism Perverted,* pp. 7, 13, 15, 21, 38-9.

36. Salt Lake City: University of Utah Press, 2007.

37. For examples of Guenter Lewy's critiques of Dadrian's writings, see "Revisiting the Armenian Genocide," *Middle East Quarterly*, Fall 2005, pp. 3-12; idem, *The History of the Armenian Genocide: Ethnic Conflict from the Balkans to Anatolia to the Caucasus* (Providence and Oxford: Berghahn Books, 1995); idem, *Warrant for Genocide: Key Elements of Turko-Armenian Conflict* (New Brunswick and London: Transaction Publishers, 1999).

38. Lewy, *The Armenian Massacres*, pp. ix, 47, 51, 83-6, 250, 253, 258, 282.

39. Edward J. Erickson, "Lewy's 'The Armenian Massacres,'" *Middle East Journal*, Spring 2006, p. 377.

40. Robert Brenton Betts, "*The Armenian Massacres in Ottoman Turkey: A Disputed Genocide*/The Armenian Rebellion at Van," *Middle East Policy*, Spring 2008, p. 177.

41. See, for example, Bernard Lewis, *The Emergence of Modern Turkey* (London: Oxford University Press, 1968), p. 356.

42. *The New York Times*, May 19, 1985.

43. Ibid.

44. Andrew Mango, *Atatürk: The Biography of the Founder of Modern Turkey* (Woodstock and New York: The Overlook Press, 1999), p. 161.

45. See, for example, Louise Nalbandian, *The Armenian Revolutionary Movement: The Development of Armenian Political Parties through the Nineteenth Century* (Los Angeles: University of California Press, 1963); Garegin Pasdermadjian (Armen Garo), *Bank Ottoman: Memoirs of Armen Garo* (Detroit: Armen Topouzian, 1990); James G. Mandalian, ed. and trans., *Armenian Freedom Fighters: The Memoirs of Rouben der Minasian* (Boston: Hairenik Association, 1963).

46. See Justin McCarthy, *Muslims and Minorities: The Population of Ottoman Anatolia and the End of the Empire* (New York: New York University Press, 1983), p. 115.

47. M. Hakan Yavuz with Peter Sluglett, eds., *War and Diplomacy: The Russo-Turkish War of 1877-1878* (Salt Lake City: University of Utah Press, 2011), pp. 1-13.

48. See Janet Klein, *The Margins of Empire: Kurdish Militias in the Ottoman Tribal Zone* (Stanford: Stanford University Press, 2011), pp. 50, 131, 183.

49. Aram Andonian, ed., *The Memoirs of Naim Bey: Turkish Official Documents Relating to the Deportations and Massacres of Armenians* (London: 1920. Reprinted, Newtown Square, Pa.: Armenian Historical Research Association, 1964). For the case against the authenticity of these documents, see Sinasi Orel and Sureyya Yuca, *The Talat Pasha Telegrams: Historical Fact or Armenian Fiction?* (Nicosia: K. Rustem and Bros., 1986). For the counterclaim that newly found Ottoman archival source material vindicates the Adonian documents see, Akçam, *The Young Turks' Crime against Human*

VIEWPOINT 3

The Armenian Question
Universidad Iberoamericana

Students who are used to the idea of forming a mock Parliament or United Nations will understand the purpose of this viewpoint, which gives background information on the Armenian Genocide so students can set set up a mock League of Nations. Through discussion, participants are expected to learn how alternate outcomes could easily have arisen during the actual events of the Armenian Genocide. The Ibero-American University is one of the most prestigious universities in Mexico and Latin America. Sponsored by Jesuits, the university is recognized for its excellence internationally. It is part of a network of eight Mexican universities, thirty-one universities and colleges in Latin America, and more two hundred world-wide facilities founded by Jesuits.

Introduction.

From 1915 to 1918 an estimated of a million and a half of the Armenian population, mainly Christians, in the Ottoman Empire died as a result of deportations through the Desert of Deir Zor, now the Syrian Desert, by the Turkish government during the First World War. During deportations people suffered from starvation and fatigue or were killed by Ottoman soldiers and civilians. This is known as the Armenian Genocide (modern definition), or the Armenian Massacre.

The delegates will discuss the topic not as members of the United Nations (UN), but as the League of Nations. The League of Nations was established in 1923 as an international organization

---

"League of Nations: The Armenian Question," Historical Security Council, Universidad Iberoamericana, 2012. Reprinted by Permission.

created after World War I. It's main objective was to reestablish peace and avoid the emergence of a new World War.

Background

Hamidian Massacres

From 1894 to 1896, before the bloodbaths of 1915, an estimated of 100,000 to 300,000 Armenians were killed in the "Hamidian Massacres". This massacres were perpetrated by the Ottoman government and the Hamidiye corps (an armed group formed by Kurds at the orders of the Sultan) during the reign of Abdul Hamid II, as acts of repression against the protests and insurrection of the Armenians.

The Armenians wanted the same rights as the muslim part of the Turkish population and were tired of paying an excessive amount of taxes. Also they were seeking autonomy and international interest for their cause.

In 1894 an armed protest took place in Sasun, organized by some of the political Armenian forces, where the Armenians refused to pay the taxes. The Armenians ought the Hamidiye corps for several weeks until the rebellion was suppressed and the Sasun villages were massacred as a punishment.

Repression in 1895 and 1896 because of protests against the violent government and the seizure of an Ottoman bank resulted in the killings of hundreds of thousands of Armenians, Kurds, civilians and Ottoman forces.

The revolutions of the Young Turks (CUP)

The Young Turks, or the Committee of Union and Progress, was a liberal political group integrated by young intellectuals and military that were against the government of the sultan Abdul Hamid II.

In 1889 the Young Turks tried to start a revolution, but they were discovered and forced into hiding. Then in 1908 they tried again, this time they got an agreement with the sultan where he restored the 1876 constitution and the parliament. From that point forward the Young Turks increased their political power in the

Empire. They took complete control of the government in 1913 by a triumvirate conformed by Talât Paşa, Ahmed Cemal Paşa, and Enver Paşa.

The Young Turks made reforms for the education and industrialization of the Empire. Also they allowed the Armenians to join the army, a privilege only for Muslim Turks. Furthermore, the Young Turks ordered the Armenian Massacre and led the Ottoman Empire into World War I.

Balkan Wars

The Ottoman Empire was in decay: losing all their territories in Africa and Europe; Bulgaria and Albania became independent; the Austro-Hungarian empire took Bosnia and Herzegovina; and Italy became the owner of Libya.

Greece, Serbia, Montenegro and Bulgaria (once a part of the Ottoman Empire and of the Balkan League alliance) declared war to the Ottoman Empire. The Balkan alliance snatched from the Turks the territories of the north of Greece, Crete, Thrace, and the southern European shores of the Black Sea.

As a result of this first war the Balkan powers started to fight about the division of one of their new territories: Macedonia. In 1913 Greece, Serbia and Montenegro allied with the Ottoman Empire against Bulgaria for the control of Macedonia. This second Balkan War allowed the Ottoman Empire to recover some of its lost territories.

First World War

When the Ottoman Empire entered to the war their main enemy was its neighbor the Russian Empire (today the Russian Federation). In the Russian contingents that entered into the Ottoman Empire were thousands of Armenian recruits, some of them deserters from the Turkish army. As a result the Armenian soldiers in the Ottoman army were disarmed and sent to labor battalions or killed.

The government made a discrediting campaign against the Armenians, accusing them of being traitors and a threat to the nation for joining the Russians.

The Massacres

In April 24 of 1915 the Ottoman government arrested, tortured and killed publicly around 250 Armenian intellectuals and community leaders in Constantinople. After that the government decided to relocate the Armenian population from the eastern of Anatolia to the provinces of the south.

The "Dead Marches"

The Ottoman government deported the Armenians from all over the Empire. The Armenians were told they were being relocated to different parts of the country. They were forced to walk long distances in difficult terrains and poor conditions. The bodies of the dead Armenians were left in the way. They died from fatigue, starvation or disease. Also the Ottoman soldiers or civilians killed them.

The government created deadly units, called the Special Organization, dedicated to kill Armenians during the deportations, while they were walking or camping.

The women and children were kidnapped or raped. The young women that were stolen were taken to the harems of rich Turks and converted into Islam.

Consequences

After the massive deportations almost all the Armenian population in the Turkish territory was exterminated or exiled. The few survivors, woman and children, were forced to embrace Islam. Others ran away from the Empire and established themselves in Europe, America and the Middle East as refugees.

In May of 1918 Eastern Armenia made the first attempt of an independent Armenian State named the Democratic Republic of Armenia. From 1918 to 1920 the Armenian Republic entered in war with the Ottoman Empire, who took large territories of the Armenian Republic. In 1920 Soviet Russia invaded the Democratic Republic of Armenia and changed its name to the Armenian Soviet Socialist Republic. That same year, during the partition of the

Ottoman territories after the First World War, Woodrow Wilson, president of the United States, was invited to delimit the new territory for an Armenian state. Borders were never draw because of the interests of the newly formed Turkey.

Conclusion

The delegates of the League of Nations will have to take actions that help the victims of these massacres, make an agreement about the validation of a possible Armenian state and its territorial delimitation. Also they will discuss the necessary measures to be applied for the responsibility of the Ottoman government and the new Turkish state on the death of Armenians during the war.

The agreements will have to secure peace between nations, the re-establishment of relations between Turks and Armenians, and their relations with the rest of the world.

Guide Questions:

What was the role of the non-Muslim population in the Ottoman Empire?

Who were the Young Turks in the triumvirate? What happened to them?

What is the history of the League of Nations? What is the position of Turkey about the Armenian massacre?

What were the topics at the Lausanne peace talks? How was the territorial delimitation of the Wilsonian Armenia? What can your delegation do to solve the Armenian refugee problem? What can your delegation do to improve the Armenian-Turkish relationship?

References:

1) "Genocidio Armenio Inicio." *GenocidioArmenio.org*. N.p., n.d. Web. 13 Sept. 2012. http://www.genocidioarmenio.org/inicio/.

2) "Ottoman Empire." *Encyclopædia Britannica. Encyclopædia Britannica Online Academic Edition*. Encyclopædia Britannica Inc., 2012. Web. 13 Sep. 2012.

http://www.britannica.com/EBchecked/topic/434996/Ottoman-Empire.

3) "Q&A: Armenian Genocide Dispute." *BBC News*. BBC, 03 May 2010. Web. 13 Sept. 2012. http://news.bbc.co.uk/2/hi/6045182.stm.

The Armenian Genocide

4) *The Armenian Genocide.* Prod. Andrew Goldberg. PBS, 2006. DVD. Web. 19 Sept. 2012. https://www.youtube.com/watch?v=1rPK6qdAcoA.

5) "Hamidian (Armenian) Massacres." *Armenian-genocide.org.* Armenian National Institute, n.d. Web. 20 Sept. 2012. http://www.armenian- genocide.org/hamidian.html.

6) "A Chronology of the Armenian Genocide." *Armenian-genocide.org.* Armenian National Institute, n.d. Web. 23 Sept. 2012. http://www.armenian- genocide.org/chronology.html.

7) "The League of Nations and the Question of Human Rights." *Humanrightsinitiative.ucdavis.edu.* UCDAVIS Humanities Institute, n.d. Web. 26 Sept. 2012. http://humanrightsinitiative.ucdavis.edu/2011/08/30/the-league-of- nations-and-the-question-of-human-rights/.

8) Watenpaugh, Keith David. "The League of Nations and the Post-Genocide Armenians of the MiddleEast: Be-tween Communal Survival and National Rights." *Scribd.* UCDAVIS Humanities Institute, n.d. Web. 26 Sept. 2012. http://www.scribd.com/fullscreen/63600363?access_key=key- 1hsc8kyqu7hppirfdum3.

9) "Mapping Armenian Genocide." *Genocide-museum.am.* Genocide Museum | The Armenian Genocide Museum-institute, n.d. Web. 27 Sept. 2012. http://www.genocide-museum.am/eng/mapping_armenian_genocide.php.

Viewpoint 4

Human Nature and Ethnic Conflict
Gregory G. Dimijian

In this viewpoint, Gregory Dimijian expounds on historical conflicts and war. For this writer, acts of war, genocide, and ethnic conflict are part of human nature. The Armenian Genocide is discussed as one dreadful event among many human events, more evil than nature's disasters. Author Gregory G. Dimijian was a psychiatrist, a scientist, naturalist, and a world traveler. As a park ranger and avid photographer, he took more than 200,000 photographs and wrote books on nature with his wife. After retiring from private medical practice, he served as a clinical associate professor of Psychiatry at University of Texas until his death in 2017.

My overriding premise in this article is that warfare, genocide, and ethnic conflict are not aberrant human nature. They *are* human nature. The dark side of human nature is fortunately only part of our nature, but it is a terrifying side; it is to be feared as much as the bright side is to be cherished. The dark side has led to heart-rending atrocities over the face of the planet, *nonstop*, over the course of human history.

The director of the United Nations Demining Program, Patrick Blagden, estimated that upward of 200 million antipersonnel landmines are scattered in 56 countries around the world (1). According to the International Committee of the Red Cross, "Most of the victims are poor farmers, women or often children who are

---

"Warfare, Genocide, and Ethnic Conflict: A Darwinian Approach," by Gregory G. Dimijian, Baylor University Medical Center Proceedings, July 2010.

collecting firewood, tending cattle or gathering food in an area that was previously a battleground" (2).

The sobering fact is that violence and warfare are characteristic of virtually all cultures throughout human history. One could even say that they are a trademark of human nature. If this is so, we cannot avoid the frightening question: Does it somehow have an *evolutionary logic*, that is, could such a tendency actually have been selected for over the course of human evolution?

We and They

One of the foremost evolutionary biologists of our time, Edward O. Wilson, has argued that a *we-they* tendency characterizes human nature. In the we-they dichotomy, people are placed inside and outside of an imaginary mental circle. Consider the following examples:

- light skin ↔ dark skin
- men ↔ women
- children: kids like us ↔ kids that are different
- Democrats ↔ Republicans
- heterosexual ↔ homosexual
- street gang #1 ↔ street gang #2
- Christians ↔ Muslims
- pro-choice ↔ pro-life
- rich ↔ poor

Those on the outside are often considered inferior, sometimes even subhuman. The boundary between *we* and *they*, however, can shift suddenly under the right circumstances.

George Orwell recounted a remarkable story in his essay "Looking Back on the Spanish War" (3). He saw a man running for his life half-dressed, holding up his pants with one hand. "I refrained from shooting at him because of that detail about the trousers. I had come here to shoot at 'Fascists' but a man who is holding up his trousers isn't a 'Fascist,' he is visibly a fellow creature, similar to your self." A mental switch flipped, and the man was instantly reclassified from *nonperson* to *person*.

During World War I, German and English troops in December 1914 laid down their arms and celebrated Christmas together. This touching story is told in the movie *Joyeux Nöel* and in a ballad by John McCutcheon, with the last line: "And on each end of the rifle we're the same" (4).

In *Humanity: A Moral History of the Twentieth Century*, Jonathan Glover described another equally poignant incident, as told to him by David Spurret, an eyewitness:

> *In 1985, in the old apartheid South Africa, there was a demonstration in Durban. The police attacked the demonstrators with customary violence. One policeman chased a black woman, intending to beat her with his club. As she ran, her shoe slipped off. The policeman was a well-brought-up young Afrikaner, who knew that when a woman loses her shoe you pick it up for her. Their eyes met as he handed her the shoe. He then left her, as clubbing her was no longer an option (5).*

In all three of these examples, a *they* person moved instantly into the inner circle. We may *humanize* our pet animals at the same time that we *dehumanize* other humans!

Preemptive Self-Protection

> *The story of the human race is war. Except for brief and precarious interludes there has never been peace in the world; and long before history began murderous strife was universal and unending. —Winston Churchill (6)*

> *We have grasped the mystery of the atom and rejected the Sermon on the Mount.... The world has achieved brilliance without wisdom, power without conscience. Ours is a world of nuclear giants and ethical infants. —General Omar Bradley (7)*

> *I know not with what weapons World War III will be fought, but World War IV will be fought with sticks and stones. —Albert Einstein (8)*

The Armenian Genocide

On the eve of the new millennium, Sir Shridath Ramphal made a chilling prediction at a United Nations conference at Cambridge University: "Humanity remains an endangered species…. On the eve of a new century and a new millennium, we probably have less reason for assurance than our ancestors had in 1900, or even the year 1000, that we are passing on to future generations the right to life" (9).

The Greek writer Thucydides, considered the greatest historian of antiquity, wrote in *History of the Peloponnesian War:* "What made the war inevitable was the growth of Athenian power and the fear which this caused in Sparta" (10).

The only option for self-protection may be to wipe out potentially hostile neighbors first in a preemptive strike. Tragically, you might arrive at these conclusions even if you didn't have an aggressive bone in your body. This Hobbesian trap is one explanation of violent conflict. If neighbors form alliances, they may become entangling, meaning that two parties with no prior animosities can find themselves at war, when the ally of one attacks the ally of the other.

The Roman philosopher Seneca imagined the Earth from space and asked, "Is this that pinpoint which is divided by fire and sword among so many nations? How ridiculous are the boundaries set by mortals" (11). Nearly 20 centuries later the American author Kurt Vonnegut observed that the Earth "looks so clean. You can't see all the hungry, angry earthlings down there—and the smoke and the sewage and trash and sophisticated weaponry"

Ingroup and Outgroup

Charles Darwin's brilliant insight that natural selection explains much of evolution was not well accepted until the early 20th century. We know now that natural selection operates on one or more of several levels, including that of the gene, cell, individual organism, or group of organisms (even an entire species).

Can group selection account for the *we-they?* Could a warlike predisposition evolve through natural selection? If we discover

Context for the Armenian Genocide

that it can, we would be one step closer to intervention. As it turns out, a study by Jung-Kyoo Choi and Samuel Bowles, published in the journal *Science* in 2007, reported the results of a theoretical analysis showing that outgroup hostility and ingroup cohesion can favor the survival of one group of people over another. The abstract of the paper states:

> *Altruism—benefiting fellow group members at a cost to oneself— and parochialism—hostility toward individuals not of one's own ethnic, racial, or other group—are common human behaviors. The intersection of the two—which we term "parochial altruism"—is puzzling from an evolutionary perspective because altruistic or parochial behavior reduces one's payoffs by comparison to what one would gain by eschewing these behaviors. But parochial altruism could have evolved if parochialism promoted intergroup hostilities and the combination of altruism and parochialism contributed to success in these conflicts. Our game-theoretic analysis and agent-based simulations show that under conditions likely to have been experienced by late Pleistocene and early Holocene humans, neither parochialism nor altruism would have been viable singly, but by promoting group conflict, they could have evolved jointly (13).*

[...]

This study throws some desperately needed light on the evolutionary roots of warfare, suggesting that a combination of ingroup cohesion and outgroup hostility can exert a group-selectionist advantage. That is, selection can favor the group, even if it doesn't favor the individual; the warrior who dies in battle testifies to this. Ingroup altruism is shown by the warrior who dies for his countrymen even if he doesn't personally know most of them.

Neither ingroup altruism nor outgroup hostility can provide benefits singly, but together they "share a common fate, with war the elixir of their success." I found a remarkable observation supporting this conclusion in an article about the Pashtun (Pushtun) people of Afghanistan: "The only time the Pashtun are at peace with themselves is when they are at war" (14).

The Pashtuns who live in Afghanistan and Pakistan, have a system of ethics that regards treachery and violence as virtues rather than vices. A man who loses his honor is ostracized, along with his family, and he is obliged to take revenge. He may kill both his daughter's lover and his own daughter.

The Elixir of Violence

In *War Is a Force That Gives Us Meaning*, journalist Chris Hedges argued that war is an elixir that envelops us with a common cause (15). War is a narcotic that can give a social group a common high, a common purpose.

The Stanford psychologist Philip Zimbardo conducted the Stanford prison experiment in 1971, in which 24 college student volunteers were randomly divided into "guards" and "inmates" and placed in a mock prison environment. Within a week the study was abandoned, as the students were transformed into sadistic guards and emotionally broken prisoners. Zimbardo has compared this to the Abu Ghraib prison event in Iraq (16, 17). In a *New York Times* interview in 2007, Zimbardo was asked: "So you disagree with Anne Frank, who wrote in her diary, 'I still believe, in spite of everything, that people are truly good at heart'?" Zimbardo answered yes, he disagreed: "Some people can be made into monsters. And the people who abused, and killed her, were" (18).

"Thrill" attacks on the homeless in US cities took a violent upswing in 2008 and 2009, when the economic recession and rising unemployment caused the ranks of street people to swell. Hate crimes, beatings, rapes, and murders were directed against these vulnerable people. A blurb appeared in an undercover publication announcing an upcoming "hobo convention" and said: "Kill one for fun. We're 87% sure it's legal." Many homeless people in Las Vegas moved to the flood tunnels beneath the streets, where flash floods occur after heavy rains. Some of these "refugees" stated that they felt safer underground in the dark, even with the risk of floods, because attackers wouldn't seek them out there (19).

Soldiers in battle and rioters in ethnic massacres report that they often kill with gusto, sometimes in a state they describe as "joy" or "ecstasy." Needless to say, this is frightening. As if to confirm this finding, an interrogator returning from a US prison in Iraq in 2005 stated, "Sadism is always right over the hill. You have to admit it. Don't fool yourself—there is a part of you that will say, 'This is fun.'" Is this a learned reaction? Or part of our animal nature?

Suicide Terrorism

Suicide attack is an ancient practice, used in early Jewish history and in the Christian Crusades. The Japanese kamikaze of World War II were young, fairly well educated pilots who understood that pursuing conventional warfare would likely end in defeat; when collectively asked to volunteer for special attack transcending life and death, all stepped forward. In the Battle of Okinawa (1945), some 2000 kamikaze rammed fully fueled fighter planes into more than 300 ships, killing 5000 Americans in the most costly naval battle in American history.

More often than not, suicide terrorists from the Middle East have been shown to have no appreciable psychopathology (mental illness) and are as educated and economically well-off as surrounding populations. Recruiting organizations enlist candidates and provide charismatic trainers who cultivate commitment to die within small cells of three to six members. The 9-11 hijackers, in keeping with these findings, were not children of deprived families, but middle-class citizens of a comparatively wealthy nation (20).

On the other hand, one study has shown a difference between men and women suicide terrorists. Whereas men showed "male-bonded coalitionary violence," collaborating closely with each other, young women seemed to act on isolated personal motives, often shame from rape or infertility (21).

The Armenian Genocide

Torture

> *Concerning Man ... he is the only creature that inflicts pain for sport, knowing it to be pain.* —Mark Twain (22)
>
> *The line dividing good and evil cuts through the heart of every human being.* —Aleksandr Solzhenistyn (23)
>
> *Torture may be worse now in Iraq than under Saddam Hussein.... Torture is at appalling levels in Iraq. Everyone, it seems, from the Iraqi forces to the militias to the anti-US insurgents, now routinely use torture on the people they kill.* —Manfred Nowak (24)

How can humans torture and kill fellow humans? Ingrid Betancourt, the Columbian-French activist who was rescued in 2008 after 6 years of captivity, said: "I think we have that animal inside of us, all of us.... We can be so horrible to the others. For me it was like understanding what I couldn't understand before, how, for example, the Nazis, how this could happen."

In the *Gulag Archipelago* (23), Aleksandr Solzhenitsyn chronicled over four decades of Soviet arrest and torture of over 10 million people. Ordinary citizens were arrested, often in the middle of the night, and deported to one of over 475 forced labor camps. There they were repeatedly interrogated and tortured and were permitted no contact with their families. They were often executed if their interrogation was considered unsatisfactory.

The unprecedented scale of human torture in the Russian Gulags forces a brute confrontation of human nature. What would you think of another planetary intelligence that perpetrated these cruelties on their own kind? How do we explain this to children?

Following is a partial list of the truly horrific torture methods used in the Soviet Gulags:

- Sleep deprivation
- Confinement in upright coffin-sized cell
- Packing in tiny cell with other prisoners so that few prisoners' feet touched the floor
- Starvation

- Humiliation
- Living cloak of blood-feeding bedbugs in a coffin-sized cell
- Standing on testicles with booted foot
- Worst of all: threats to prisoner's family

Humans have *justified* torture in a variety of ways:

- Claiming *moral* authority (dehumanization): *They are degenerates, infidels, cockroaches.*
- Displacing responsibility: *We are just carrying out orders.*
- Diffusing responsibility: *Everybody does it.*
- Blaming the victims: *They deserved it; they asked for it; they had it coming.*
- Renaming torture: *We use aggressive interrogation.* Does this sound familiar?

Physicians participated to an extraordinary extent in the Nazi exterminations of the 1930s and 1940s. Some 50% of German physicians collaborated in the sterilizing of Jews, infants born with deformities, gays, and patients at mental institutions, all of whom were compared to infectious disease organisms seen through the microscope. Tens of thousands of prisoners lost their lives in medical experiments performed on them, such as freezing with attempts to revive them with warming, hyperbaric compression, wound creation, infectious disease experiments with malaria and typhus, and poisonous chemical warfare experiments. How does one explain the approval and collaboration of so many physicians, who used their skills to torture, kill, and perform inhumane experiments on the prisoners?

I can find no evidence of similar physician participation in the atrocities of the Gulag, perhaps because the Gulag was intended to exterminate *political* enemies, in contrast to the Nazi extermination of "inferior" humans.

War seems to be open season for rape, often mass rape of thousands. This is not an exaggeration. Read about almost any war, any genocide, and you will gasp at the victimization of women and children. It becomes obvious that this is less about sex than about power, humiliation, and conquest, using sex as a weapon. Men seem to feel a kind of narcotic power in war, at a time when women have lost their male partners. In the ethnic conflict of the Democratic Republic of Congo in 2008, rape was described as the norm by a refugee survivor. Women were raped, brutalized, and murdered. Survivors were abducted by the invaders. This is not just one more form of torture and murder. It is also a reflection of an asymmetry in the way the sexes have treated each other across cultures and through human history. The difference in strength between a man and a woman cannot be the only explanation. There is an underlying evolutionary dynamic that reflects a fundamental difference in gender identity and aggression, encoded in behavioral predispositions.

[…]

Mobs and Militias

We need look no further than to pre–civil rights America for some of the most dramatic examples of dehumanization, when blacks were hanged and burned publicly in savage rituals. Photographs of the "barbeques," as they were called, with children looking on, were sent to relatives on postcards.

In some ethnic conflicts, which may or may not be labeled *genocide*, children have been conscripted into the killing armies. Ishmael Beah, a child ex-soldier himself, chronicled his story, which was published in 2007. He grew up in Sierra Leone, West Africa, and had a nonviolent childhood until age 12, when his world fell apart. His family was murdered in front of his eyes, and he was conscripted into a militant army for 2 years. During this time he learned to murder with impunity and enjoyed torturing his captives before killing them, having learned that he should view them as the ones who killed his family.

Here is a painful example of E. O. Wilson's *we-they*. Ishmael described burying captives alive after forcing them to dig their own graves. In the course of his rehabilitation at age 15 he lived through flashbacks of the torture he once enjoyed imposing on his victims.

> *The idea of death didn't cross my mind at all and killing had become as easy as drinking water. My mind had not only snapped during the first killing, it had also stopped making remorseful records, or so it seemed. I joined the army really because of the loss of my family and starvation. I wanted to avenge the deaths of my family. I also had to get some food to survive, and the only way to do that was to be part of the army. It was not easy being a soldier, but we just had to do it.... I am not a soldier any more.... What I have learned is that revenge is not good.... If I take revenge, I will kill another person whose family will want revenge; then revenge and revenge and revenge will never come to an end (26).*

Ishmael described his own deviant and disturbed behavior. How do we view such behavior on the scale of an entire culture engaged in genocide or warfare? Where do we draw a line between *human nature* and deviant individual behavior? No one knows how to draw such a line, but the question must be addressed, because we must try to understand where cultural group behavior ends and sick, disturbed individual behavior begins, even if we can't draw a fine line. Human nature is part of this equation, and we must understand how it has evolved if we ever expect to do anything about it. Otherwise the cycle will go on and on, as Ishmael Beah warned.

Genocide and Ethnic Conflict

Genocide is the deliberate and often systematic destruction of an ethnic, religious, or racial group. As in warfare, one side often dehumanizes the other side, but unlike warfare, genocide is often waged by one group against another and not the other way around. Some consider the Holocaust the mother of all genocides. A close second was the Gulag, involving systematic capture, punishment, and often execution of millions of supposed political opponents.

A survivor of Auschwitz wrote poignantly in 2010:

> *The fury of the Haitian earthquake, which has taken more than 200,000 lives, teaches us how cruel nature can be to man. The Holocaust, which destroyed a people, teaches us that nature, even in its cruelest moments, is benign in comparison with man when he loses his moral compass and his reason (27).*

The Holocaust and Gulag each claimed over 10 million lives, the equivalent of 100 Haitian earthquakes.

In 1994, extremist Hutus in Rwanda slaughtered 8000 Tutsies a day for 100 days, calling the Tutsies "myenzi" (cockroaches). The violence became so maniacal that neighbors and even relatives slaughtered each other. The nightmare is described in lurid detail by Paul Rusesabagina in his excellent documentary, *An Ordinary Man*, written in 2006 (28).

In an equally gripping book, a near-victim of the Rwandan genocide, Immaculée Ilibagaza, told her story. She was hidden in a bathroom for months, along with a few friends, and given food and water. Hundreds of people surrounded the house, many of whom were dressed like devils, wearing skirts of tree bark, and some had goat horns strapped onto their heads. Their faces were easily recognizable, and "there was murder in their eyes." They jumped about, waving spears, machetes, and knives in the air. They chanted a chilling song: "Kill them, kill them all, kill the old and the young.... A baby snake is still a snake, kill it, too, let none escape, kill them, kill them all!" Immaculée Ilibagiza commented:

> *It wasn't the soldiers who were chanting, nor was it the trained militiamen who had been tormenting us for days. No, these were my neighbors, people I'd known since childhood. He was a high school dropout my dad had tried to help straighten out. I saw Philip, a young man who'd been too shy to look anyone in the eye, but who now seemed completely at home in this group of killers. At the front of the pack I could make out two local schoolteachers who were friends of Damascene. I recognized dozens of Mataba's most prominent citizens in the mob, all of whom were in a killing frenzy, ranting and screaming for Tutsi blood. The killers leading the group pushed their way into the pastor's house, and suddenly the chanting was coming from all directions (29).*

If you don't think genocide will go on and on, consider Jared Diamond's list of genocides (30):

- Tens of millions of American Indians killed by Spanish and English colonists of North, Central, and South America from the 15th through the 19th centuries
- Over 1 million Armenians killed by Turks in 1915
- Over 10 million Jews killed by Nazis in Occupied Europe between 1939 and 1945
- 8000 Tutsies killed per day for 100 days by extremist Hutus in Rwanda in 1994
- Hundreds of thousands of Darfurians killed since 2003

The *New England Journal of Medicine* called Darfur the "first genocide of the 21st century" (31). The killing in Sudan became so chaotic in 2007 that Arab tribes began fighting other Arab tribes and rebels began fighting rebels. Armed men who seemed to have no allegiances were attacking anyone who crossed their path. It appeared that in places the *we-they* becomes so arbitrary that almost anyone else could be considered *they*.

Human Nature Versus Individual Psychopathology

Teenagers in Los Angeles flaunt their gang sign and play with loaded guns. There is a subculture of violence in the toughest neighborhoods, in which gangs are like rival armies. A Jesuit priest in Los Angeles said, "I've buried kids I loved who were killed by kids I love" (32).

If we consider that violence is inherent in human nature, how do we distinguish between *normal* violent behavior and pathological (sick) violent behavior? Consider these categories: soldiers in war, genocide, violent ethnic conflict, street gangs, terrorist activity, and torture.

Where do we draw the line between *normal* and *abnormal* forms of abuse and violence? Unfortunately, this is an unanswered question and a painful confrontation. Many violent individuals are clearly mentally ill. These are singled out and treated, and often incarcerated. Yet many persons who commit violent acts, such as soldiers in warfare, are not considered emotionally ill and may be rewarded for their courage in killing. This is true in ethnic conflicts as well.

A person with no history of violence can be trained to be violent and abusive, if this is systematically carried out in a social setting where it is encouraged and rewarded. The Stanford experiment by Philip Zimbardo showed this, as did the prison experience at Abu Ghraib. Such training can also be effective even if it is abrupt and highly traumatic, as in the case of Ishmael Beah, who became a shadow of his former self, finding it exciting and fun to torture and kill. There are examples of men who have tortured prisoners during their daily jobs and returned in the evening to their families, living as good family men and neighbors (personal communication, Ryan F. Estévez, MD, PhD, MPH). Suicide bombers are often remembered as well respected and well adjusted.

The behavior of other animals is reminiscent of our own. Aggression against a perceived enemy, whether of the same or another species, has evolved in the interest of personal and in-group survival.

Posttraumatic stress disorder (PTSD), now recognized as a common and tragic result of the emotional trauma of war, is not a human exclusive. It has also been documented in elephants, with symptoms typical of human PTSD: abnormal startle response, apparent depression, unpredictable asocial behavior, and hyperaggression. They were studied by veteran researchers Cynthia Moss and Joyce Poole, among others, who described their startling behavior:

> The air explodes with the sound of high-powered rifles, and the startled infant watches his family fall to the ground, the image seared into his memory. He and other orphans are then transported to distant locales to start new lives. Ten years later, the teenaged orphans begin a killing rampage. A scene describing post-traumatic stress disorder in Kosovo or Rwanda? The similarities are striking— but here, the teenagers are young elephants and the victims,

rhinoceroses.... Now, studies of human PTSD can be instructive in understanding how violence also affects elephant culture (33).

A raging elephant matriarch can be a frightening sight. The matriarch would have almost certainly overturned the vehicle and tried to kill us had we not outdistanced her. We had startled her and her bond group the day before, when they suddenly discovered us parked in the forest close beside the river they were playing in, and they didn't forget who we were.

Preventing War and Genocide

The psychoanalyst Vamik Volkan has spent much of his professional life studying ethnic and political strife in the Middle East. He has taught arbitration and conflict resolution to cultural and political leaders, using his skills as a psychoanalyst in a group setting. In *Killing in the Name of Identity* he wrote:

> *Despite some pessimism about human nature, especially as it is manifested in large groups, I believed that we could be successful in certain areas of international conflict if we were to spend extended periods of time—as a psychoanalyst spends years in treating an analysand—opening dialogues between enemies and providing actual examples of peaceful coexistence.... I knew we could not change human nature in general, but perhaps we could manage to tame massive aggression in certain locations (34).*

In an earlier book, *Blood Lines: From Ethnic Pride to Ethnic Terrorism*, Volkan wrote that most Jewish people share a legacy "to never forget," and he asked the poignant question: "How do members of a group adaptively mourn past losses ... so that they do not induce feelings of anger, humiliation, and the desire for revenge?" (35).

Although Volkan's studies and teaching reflect a state-of-the-art understanding of warfare and ethnic conflict, not once in his books have I found a discussion of evolutionary aspects of human behavior. He covers cultural, developmental, and psychoanalytic aspects of the *we-they* tendency inherent in human nature, but fails to address the critical need of understanding human nature in a fundamentally biological light.

How did a *we-they* tendency evolve and become so powerful? Has it had Darwinian adaptive value over the course of our evolution? If so, at what level(s) of selection did it evolve—gene, individual, and/or group?

Much has been written about how to intervene in ethnic conflicts—how to stop genocide from escalating and "spilling out of control"—but the challenge is like sweeping back the ocean with a broom. If we wait until feelings are at the breaking point we may have lost the chance to intervene by arbitration. Instead, I would argue that we are "missing the boat" in the search for a solution to genocide.

Teaching Children

The ready availability of lethal weapons has not made violent behavior any easier to manage. An AK-47 is easy to learn to use; in half an hour a 10-year-old can learn the basics and have as much firepower as a Civil War regiment.

In a 2007 article, Hamza Hendawi described Iraqi children playing make-believe war games inspired by the Shiite-Sunni conflict in Baghdad's Shiite enclave of Sadr City, Iraq. He wrote:

> "Playing such games is normal," said a schoolteacher in Baghdad. Violence has become part of children's lives. A toy store owner said that most of the children who visit his store are looking for the "biggest and most harmful toy guns. Ninety-five percent of the toys I sell are guns." A policeman said he tries to discourage his two sons from playing, and talks to them about Shiites and Sunnis living in peace, but "they keep going back to the same game" (36).

We have neglected to teach the evolution of human nature to children—very young children—when they are forming their fundamental ideas about human behavior. We now know that the *we-they* dichotomy is a feature of human nature in all cultures and across history, and we are beginning to see how it may have evolved through group selection. If we teach children that outgroup hostility is a product of evolutionary *logic*, there is hope that they will see it as a deep-rooted behavioral predisposition to be always aware of.

The golden opportunity to teach children about the dangers of *we-they* comes in their school years when they see examples all around. In schools one sees arbitrary social divisions created by the children themselves, based on clothing styles, ethnic identity, academic standing, skin color, sports team, fraternities, sororities, even the kind of car an older child drives.

The Nazis used their educational system to demean, even to dehumanize, Jews, by incorporating their xenophobia into the everyday life of their children.

"Look around you," we can tell them. These are the seeds of dangerous adult conflicts which cross every conceivable boundary. Very graphic examples are in the news every day and in the personal family histories of many. The teaching must be sensitively planned and pursued year after year.

This is no easy task if a child goes home and reports that he is being taught to respect and appreciate all other people, even if a clear distinction is made between respecting another person but not respecting their behavior. What if his family harbors a deep bitterness toward another ethnic or political group? Is he supposed to defy his own family's values? Family intervention may become a necessary part of the educational challenge.

It may take generations before the reality sinks in that the *dark side* of human nature is to be feared and taken seriously—in everyone, including you and me. Our large brains are unique in nature in being endowed with the ability to understand what's wrong with them and to work to overcome destructive behaviors that have been chiseled into them by natural selection. "Nature, Mr. Allnutt, is what we were put in this world to rise above."

Our very nature embodies our hope.

Closing Thoughts

In *The Youngest Science*, Lewis Thomas argued that civilization would be much improved if men retired for 100 years and allowed women to run everything.

> *I am, in short, swept off my feet by women, and I do not think they have yet been assigned the place in the world's affairs that they are biologically made for. Somewhere in that other X chromosome are coils of nucleic acid containing information for a qualitatively different sort of behavior from the instructions in the average Y chromosome. The difference is there, I think, for the long-term needs of the species, and it has something to do with spotting things of great importance (37).*

I would like to see Thomas's wish come true. There is a caveat, however. If violent traits are more characteristic of men than of women, and if they are represented in genetic predispositions toward violence, how did those traits evolve? If they evolved by female choice (intersexual selection), then women have played a role. Could women have consciously or unconsciously (or both) favored mating with men who were strong and more aggressive, thus contributing to the spread of such predisposing genes, especially in their sons?

Or instead, did male-male competition (intrasexual selection) favor violence in men? Could men who were more inclined to be violent have more reproductive success than other men? Could both inter- and intrasexual selection have worked together to predispose men to violence? In addition, there is still the possibility of group selection, as discussed above, contributing to 1) ingroup cohesion and altruism and 2) outgroup hostility, in both men and women.

Powerful reasons exist, then, to consider evolutionary predispositions to warfare, genocide, ethnic conflict, and any other kind of we-they segregation. If these innate predispositions exist, we must acknowledge and understand them to combat their devastating consequences. We have come full circle to the three-tiered bridge of biology, culture, and development. We disregard any of these levels at our peril.

Humans bond, love, spend a lifetime giving to others, yet can also be cruel and commit atrocities on a vast scale. The paradox of a bright side and a dark side coexisting in human nature is deeply buried in ignorance, ignorance born of turning our head the other way when there are rich opportunities to understand the evolutionary origins of the paradox.

References

1. Summary of United Nations Demining Report Presented by Patrick M. Blagden, United Nations Demining Expert. In ICRC Symposium on Anti-Personnel Mines, Montreux 21-23 April 1993 Geneva, Switzerland: International Committee of the Red Cross, 1993:117.

2. Parlow A. Toward a global ban on landmines. International Review of the Red Cross. 1995;307:391–410.

3. Orwell G. Looking back on the Spanish War. New Road, 1943. Available at http://www.orwell.ru/library/essays/Spanish_War/english/esw_1; accessed March 19, 2010.

4. McCutcheon J. Winter Solstice. Burlington, MA: Rounder; 1984. Christmas in the trenches [song]

5. Glover J. Humanity: A Moral History of the Twentieth Century. New Haven, CT: Yale University Press; 2000.

6. Churchill W. Shall we all commit suicide? Nash's Pall Mall Magazine, June 1924.

7. Bradley ON. The Collected Writings of General Omar N. Bradley. Vol. 1. Washington, DC: Government Printing Office; 1967.

8. Einstein A, Calaprice A, editors. The New Quotable Einstein. Vol. 173. Princeton, NJ: Princeton University Press; 2005.

9. Ramphal S. Second Global Security Lecture Cambridge University, June 1995.

10. Thucydides. The Peloponnesian War Book 1, Chapter 23.

11. Seneca, Lucius Annaeus. Natural Questions Book 1, Pref. 7-11.

12. Cockell C. Year of astronomy: visions of ourselves. Nature. 2009;456(7725):30.

13. Choi JK, Bowles S. The coevolution of parochial altruism and war. Science. 2007;318(5850):636–640. [PubMed]

14. McGirk T. On bin Laden's trail. National Geographic, December 2004.

15. Hedges C. War Is a Force That Gives Us Meaning. New York: Public Affairs; 2002.

16. Stannard MB. Stanford experiment foretold Iraq scandal: 'inmates' got abused in psychology study. San Francisco Chronicle, May 8, 2004.

17. Zimbardo PG. Stanford Prison Experiment: A Simulation Study of the Psychology of Imprisonment Conducted at Stanford University [website]. Stanford, CA: Stanford University, 1999. Available at http://www.prisonexp.org/; accessed March 19, 2010.

18. Dreifus C. A conversation with Philip G. Zimbardo: finding hope in knowing the universal capacity for evil. New York Times, April 3, 2007.

19. Lichtblau E. Attacks on homeless bring push on hate crime laws. New York Times, August 7, 2009.

20. Carter AB. International affairs: a prescription for peace. Science. 2003;300(5624):1374.

21. Jenkins B. Sex and death. Science. 2006;313(5794):1711.

22. Twain M, Bender P, editors. What Is Man? And Other Philosophical Writing. Berkeley, CA: University of California Press; 1973.

23. Solzhenitsyn AI, Whitney TP. The Gulag Archipelago, 1918–1956: An Experiment in Literary Investigation (Volume One) New York: Harper & Row; 1973.

24. Iraq torture "worse after Saddam." BBC, September 21, 2006.

25. Mailer N. The white man unburdened. New York Review of Books, July 17, 2003.

26. Beah I. A Long Way Gone: Memoirs of a Boy Soldier. New York: Sarah Crichton Books/Farrar, Strauss & Giroux; 2007.

27. Pisar S. Out of Auschwitz. New York Times, January 29, 2010, p. A19.

28. Rusesabagina P, Zoellner T. An Ordinary Man: An Autobiography. New York: Viking Penguin; 2006.

29. Ilibagiza I, Erwin S. Left to Tell: Discovering God Amidst the Rwandan Holocaust. Carlsbad, CA: Hay House; 2006.

30. Diamond J. Rise and Fall of the Third Chimpanzee: How Our Animal Heritage Affects The Way We Live. Santa Fe, NM: Radius; 2000.

31. Fowler J. Beyond humanitarian bandages—confronting genocide in Sudan. N Engl J Med. 2004;351(25):2574–2576. [PubMed]

32. Herbert B. L.A.'s streets of death. New York Times, June 12, 2003.

33. Bradshaw G, Schore AN, Brown JL, Poole JH, Moss C. Elephant breakdown. Nature. 2005;433:807. [PubMed]

34. Volkan V. Killing in the Name of Identity: A Study of Bloody Conflicts. Los Angeles: Pitchstone Publishing; 2006.

35. Volkan V. Bloodlines: From Ethnic Pride to Ethnic Terrorism. Boulder, CO: Westview Press; 1998.

36. Hendawi H. Iraqi kids play make-believe war games *Associated Press*, February 24, 2007.

37. Thomas L. The Youngest Science: Notes of a Medicine-Watcher. New York: Viking; 1983.

Viewpoint 5

Remembering a Genocide Survivor
Michael J. Stone

The following viewpoint is from the Toronto Globe and Mail's Lives Lived *section. This moving obituary tells the life story of Knar Yemenidjian, a survivor of the Armenian Genocide. Her life was profoundly affected by her experience during that turbulent time. As her deeply personal story illustrates, there were lasting consequences even for those survivors who escaped physical injury. The author Michael J. Stone is a Canadian journalist and artist living in Montreal, Quebec. Stone writes for magazines and the Canadian Broadcasting Corporation,* Globe and Mail, *and on health-related matters for websites.*

She was one of Canada's last living links to an atrocity that occurred more than 100 years ago. Although Knar Yemenidjian, who died on Jan. 19, reached the age of 107, her childhood was marred by unfathomable violence that nearly ended her life.

"We're all grieving with the family," Armen Yeganian, Armenia's ambassador to Canada, commented after Ms. Yemenidjian's death. "But she was also a bigger symbol, I would imagine, for the Canadian Armenian community and for Armenian people in general."

She was born Knar Bohjelian on Feb. 14, 1909, in Caesarea, a city in central Turkey now known as Kayseri. Less than a year earlier, a group of Turkish reformers known as the Young Turks overthrew Sultan Abdul Hamid and established a constitutional

---

"Remembering Knar Yemenidjian, Survivor of the Armenian Genocide," by Michael J. Stone, February 22, 2017. Reprinted by Permission.

The Armenian Genocide

government. Although the Armenian population of Turkey was initially optimistic about the new regime, they were caught off guard by the xenophobia of the Young Turks and their targeted hatred aimed at Christians and non-Turks who they believed were a threat to the Islamic, "pure Turkish" state they envisioned.

When the Young Turks began their campaign of mass murder on April 24, 1915, the first order of action was arresting and executing several hundred Armenian intellectuals. After that, other Armenians were either systematically slaughtered by marauding killing squads or forced on death marches across the Mesopotamian desert without food or water.

Six-year-old Knar and her family survived the first wave of violence by seeking sanctuary in a barn. Ms. Yeminidjian's niece Nazar Artinian told CTV News that the family survived only because Knar's father had been warned by a Turkish friend that "all the Armenians were going to be killed."

According to Ms. Artinian, the family friend insisted, "if you want to live, leave your house, take your family and go to this farm and hide yourselves there." So the family hid among the livestock. They were besieged by typhoid and had barely enough food to sustain themselves, but they survived.

When the violence subsided, Knar and her family returned to find many of their neighbours murdered, and all the Armenian homes—including theirs—burned to the ground.

The family's only hope for continued survival was converting to Islam. So, after they left the barn they adopted Turkish names and Muslim identities. Ms. Artinian said that a great aunt convinced them that it was their only salvation. "It is better to change your religion and live longer than remain Christians and die." So they rebuilt the family home and lived under Muslim identities in Caesarea for 10 years.

Despite their conversion, the family lived in constant fear. In an interview with humanities professor Lalai Manjikian in 2015, Ms. Yemenidjian confided that while growing up, she remembered how her mother would wrap a scarf around her brother's head, "so that he might pass for a girl, given that all the men were being rounded up or killed."

Joseph Yemenidjian, Ms. Yemenidjian's son, told the *Globe and Mail* about an incident that long haunted his mother: "A half-dozen years after the genocide first started, my mother was walking with her aunt, who was only a few years older than her, down a street in Caesarea." When they turned a corner they happened upon soldiers who were dragging the body of a dead man by his feet. "He was a victim of the government-sanctioned violence. When my mother's aunt, who was already suffering from jaundice, witnessed the scene, she collapsed with terror. She never recovered, dying just a few days after the incident."

As the genocide continued, Knar got older and began attracting potential suitors, Joseph said. During the family's remaining years in Turkey, however, her father refused all requests for her hand. "My grandfather was desperate to leave Turkey," he said, "and he had no intention of leaving his daughter to fend for herself in such a place."

Once a ceasefire was established, the family fled the region. They travelled to Ankara in 1928, then Istanbul. Eleven months later, they headed to Greece by boat before immigrating to Alexandria, Egypt.

Even after they settled into their new home, Knar's father continued to reject the suitors who pressed for his permission to marry her. Joseph said that his grandfather insisted that she marry into a respectable family. In the end, his prudence paid off. "My mother was 34 when she finally met my father, who had a family member who was already connected to my mother's family via marriage." Once the family patriarch deemed Jean Yemenidjian acceptable, the couple married in 1943.

Joseph explained that his father believed that meeting Knar was fate. "He was already 41 and a goldsmith whose extended family was left destitute following the genocide. The welfare of his family fell upon his shoulders." Joseph noted that his father worked around the clock and had confessed that until Knar stole his heart, he had given up on romance.

"I never heard either of my parents utter a negative word about the other. It was just the opposite, in fact." Joseph said that his father's love for his wife and children inspired him to bless others with a singular wish. "I hope that you are lucky enough to find yourself with a family just like mine."

The couple lived happily in Egypt until 1956, when the Armenian community in Egypt once again found itself the scapegoat as a result of the Suez Canal crisis.

Arab nationalism swept the country, inciting rage and intimidation that was directed at Armenians. As a consequence, Ms. Yemenidjian's two sons, Joseph and Noubar, left for Canada and settled in Montreal.

While paying a visit to Montreal during Expo 67, Ms. Yemenidjian was wooed by the city's charms, and the couple settled there permanently in 1971.

A few years ago, she required the type of assistance that only a nursing home could provide, Joseph said. "When she moved in, and we met the medical staff, they inquired about the medications she was taking. They couldn't believe that a person might reach the age of 106 without prescription medication."

Ms. Yemenidjian's son said that his mother had a wonderful, self-effacing sense of humour. He noted that, although she spoke very little English or French, the other residents surprised him one day, when they remarked to him how funny his mother was. "We can't understand her and she can't understand us, they told him, but does she ever make us laugh!"

In 2004, Canada was among the first countries to officially recognize the genocide.

At the age of 106, Ms. Yemenidjian was among a handful of Armenian-Canadians who attended a special ceremony on Parliament Hill in 2015 to mark the centennial of the start of the genocide.

To this day, despite widespread agreement among historians, the Turkish government denies that an Armenian genocide occurred. Since 2003, Turkish teachers have been forbidden to use the term "genocide" in the classroom.

Last year, the country recalled its ambassador from Germany after the German parliament voted to recognize the genocide.

Historians conclude that approximately 1.5 million Armenians were killed during the genocide, but Turkey says the death toll has been exaggerated and considers those who were killed as casualties of a civil war.

Knar Yemenidjian leaves her two sons, Joseph and Noubar, three grandchildren and five great-grandchildren.

CHAPTER 3

Lasting Effects of the Armenian Genocide

Chapter Preface

As the viewpoints presented here discuss, more countries and institutions around the globe are recognizing that the Armenian Genocide did occur. Even Pope Francis acknowledged the genocide at a 2015 service in Rome, saying: "Concealing or denying evil is like allowing a wound to keep bleeding without bandaging it."

Still, even in the United States, there is more to be done. As late as 2013, Armenian-Americans requested that President Obama allow the Smithsonian Institute to display the Armenian Orphan Rug, a carpet woven by orphans of the genocide. And, as one viewpoint details, college students in California took to the streets in 2015, demanding acknowledgement of the Armenian Genocide to coincide with the hundred-year anniversary of the terrible events.

Another writer in this chapter speaks out about ending Turkey's denial of the Armenian Genocide—not only because the ongoing denial causes harm in Turkish society, but because this bad example has set an international precedent for denial of responsibility.

Authors of another viewpoint observe that traumatic events of the Armenian Genocide and the Holocaust have measurable lasting effects not only on survivors but their children and through epigenetics on following generations.

Looking across history and around the world—at several 20th century genocides and the various ways these events were brought to an end—it is clear that the impact of genocide is deep and wide, leaving a crater not only in global history, but in personal histories as well. Without acknowledgement, remembrance, and change, such genocidal events are bound to continue.

Viewpoint 1

Trauma Reverberates Through the Generations

Anie Kalayjian and Marian Weisberg

In this viewpoint, the authors discuss how trauma from the Armenian Genocide is transmitted to younger generations. The experience of surviving Armenians is likened to and compared with Jewish survivors of the Holocaust. People participating in a study and workshop are discussed in psychological terms that will be easily understood. Dr Anie Kalayjian is the child of parents who survived the Armenian Genocide. She is an author, educator, and therapist and an internationally renowned expert on the effects of trauma on disaster victims. Marian Weisberg is an clinical social worker and therapist working in New York City.

The attempted destruction of the Armenian people by the Ottoman Turkish Government from 1895–1915 not only cost one-and-a half million Armenian lives but created massive trauma for many of those who survived. This chapter explores the physical, psychosocial, and spiritual impact of Genocide on the offspring of survivors. Concomitantly, the authors utilize therapeutic modalities to work with this form of generational transmission of mass trauma.

Introduction

Articles addressing the generational transmission of the Genocide of the Armenians began to be published in early 1980s. In

"Generational Impact of Mass Trauma: The Post-Ottoman Turkish Genocide of the Armenians," by Anie Kalayjian and Marian Weisberg. Reprinted by Permisison.

about two decades there have been only a handful of research articles addressing this transmission. By contrast, over the past three decades, several hundred articles and dozens of doctoral dissertations have been written and published on the transmission of the effects of the Holocaust on further generations.

This chapter presents a review of the findings of an exploratory study conducted by the authors with second and third generation survivors of the Ottoman Turkish Genocide of the Armenians living on the East Coast of the United States of America.

Since the Armenian plight is not well known to many, the authors will present a historical background cited from both Armenian and non-Armenian perspectives, in an attempt to provide a balanced review.

Historical Background

Armenia is an ancient nation which occupied the region of historic Armenia, including what is now northeastern Turkey, from before 500 B.C.E. until their attempted annihilation in 1915 (Walker, 1991). Armenia was the first nation to accept Christianity as its state religion in 301 C.E., while the surrounding Ottoman nation accepted Islam around 648 C.E..

Armenia was one of many nations conquered by what was eventually consolidated as the Ottoman Empire. Ottoman Turks considered Armenians, the non-Muslim minority, as second-class citizens and for centuries subjected them to oppression. For example, Armenians and other Christians had to pay special taxes, including child levies (Housepian, 1971; Hovannisian, 1985; Reid, 1984), and were forced to give Muslims and their herds free room and board for up to 6 months under the hospitality taxes (Housepian, 1971). In some areas, Armenians were barred from speaking Armenian except when praying (Hovannisian, 1985), and the first author researching the survivors of the Genocide interviewed a woman who had known Armenian men in her village whose tongues had been cut out for speaking in Armenian. Armenians were subjected to forced migration, enslavement (Reid,

1984), and repeated massacres (Dadrian, 1995; Lidgett, 1897). Armenians were also barred from giving legal testimony or bearing arms, leaving them no legal recourse or self-defense against gun-bearing Muslim neighbors (Hovannisian, 1985; Kalfaian, 1982).

When Sultan Abdul-Hamid II, known in history as the Damned or the Bloody Sultan, came to the throne in 1876, he created the Hamidiye, an irregular cavalry modeled after the Russian Cossacks, to carry out pogroms against the Armenians just as the Tsar used his irregulars to persecute the Jews. Hamid massacred hundreds of thousands of Armenians during his reign, in 1894 in the Sassun villages, in 1895–1896 throughout the Turkish Empire, in 1904 again in Sassun, and there is suspicion that he was behind the 1909 massacre in Adana and Cilicia, which coincided with the attempted coup d'état in Constantinople (Istanbul) (Papazian, 1993).

Enlightened Turks were distressed by the misrule of Abdul-Hamid, as were the Armenians or the European powers. These Turkish patriots began to organize a revolutionary movement called the Committee for Union and Progress (CUP). This group was well known in Europe and America as the Young Turks. These Young Turks were successful in seizing the Sultan's power by revolution and reinstating the liberal constitution of 1876. Having managed a successful revolt against the Sultan, the Young Turks then turned on the Armenians, claiming Turkey for the Turks. The new implication of the racist policy was that the minorities, especially the Armenians, had to be eradicated (Papazian, 1993).

Lord Bryce's "Blue Book," *The Treatment of the Armenians in the Ottoman Empire, 1915–1916*, edited by Arnold Toynbee, is one of the most damning single early sources of the eyewitness accounts of the Genocide of the Armenians, 1915–1916. According to Toynbee (1916), in the Genocide of the Armenians the criminals had been members of the Committee of Union and Progress, above all, perhaps Talaat, the most intelligent of the ruling triumvirs. In the course of the seven years spanning 1909-15, the leaders of the CUP had apparently degraded from idealists into ogres. How

Lasting Effects of the Armenian Genocide

was one to account for this sinister metamorphosis? According to Toynbee, the deportations of the Armenians had been carried out by orders from the Government in Istanbul. The Turkish gendarmes and soldiers executed these orders without having any personal connections with the localities.

Exploiting the international confusion created by World War I (1914–18), the Turkish authorities declared the native minority Armenians as Christians and therefore enemies of the Ottoman Empire (Kazanjian, 1989). Adult males, especially those identified as potential leaders, were arrested, escorted to desolate spots, and shot (Krieger, 1989). This process was designed to deprive Armenians of leadership and representation so that forced deportations might proceed with less resistance (Kuper, 1981). Henry Morgenthau, the American Ambassador to the Ottoman Empire from November 27, 1913–February 1, 1916, provides detailed descriptions of the forced marches, rapes, pillaging, and destruction of life. Morgenthau writes that "I called on Talaat, I argued in all sorts of ways with him but he said that there was no use; that they [the Turks] had already disposed of three-fourths of them [the Armenians], that there were none left in Bitlis, Van, Erzeroum, and the hatred was so intense now that they have to finish it. He said that he wanted to treat the Armenian like we treat the Negroes, I think he meant like the Indians. I told him three times that they were making a serious mistake and would regret it. He said we know we have made mistakes, but we never regret" (Journal entry of August 8, 1915, in Lowry, 1990).

Missionary reports all tell the same general story: Armenians all over Anatolia were expelled from their homes, slaughtered and massacred, and the remnant driven into the Syrian Desert to die. Thousands of these reports are on file in the archives of the American Board of Commissioners for Foreign Missions, which are now deposited in the Houghton Library at Harvard University and open to scholars (Papazian, 1993). According to Papazian (1993), American Consul Leslie Davis of Kharpert wrote on July 11, 1915 that the entire movement seemed to be the most thoroughly

The Armenian Genocide

organized and effective massacre Turkey had ever seen. Davis wrote dozens of reports to Morgenthau telling essentially the same story of mass murder on a horrifying scale (Papazian, 1993). Davis's report to the State Department detailed how few localities could be better suited to the fiendish purposes of the Turks in their plan to exterminate the Armenian population than the peaceful lake Goeljuk in the interior of Asiatic Turkey. That which took place around beautiful Lake Goeljuk in the summer of 1915 was almost inconceivable. Thousands and thousands of Armenians, mostly innocent and helpless women and children, were butchered on its shores and barbarously mutilated (Davis, 1915).

The Genocide was planned and premeditated by the leaders of the Committee of Union and Progress; and was carried out by a covert and secret Special Organization (Teskilati Mahsusa) established by the CUP. German officials stationed in Turkey reported that the campaign had killed 1.5 million Armenians, including 98% of the Armenian male population and 80-90% of the total Armenian population of Turkey (Compiled in English in Dadrian, 1994).

The Armenian presence in Asia Minor has been recorded over three Millennia. Armenians, Ottomans, Persians, Greeks and Arabs lived there, side-by-side. Although there were many stories of neighborly collaboration, love, and sharing, politically, there was a constant struggle for dominance. There were many relatively minor campaigns by the Ottomans to destroy Armenians, but none as vast and heinous as the systematically planned and executed Genocide of 1915.

Immediately prior to World War I, Armenians comprised the elite in Anatolia. Armenians were the educated physicians, attorneys, architects, and even numbered among the high-ranking Ottoman Empire officials. In 1915, during World War I, as the Ottoman Empire was on the brink of disintegration, there was overwhelming fear and hysteria in the land. In that panic, the Ottomans needed to identify an enemy. Armenians were the easy targets right in their backyards; especially since Armenians were

Christians, and for Turks, all those who are not Muslims are not to be trusted, and are called "gavour," meaning "faithless."

Feelings of inadequacy, rivalry, and therefore anger increased among the Ottomans. Armenians were the ones going to Europe and receiving higher education, and coming back home with a new philosophy of democracy and human rights. So long as the Turks remained dependent on the Armenians they were filled with a sense of inadequacy and rage.

The Turks assaulted the Armenian intelligentsia first, rounding them up and summarily executing them. Then they destroyed the churches, schools, and educational centers. Then they collected all weapons that Armenians might use to defend themselves. And lastly, they raped the women, killed the children, and drove the rest out of their homes and into forced death marches.

Common to most cases of genocide is the projection of a perpetrator's own intentions onto the group targeted for genocide. In this case, the Ottomans claimed that the Armenians would be siding with Russia and taking over the Ottoman Empire, just as Hitler claimed that the Jews were out to rule the world, when he was planning his own world conquest.

Armenians in Diaspora

The surviving remnants of the Armenians were scattered throughout the globe after World War I, to whatever countries would accept refugees. Outside the Middle East or Russian Armenia, these refugees were often the first and only Armenians, and even there, the pre-existing community's resources were vastly overwhelmed by the survivors' extraordinary destitution (Kupelian, Kalayjian & Kassabian, 1998).

In the United Sates, these new immigrants frequently settled in tight-knit urban communities (Mirak, 1983). Their world was starkly split between the outside world of strangers and their inner, shared world of intimate community. Their American neighbors were asked to bring in a nickel per person to help the starving Armenians without knowing why they were starving. The Great

Depression and the new horrors of World War II followed, which relegated the Genocide of the Armenians to historical obscurity, and swept up the traumatized remnants of the Armenian people with everyone else. Frequent denial of their plight surrounded Armenians with mixed feelings: indifference vs. over involvement, and anger and rage vs. peaceful interventions.

Currently, there are approximately one million Armenians living in the United States of America, with the majority settled on the West Coast; 90% of those who did not migrate from previously Soviet Armenia are offspring of the Genocide survivors.

Purposes of the Study

Whereas research focusing on the survivors of the Holocaust of the Jews is vast, very few studies have been conducted to explore the impact of the Genocide of the Armenians on its survivors and their descendents. The descendants of the Genocide survivors have only recently turned to conducting studies relevant to understanding intergenerational issues. When Armenians first emerged from their catastrophic trauma after World War I, psychology was in its infancy; there was world silence around this issue, and there was no impetus for collecting this group's personal data, in contrast to the reparation requirements that produced much of the early literature on Holocaust survivors (Kupelian, Kalayjian & Kassabian, 1998).

The purposes of this study are to explore: (1) the intergenerational impact of the Genocide on the Armenian offspring, (2) the physical, emotional and spiritual effects of the Genocide on the offspring, (3) how participants dealt with their emotions, re. the Genocide, and (4) the effectiveness of group techniques in facilitating the processing and integration of those feelings.

Study Method

The Armenian American Society for Studies on Stress & Genocide (AASSSG) organized a workshop for the children and grandchildren of survivors of the Ottoman Turkish Genocide of the

Armenians. This workshop was open to all those whose lives had been directly or indirectly impacted by the collective trauma of the Genocide. Participants were given two questionnaires: the first 18-item questionnaire elicited demographic information. The second 8-item pre-workshop questionnaire elicited specific emotional reactions, ways used to cope with those reactions, feelings, and reactions regarding the Turkish denial and involvement in the Armenian-American community. At the end of the workshop the participants were retested with the same questionnaire to elicit the impact of the workshop.

Announcements regarding this workshop were placed in Armenian-American newspapers, as well as on websites. Interested participants were encouraged to register. There were no fees charged to register. There were approximately eighteen telephone inquiries; and eight people participated in the workshop. The workshop took place at a University in New York City. It was a full day workshop. Workshop facilitators were experienced group leaders, who had worked in the field of Genocide and trauma studies for over a decade. They were both offspring of the Genocide and Holocaust survivors. Adjunctively, a chiropractor who specialized in psychosomatic manifestations and non-verbal body language was invited to assist the participants in gaining a greater awareness of how emotions effect body sensations. He too was a child of a Genocide survivor. Kalayjian's six-step Bio-Psychosocial and Spiritual model was utilized. The following are the six-steps of this model: 1) assessment, 2) expression of feelings, 3) empathy and validation, 3) discovery of positive meaning, 4) information dissemination, 5) diaphragmatic breathing exercises and 6) being mindful of the body. These different steps address the mind-body-spirit continuum and several aspects of the traumatic event. The model attempts to assess, validate, empathize, inform, and engage in a discussion of rediscovery of meaning, and provides physical relaxation (Kowalski & Kalayjian, 2001).

Style of leadership included self-disclosure with the intention of providing positive role modeling. At the conclusion of each step, the facilitators offered ego-supportive strategies, when deemed appropriate.

The facilitators and body specialist reviewed the results of each question to identify categories of themes for developing a method for content analysis.

Study Results

Part 1: Sociodemographic and Socioeconomic Characteristics of Respondents

Respondents ranged in age from twenty-two to seventy-eight. There were two males and six females. Educational background included a minimum of a Bachelors degree with one in progress. Three were children of survivors, the remaining five were the grandchildren of at least one survivor grandparent. Five of the participants were born in the United States, two in Lebanon, another in Iran. For those who were born outside of the US, the year of entry ranged from 1946 to 1997.

Four of the participants were single, two widowed, one divorced, and one married. Three of the participants were college students, three were retired, two employed.

Part 2: Pre-Workshop Questionnaire

In response to the first question, eliciting the earliest history or a picture regarding the Genocide, each participant recalled stories of their traumatized and wounded parents or grandparents, including physical scars from being shot while attempting to escape. There were also psychological wounds from the massive loss of family members. The feelings characterizing these memories were combinations of anxiety, confusion, and curiosity. In recalling these memories, participants expressed deep sadness, helplessness, a sense of being overwhelmed, paralyzed, and experienced intense psychic pain.

When asked about the ancestors involved in the Genocide, responses ranged from eleven siblings of their mother to parents

Lasting Effects of the Armenian Genocide

and grandparents. All of the participants recalled a memory of the murder of a primary family member.

When asked how their own memories affected them personally, responses ranged from such violence being a major factor in shaping their identity, to making them cynically angry, and intensely curious about the tragic past. In addition they expressed mixed feelings, re. their relationship to the larger Armenian community. On the one hand they felt closer to the Armenian-American community, hoping to keep the memories alive; on the other hand there were feelings of being burdened and wishing to distance themselves from the community.

In response to the impact of the Genocide on the survivors, responses ranged from it having a devastating effect on their ability to live a normal emotional life, burdening them with sadness, being forced to live in the past, to living in a continuous state of trauma. In response to the impact of the Genocide on the Armenian people in general, responses included protracted suffering, deep sadness, and distrust of outsiders, especially in light of the continued world denial of the Genocide.

One participant observed that there is a connection between the legacy of survivorship and their relationship to food and starvation. She recalled experiences with her own father who was a survivor, expressing extreme disturbance when there was food uneaten. It was defined as a sin. The first author recalled one of her American professors stating that while she was growing up in the 1930s she was told to bring in a nickel for the starving Armenians, never knowing what caused their starving. The second author recalled similar issues around food with Holocaust survivors in concentration camps.

When asked if there were things they did or avoided doing regarding the Genocide, the following was expressed: there was general paralysis and a deep sense of helplessness, especially in regard to the Turkish denial, and the search for finding a proactive stance. When asked with whom they have spoken about their memories of the Genocide, fifty percent had spoken to no one before the workshop, and most were surprised at how strongly they felt about this topic without having verbalized it before. Three spoke with friends, one person spoke with her mother and grandmother, and another with a therapist.

Regarding the ongoing Turkish denial of the Genocide, all participants expressed experiencing feeling an attack on their personhood, feeling like a non-person. Others voiced generalized pain and confusion. One participant suggested that perhaps Armenians were not strong enough to unite and counter this denial in an appropriate fashion.

With regard to the meaning of Turkish acknowledgment of culpability for the Genocide, participants expressed the following: the need to foster a historical identity, to experience psychological relaxation, to receive compensation after an admission of the truth, and the ending of all Genocide.

When asked what would be considered an adequate compensation for their family losses and sufferings, the following reactions were expressed: two-thirds of the participants indicated that acknowledgment of the truth and a return of Armenian lands was important. One person expressed hopelessness as exemplified by the following statement: "past losses cannot be made up; they can't bring all my relatives back; we need a long time for rehabilitation." Another pointed out the importance of compensation as well as improved political relationships of the two countries.

In response to their experiences with the Armenian-American community there were mixed but strong feelings ranging from over-involvement, on the one hand, to negative feelings and withdrawal on the other. A few respondents stated their skepticism, re. parochialism. A few others expressed how different these Armenian communities were depending on the host country, i.e., Lebanon, Syria, Iran and the United States. Two others expressed anger at not being accepted by the Armenian-American community due to their lack of proficiency in the Armenian language, or their mixed ethnic family background.

Part 3: Facilitators' Observations

The facilitators observed that participants maintained some level of distancing as evidenced by their coolness and resistance. For example, group members did not console or reach out to one other when given an opportunity to do so. Participants did not interact cohesively. The facilitators speculated that, contributing to this lack of cohesion were: (1) diversity of age, resulting in two generations represented in the group (2) diversity of birthplace, as the group consisted of both foreign born and native born, and (3) diversity in ethnicity, resulting in two members with mixed Armenian and non-Armenian parentage.

For example, connectedness between group members through eye contact was fair but not well-sustained or continuous. Male participants would look at objects around the facilitation space without looking at the others. Female participants usually looked at the facilitators or down at a table. Sustained visual contact with slow and well-paced speech suggested emotional responses of anger or sorrow in most participants. Some spoke quickly as if they were reporting a story without any emotional response.

Initially, participants had difficulty in establishing rapport with one another. This improved throughout the day. Body posture and eye contact were noticeably improved as participants listened to each other's tragic stories and shared their own feelings. Facilitators noticed an undertone of anger, which was displaced and projected at certain emotional points. One intervention was shifting awareness to feelings and thereby assisting participants in expressing those feelings, through emotional openness, acknowledgement, and finally through tears.

At the end of the workshop, members of the group expressed appreciation and gratitude for the opportunity to participate. They also expressed how instrumental the workshop had been in assisting them in talking about difficult issues that most of them had not shared with others previously. They concluded by asking for future similar opportunities.

Part 4: Results of Post-Workshop Questionnaire

In response to question one, related to the earliest memory regarding the Genocide, although participants expressed having some of the same memories, they reported a change in their feelings and attitudes associated with those memories. One respondent stated that she was more conscious of feelings that she had not acknowledged before. The feelings included sadness, helplessness and anger. Another respondent, who had not been able to recall a picture, was then able to for the first time. The picture was of her father's obsession with finding family members, since he was taken away from them and forced on the death march. A third participant stated that his confusion cleared up after the workshop, but he kept his pride associated with his identity as an Armenian. His confusion was related to his belonging to a hated Christian minority. A fourth respondent expressed being much more connected to the memories of the Genocide. She described a sense of awareness which was absent beforehand. She also expressed feelings of guilt at being safe, secure, and economically stable, while at the same time carrying around these Genocide memories.

When asked what effects they thought the Genocide had on them, most of the respondents were consistent with the expressions of the pre-workshop questionnaire. One respondent had yet an additional memory of being seven years of age and torn over her feelings of love for a Turkish classmate, whom she found defined as the enemy. Another respondent expressed a sense of purpose, which was missing in his pre-workshop response.

When asked if there was anything the participant did or did not do regarding the Genocide, the majority did not express excessive concern. One respondent was plagued by her feelings about death as she raised questions regarding her wish to make up for the lives of the ten people who were taken away from her family during the Genocide. When asked about the continuing Turkish denial, all respondents expressed sadness, hurt, anger, and helplessness.

In response to what they considered adequate compensation, most of the participants still felt that no one could compensate for the loss of their family members and loved ones, yet at the same time there were strong ideas about the following possible options: an offer of an apology, normalization of relations with the Republic of Armenia, restoration of all Armenian monuments in Turkey, payment of compensation, and removal of the blockade. Two strongly stated the necessity to return lands taken.

In response to their experiences with the Armenian-American community the majority expressed a degree of involvement, ranging from low to high commitment. Some noted the fragmentation of the Armenian community, attributing it to cultural differences in different parts of the Diaspora.

Discussion and Analysis

According to Niederland (1981), the physical and psychological trauma of persons brutally persecuted, incarcerated, and tortured, rarely heal. Shoshan (1989) confirms that children of survivors react to the lack of memories and absence of dead family members. This was a problem to a few of the participants in this research, where they stated feeling like orphans: no roots, no relatives, no uncles and great aunts—not by choice, but by force.

The majority of the respondents in this study expressed feeling burdened by having to carry emotional memories of previous generations. They were thus saddled with a sense of forced responsibility for carrying the memories and helping their ancestors. Most of these participants felt this was an infringement on their freedom, and some second-generation respondents reported resentment. This is consistent with then reflections of Aaron Hass, a child of Holocaust survivors. According to Hass (1990), the most important event in his life occurred before he was born. Others of second generations report being drawn to memories and descriptions of genocide and therefore expressing their parents' unexpressed sadness and rage. This confirms Israeli Psychologist Shoshan's (1989) assertions, after studying Holocaust survivors and their children, that longing and mourning are transmitted from generation to generation. This sense of being burdened is also found as one reaction to the magnitude of the survivor's loss, leading to the tremendous onus of expectation on the children of the Holocaust survivors. The parents often looked to the children as magical reincarnations of their lost worlds (Freyberg, 1980; Kestenberg, 1972; Sigal, 1971).

Among the workshop participants, some expressed this sense of oppressive burden forced upon them and responded by cutting their ties to the Armenian-American community, which they described as a sense of obligation; while forcing involvement, others get over-involved with their community. This latter group attempted to sublimate their negative feelings into positive actions as reflected in their careers, i.e. studying Armenian Literature, making Armenian movies, participation in their community through volunteering, lobbying, and transcending the traumatic sequelae. This was consistent with the study by Boyajian and Grigorian (1982) of the children of the Armenian survivors.

Distrustfulness was another major theme expressed by those who were told not to trust anyone outside their own families. This is consistent with some post-Holocaust families (Hass, 1990). According to Hass, for the children of survivors the world is hostile, as their parents impart to listeners firsthand observations of man's savagery. Historically, the message given was that the outside world is not to be trusted. Post-Genocide Armenian families continued living in fear of the outside world, since the threat to their lives continued due to geographically widespread Ottoman oppression even in those countries where they took refuge. According to Epstein (1979), children of Holocaust survivors also share varying degrees of over-responsibility to their parents, and distrust the world.

Participants expressed deep and intense feelings of helplessness on many levels: personal, collective, and global. Most of this helplessness centered on the persistent Turkish denial of the Genocide. This is consistent with research findings of Kalayjian and Shahinian (1998), where 39% of the Armenian survivors reasserted the evidence that they had witnessed the Genocide. When asked to express their feelings about the Turkish denial, typical responses included: "I saw with my own two eyes how hundreds of people were placed in a big hole in the ground and burned to death." "What then happened to my clan? Out of 90 relatives, only three have survived." "What of my sister who was raped by a group of Turkish Gendarmes and then set on fire in front of my eyes?" According to Kalayjian (1995), other offspring of the Genocide survivors—who also experienced the 1988 earthquake in Armenia—also reported having nightmares involving similar images of the Ottoman-Turkish atrocities. This helplessness was also expressed in anger. Feelings of anger were turned both inward and outward. Anger turned inward was expressed in self-criticism. This was apparent in the workshop, as participants struggled with an object for their anger, and a means by which they could work it through. Workshop facilitators became increasingly aware that initially, participants had no mechanisms to process their anger. This was interpreted as complex anger, as part of it was no doubt inherited from their parents and grandparents who survived the Genocide.

Anger that was not expressed internally was expressed horizontally: toward one another, to other Armenians, toward the facilitators in the workshop. According to Kalayjian (1999), this is a common phenomenon when Armenians as oppressed people, failing to process their inherited anger, therefore, cope by displacing it horizontally onto their fellow Armenians.

In response to communicating these feelings with others, over fifty percent of the participants expressed problems with communication. This is consistent with some findings in post-Holocaust Jewish families, where some parents did not talk so as to protect their children. According to Danieli (1985) and Peskan et al. (1997), the issue of communication (literally knowing another and ultimately knowing oneself) thus becomes a focal theme for many children of survivors. This is also consistent with research findings by Kalayjian et al. (1996), who found that three out of four Armenian survivors interviewed asserted that they did not talk to anyone about their experiences of the Genocide. Most of these survivors did not communicate for fear of continued persecution and with the overhanging threat of death to self and the remaining loved ones. This general lack of communication suggests their traumas were not resolved (Kalayjian et al., 1996).

Cahn (1987) has found a correlation between the ability of Holocaust survivors to communicate/symbolize their experiences of traumatic events and their posttraumatic health. Her work suggests that in order to cope with an affectively intense experience such as genocide in the healthiest possible manner, one would need to modulate affect with cognition by talking about the experiences. The review of the Holocaust literature confirms that those parents who refrained from ever mentioning their Holocaust experiences (usually in an attempt to shield their children from the pain), reported more disturbances in their children (Epstein, 1979; Kestenberg, 1982; Link, Victor, & Binder, 1985). One hypothesis is that a lack of actual information leaves a vacuum filled by horrifying fantasies, and because the horror is not grounded in history, it is experienced as part of the child's self (Lipkowitz, 1973). Those parents who are able to share their history with appropriate affect, and in controlled doses, do not seem to harm their children (Kupelian, 1991). These parents have likely integrated their experiences more effectively, and their stories are told with sensitivity to the listeners. These findings are in line with a study by Rosenheck (1986), which found that children of World War II combat veterans with chronic longstanding PTSD were adversely affected by too much or too little discussion of their father's war experiences, while those who discussed it in controlled doses were not adversely affected.

Cultural differences account for some varied responses in the two groups of Holocaust and Genocide survivors. For example, survivor guilt has been described as a major manifestation of the survivor syndrome among Jewish survivors of the Holocaust (Krystal & Niederland, 1968; Niederland, 1981). Danieli (1985) has described various defensive and coping functions of survivor guilt for this population, including a commemorative function. In this function, guilt serves to maintain a connection and a bridge of loyalty to those who perished, and to metaphorically provide the respectful regard of a cemetery that these victims were denied.

However, this guilt experience is not documented in the Armenians. According to Kalayjian, et al. (1996), survivors did not express feelings of guilt for survival. This accords with a study done by Boyajian and Grigorian (1982), which found that only a few respondents talked about guilt, which was associated with duties to the living (i.e., not having done enough for the Armenian community), and, among the second generation, not having done enough for their survivor parents. In this current study, only one participant expressed guilt over leaving, being economically stable, and living in a democratic country, while her ancestors suffered persecution.

Although scholarship in this area places emphasis on the importance of not generalizing survivorship, the authors are recommending here not to generalize nor pathologize generational transmission as well.

Conclusion

This study began with a group of second and third generation Armenian-American survivors of the Ottoman-Turkish Genocide. Participants were frozen and non-cohesive at first and grew into a cohesive group whose members were able to not only process their own unexpressed feelings, but also to support one another.

According to Courtois (2001), working with the psychosocial impact of trauma through the group medium offers an opportunity to restore a sense of reality, a catalyst and context for the exploration of feelings, and a challenge to one's emotions and beliefs. Groups give an opportunity to talk about and bear witness to the trauma, to grieve, to restructure the assumptive world, and to restore trust.

This is consistent with the observations of the facilitators that the group was instrumental in reaffirming one's identity, as well as providing an opportunity to collectively explore ways of coping. According to Yalom (1985), the group is a social support for exchange between members, offering catharsis, hope, and an examination of life's existential factors. Yalom also notes the existential factors that group members address collectively: recognizing that life is at times unfair and unjust. There is no escape from life's pain, and fearing the basic issues allows living life more honestly.

Research indicates that mental and emotional stresses are felt and held in the body (van der Kolk, 1992). Assessment of the body revealed tension and sadness in their neck and shoulders as well as their voices. Attentive and gentle work with body awareness techniques opened opportunities for healing conflictual mental and emotional stresses and transmitted traumas. Thus, through the utilization of body messages one may accelerate the healing process and free the individual of long held tensions.

As the facilitators measured the impact of the group process, they noted that the group struggled with the existential question of rapprochement with the Turkish perpetrators of the genocide, their current offspring. The group also struggled with the current refusal of the Turks to acknowledge that the Genocide occurred. A particular anger, similar to that of the second generation of the Jewish Holocaust, is generated by this question, as members brought out their frustrations about unwanted victimization. The anger is an outcome of feelings of helplessness and powerlessness.

Compared to the German Government, which made reparations, the Turks have not evidenced any admission of culpability. They repeatedly blame their atrocities on the Armenians themselves. The sting of this anger appears to move the group process to a type of hopelessness and melancholy. This discussion at the same moment increased group cohesion, since all members shared a similar outrage, and were able to validate one another. Yalom (1985) confirms the curative factors of this cohesiveness, where individuals no longer feel alone. Also cited by Courtois (2001), the joint sharing of trauma tends to most closely approximate group catharsis. Catharsis can relieve long held anger, which this group addressed in this first meeting. According to

Sullivan (1953), validation of a traumatic experience is an essential step toward resolution and closure. In addition to such group validation, the group decided that an explicit expression of remorse by a perpetrator, or the next generation, would have enormous healing value, as was reinforced by Staub (1990).

Recommendations

The authors recommend further research to explore feelings of generational transmission of trauma in Armenians as well as non-Armenian offspring of mass trauma. In this group, the opportunity to process feelings was well utilized when the group melancholy was transformed into hope, as expressed by the wish for further workshops. According to Yalom (1985), groups can instill hope by seeing how others can get better and solve similar issues. By the end of the workshop, the group interacted with hope, which facilitators attributed to the release of sadness shared so that their individual isolation was dismantled. One example is the South African Truth Commissions, where by the acknowledgement of crimes against humanity, the world witnessed and therefore validated the fact that an injustice had been perpetrated. Henceforth was the beginning of an attempt at reconciliation and healing.

When the trauma is properly processed emotionally there is a cathartic effect. When the facilitators can validate each participant's feelings, and offer empathy, this will help reintegrate the trauma into one's personality in a more effective, therapeutic, healthy, and meaningful way.

Bibliography

Boyajian, K. & Grigorian, H. (1982, June 20-24), Sequelae of the Armenian Genocide on Survivors. Paper Presented at the International Conference on the Holocaust and Genocide, Tel Aviv, Israel.

— (1988), Psychosocial Sequelae of Genocide of Armenians. In R. G. Hovannisian (Ed.), *The Armenian Genocide in*

Perspective. New Brunswick, NJ: Transaction Publishers, pp. 177-185.

Cahn, A. (1987, August). *The Capacity to Acknowledge Experience in Holocaust Survivors and their Children*. Paper presented at the 95th Annual Convention of the American Psychological Association, New York, NY.

Courtois, C. (Nov. 9, 2001), Group Therapy of Trauma. Presentation at the Eastern Regional Group Psychotherapy Association Meeting. New York, NY.

Dadrian, V. (1994*), The Secret Young-Turk Ittihadist Conference and the Decision for the World War I Genocide of the Armenians*. Journal of Political and Military Sociology, 22 (1): 173-202.

Dadrian, V. (1995), *The History of the Armenian Genocide: Ethnic Conflict from the Balkans to Anatolia to the Caucasus*. Providence, RI: Berghahn Books.

Danieli, Y. (1985), The Treatment and Prevention of the Long-Term Effects of Intergenerational Transmission of Victimization: A Lesson from Holocaust Survivors and their Children. In C. Figley (Ed.), *Trauma and Its Wake*. NY: Brunner-Mazel, pp. 295-313.

Davis, C. (1915). U.S. Department of State, Record Group 59, International Affairs of Turkey, 1910-1929 (Microfil Publications) Microcopy 353: 88 reels, especially 867.4016/1-1011, reels 43-48.

Epstein, E. (1979), *Children of the Holocaust*. NY: G. P. Putnam's Sons.

Hass, A. (1990), *In the Shadow of the Holocaust*. Ithaca, NY: Cornell University Press.

Housepian, M. (1971), *The Smyrnia Affair: The First Comprehensive Account of the Burning of the City and the Expulsion of the Christians From Turkey in 1922.* NY: Harcourt Brace Jovanovich.

Hovannisian, R. (1985), The Armenians Question, 1878-1923. In G. Libaridian (English Lang. ed.), *A Crime of Silence: The Armenians Genocide.* Bath, UK: Pitman Press, pp. 11-33.

Freyberg, J. T. (1980), Difficulties in Separation-Individuation as Experienced by Offspring of Nazi Holocaust Survivors. *American Journal of Orthopsychiatry*, 50: 87-95.

Kalayjian, A. S. (1995), *Disaster & Mass Trauma: Global Perspectives in Post Disaster Mental Health Management.* Long Branch, NJ: Vista Publishing.

—— & Shahinian, S., Gergerian, E., & Saraydarian, L. (1996), Coping with Ottoman Turkish Genocide: An Exploration of the Experience of Armenian Survivors. *Journal of Traumatic Stress*, 9 (1): 87-97.

—— & Shahinian, P. (1998), Recollections of Aged Armenian Survivors of the Ottoman Turkish Genocide: Resilience Through Endurance, Coping, and Life Accomplishments. *Psychoanalytic Review*, 85 (4): 489-504.

—— (1999), Forgiveness and Transcendence. *Clio's Psyche*, 6 (3): 117-119.

—— & Kanazi, R. L. & Aberson, C. L. (2002), Cross-Cultural Study of the Psychosocial and Spiritual Impact of Natural Disasters. *Journal of Group Tensions*, (in press).

Kalfaian, A. (1982), *Chomaklou: The History of an Armenian Village* (Trans. K. Asadourian). NY: Chomaklou Compatriotic Society.

Kazanjian, P. (1989), *The Cilician Armenian Ordeal.* Boston: Hye Intentions.

Kestenberg, J. S. (1972), Psychoanalytic Contributions to the Problem of Children of Survivors from Nazi Persecution.

The Israel Annals of Psychiatry and Related Disciplines, 10: 311-325.

Kestenberg, M. (1982), Discriminatory Aspects of the German Indemnification Policy: A Continuation of Persecution. In M. S. Bergmann & M. E. Jucovy (Eds.), *Generations of the Holocaust*. NY: Basic Books.

Kowalski, K. M. & Kalayjian, A. (2001), Responding to Mass Emotional Trauma: A Mental Health Outreach Program for Turkey Earthquake Victims. *Safety Science*, 39: 71-81.

Kreiger (1989), The Armenian Genocide: An Outline. *The Armenian Church*, 8.

Krystal, H. & Niederland, W. (1968). Clinical Observations on the Survivor Syndrome. In H. Krystal (Ed.), Massive Psychic Trauma. NY: International Universities Press, pp. 327- 348.

Kupelian, D. (1991). Inter-generational Transmission of Trauma: The Case of the Holocaust. Unpublished paper, American University, Washington, DC.

Kupelian, D., Kalayjian, A. S., Kassabian, A. (1998), The Turkish Genocide of the Armenians: Continuing Effects on Survivors and their Families Eight Decades After Massive Trauma. In Danieli, Y. (Ed.), *International Handbook of Multigenerational Legacies of Trauma*. NY: Plenum Press, pp. 191-210.

Kuper, L. (1981), *Genocide: Its Political Use in the Twentieth Century*. NY: Penguin Paperback.

Lidgett, E. (1987), *The Ancient People*. London: James Nisbetter.

Link, N., Victor, B., & Binder, R. L. (1985), Psychosis in Children of Holocaust Survivors: Influence of the Holocaust in the Choice of Themes in their Psychoses. *The Journal of Nervous and Mental Disease*, 173: 115-117.

Lipkowitz, M. H. 1973), The Child of Two Survivors: A Report of an Unsuccessful Therapy. *The Israel Annals of Psychiatry and Related Disciplines*, 11: 141-155.

Mirak, R. (1983). *Torn Between Two Lands: Armenians in America, 1890 to World War I.* Cambridge, MA: Harvard University Press.

Morgenthau, H. (1975), *Ambassador Morgenthau's Story*. NY: Doubleday Pope & Co (1918, First Print, Garden City, NY: Doubleday, Page); Plandome, NY: New Age Publishers.

Neiderland, W. G. (1981), The Survivor Syndrome: Further Observations and Dimensions. *Journal of American Psychoanalytic Association*, 29 (2): 20-31.

Peskin, H., Auerhahn, A.C. & Laub, D. (1997), The Second Holocaust: Therapeutic Rescue When Life Threatens. *Journal of Personal and Interpersonal Loss*, 2: 1-25.

Papazian, D. R. (1993). Misplaced Credulity: Contemporary Turkish Attempts to Refute the Armenian Genocide. In *Genocide & Human Rights: Lessons Learned From the Armenian Experience*. Belmont, MA: Armenian Heritage Press. Special Issue of the *Journal of Armenian Studies*, 4 (1 & 2), pp. 227-256.

Reid, J. (1984), The Armenian Massacres in Ottoman and Turkish Historiography. *Armenian Review*, 37: 22-40.

Rosenheck, R. (1986), Impact of Posttraumatic Stress Disorder of World War II on the Next Generation. *The Journal of Nervous and Mental Disease*, 174: 319-327.

Shoshan, T. (1989), Mourning and Longing From Generation to Generation. *American Journal of Psychotherapy*, 43 (2): 193-207.

Sigal, J. J. (1971), Second-Generation Effects of Massive Psychic Trauma. In H. Krystal and W. G. Niederland (Eds.),

Psychic Traumatization: After Effects in Individuals and Communities. Boston: Little, Brown & Co.

Staub, I. (1990, April), Denial of the Armenian Genocide: Compounding the Crime. Conference Presented by the Armenian Center at the School of International Affairs, Columbia University, NY.

Sullivan, H. S. (1953), *The Interpersonal Theory of Psychiatry.* NY: W. W. Norton & Co.

Toynbee, A. J. (1916). *The Treatment of the Armenians in the Ottoman Empire.* London: Sir Joseph Causton and Sons.

Niederland, W. G. (1981), The Survivor Syndrome: Further Observations and Dimensions. *Journal of American Psychoanalytic Association,* 29 (2), 413-425.

van der Kolk, B. A.(1992). Group Psychotherapy With Post Traumatic Stress Disorder. In H. Kaplan & B. Sadock (Eds.), *Comprehensive group psychotherapy.* Baltimore, MD: Williams & Wilkings, pp. 550-560.

Walker, B. (1991, Apr. 5). *Armenia at Crossroads.* (Television News Broadcast). Las Angeles: CBS News.

Yalom, I. (1985), *The Theory and Practice of Group Psychotherapy.* NY: Basic Books.

Viewpoint 2

How Ending Genocide Denial Will Help Turkey
David Tolbert

The Turkish government has never acknowledged responsibility for the Armenian Genocide. This viewpoint from 2015 discusses not only how Turkish denial is harming Turkish society, but how it has set a terrible precedent internationally. Other genocidal events in countries around the world have similarly lasting effects. How can a society move beyond denial to some kind of resolution? Author David Tolbert is president of the International Center for Transitional Justice, a global human rights organization. After beginning his law career in the USA, Tolbert taught international law and human rights in the UK. He has been an international advisor and written extensively on international justice and human rights.

On April 24, we commemorate the 100th anniversary of the Armenian genocide. On that date in 1915, some 250 Armenian political leaders and intellectuals were arrested and subsequently tortured and murdered by Ottoman Turkish authorities, effectively launching the genocide in which approximately 1.5 million Armenians were systematically murdered. This grim centenary marks not only the crime itself but also a century of its denial by the Turkish state and wide swaths of Turkish society.

Denial is the final fortress of those who commit genocide and other mass crimes. Perpetrators hide the truth in order to avoid

---

"The Armenian Genocide: 100 Years of Denial (And Why It's In Turkey's Interest to End It)," by David Tolbert, International Center for Transitional Justice, April 24, 2015. Reprinted by Permission.

accountability and protect the political and economic advantages they sought to gain by mass killings and theft of the victims' property, and to cement the new reality by manufacturing an alternative history. Recent studies have established that such denial not only damages the victims and their destroyed communities, it promises a future based on lies, sowing the seeds of future conflict, repression and suffering.

The facts of the Armenian genocide are well known and documented, and any honest debate is not about whether the genocide happened but about the exact number of murdered, the worth of their stolen property and the long-term impact of this crime.

The Ottoman authorities of the day (the government of the Committee of Union and Progress (CUP), often referred to as the Young Turks) and their allies carried out the systematic murder of some 1.5 million Armenians between 1915 and 1917, destroying a large percentage of the Armenian population in the Ottoman Empire at that time. Then, from 1918 to 1923, many of the surviving Armenians and others, including Greeks and Assyrians, were driven from their homes, robbed of their remaining possessions, starved, and murdered.* Like other genocides, the mass killing of Armenians was hardly spontaneous. It was planned and executed with efficiency, without mercy.

Turkey's Culture of Denial and its Spoils

A hundred years on, despite a mountain of evidence, there remains a culture of official denial in Turkey. In a pallid public statement "on the events of 1915," President Recep Tayyip Erdoğan recently extended "[Turkey's] condolences to [the] grandchildren" of the Armenians "who lost their lives in the context of the early twentieth century." Rubbing salt in the wounds, he trivialized the suffering caused to Armenians at the time by equating them to that of "every other citizen of the Ottoman Empire."† Considering the scale of the slaughter and the nature of the genocidal effort directed at Armenians, Erdogan's attempts to equate their suffering to that of "every citizen of the Ottoman Empire" constitutes a form of denial in itself.

Although such rhetoric is not new, the culture of denial in some respects has intensified in Turkey over the years. In 1919, albeit under international pressure, the Ottoman authorities established a tribunal that convicted two senior district officials for deporting Armenians and acting "against humanity and civilization". The tribunal found that the perpetrators and their co-conspirators had executed a top-down, carefully crafted plan, specifically finding:

> The disaster visiting the Armenians was not a local or isolated event. It was the result of a premeditated decision taken by a central body; [...] and the immolations and excesses which took place were based on oral and written orders issued by that central body.‡

However, a few years later, after a new government was formed in Ankara, the Nationalists annulled all of the sentences.§ Moreover, in another crime against humanity,‖ pursuant to the orders of Kemal Ataturk, who later became the President of the Republic of Turkey, Armenians who remained in the western Cilicia region of Turkey were expelled, along with the Greek and Assyrian populations. Several high-level perpetrators of the genocide became senior leaders in Turkey and others were celebrated as national heroes.

While it is argued that the culture of denial arose as a result of the close connection that the Armenian genocide has with the birth of modern Turkey,** this is an explanation of possible causes, not a justification for the most serious of crimes. A parallel can be drawn with the conquest of the Americas by the United States and the continental powers in their multitudinous abuses and genocidal killings of Native Americans: the explanation may be the rapacious hunger for land, but it is not a defense for the crimes committed. Looking for such justification for these systematic crimes amounts to a strategy of normalization and denial.

However, a few years later, after a new government was formed in Ankara, the Nationalists annulled all of the sentences.§ Moreover, in another crime against humanity,‖ pursuant to the orders of Kemal Ataturk, who later became the President of the Republic of Turkey,

The Armenian Genocide

Armenians who remained in the western Cilicia region of Turkey were expelled, along with the Greek and Assyrian populations. Several high-level perpetrators of the genocide became senior leaders in Turkey and others were celebrated as national heroes.¶

While it is argued that the culture of denial arose as a result of the close connection that the Armenian genocide has with the birth of modern Turkey,** this is an explanation of possible causes, not a justification for the most serious of crimes. A parallel can be drawn with the conquest of the Americas by the United States and the continental powers in their multitudinous abuses and genocidal killings of Native Americans: the explanation may be the rapacious hunger for land, but it is not a defense for the crimes committed. Looking for such justification for these systematic crimes amounts to a strategy of normalization and denial.

This twisting of legal language is hardly limited to Turkey. It has many imitators, from the Nazis to the Khmer Rouge.

Another of Turkey's tactics is to pressure other states not to recognize the genocide. In the latest development, Turkey recalled its ambassador to the Vatican for "consultations" just hours after Pope Francis referred to the mass killing of Armenians as the "first genocide of the twentieth century." Turkey was successful in lobbying members of the U.S. Congress during the Reagan and Bush administrations to defeat congressional resolutions that would have made April 24 a national day of remembrance.§§ However, it is noteworthy that such pressure failed in other cases, and dozens of countries, including Argentina, France, Greece and Russia, have all officially recognized the Armenian genocide, despite Turkey's threats and reprisals.

Another ploy in the denier's bag of tricks is to manipulate statistics, downplaying the number of victims (or, in this case, the number of Armenians who lived in the Ottoman Empire in 1915), and destroy official documents.

The genocide of the Armenians proved to be an opening act in a century replete with mass extermination: from the furnaces of Auschwitz to the killing fields of Cambodia to the genocide in

Rwanda (marked earlier this month by its 21st anniversary) to the slaughterhouse of Bosnia and to much of the barbarity that we see in the world today. The butchers have learned the lessons all too well.

Hitler himself took succor in the genocide of the Armenians and famously remarked: "Who, after all, speaks today of the annihilation of the Armenians?"‖ Hitler learned the lessons of the Armenian genocide well and drew on them as he planned the extermination of Jews and other groups that stood in the way of his murderous vision of "Aryan superiority".

Consequences of Denial and Benefits of Acknowledgement

The consequences of denial are deep and lasting, not only for the descendants of the Armenians, but also for Turkey itself, in large and small ways. Putting perpetrators of genocide in the Turkish pantheon of national heroes has its price.

While we must be careful not to draw too direct a line from the Armenian genocide to all of Turkey's current problems, we would be remiss not to take account of Turkey's poor current human rights record and its history of substandard treatment of minorities within its borders.

Indeed, Turkey today bears the dubious distinction of having the highest number of judgments for violation of human rights rendered against it by the European Court of Human Rights.*** It is criticized for legislating such vague and groundless crimes such as "insulting Turkish identity,"††† which has now been reformed to "denigration of the Turkish nation, the state of the Republic of Turkey, the Turkish Parliament (TBMM), the government of the Republic of Turkey and the legal institutions of the state".

Even Orhan Pamuk, the Turkish Nobel Laureate, faced an official order for his books to be removed from the shelves of public libraries and burned after he referenced the Armenian genocide to a Swiss newspaper. These are not actions of a state grounded in the rule of law and human rights.

There is a different path to follow, one traveled by other countries with as heavy or heavier burdens of history, and it points to approaches that might be useful for Turkey.

The first step includes ending the politics of denial and embracing acknowledgement. One need only think of the experience of post-war Germany, which, despite the Nuremberg trials, spent several decades (at best) ignoring, if not denying, the massive crimes of the Nazi period. Over time though, West Germany and then a reunited Germany began to deal with the horrendous crimes of the Holocaust through important trials, such as those held in Frankfurt in the 1960s, which exposed the awful crimes committed in Auschwitz in chilling detail.

The German government opened up archives to the public, provided reparations to victims (or their descendants) and constructed memorials to affect public remembrance and acknowledgement.

Over time, it began to remove some of the culprits from the police, military and political ranks, and importantly reformed its political legal institutions. In one of the most iconic acts of acknowledgement, Chancellor Willy Brandt went to his knees in front of a monument dedicated to victims of the Warsaw Ghetto. It was a symbolic act that spoke of contrition and apology; it carried enormous significance and meaning for the victims and their survivors as well as the world at large.

Germany is not alone, other countries have moved past the stage of denial, whether expressed or implied, to address the violations of the past. We are now celebrating the 30th anniversary of Nunca Mas ("Never Again"), the final report of an official effort to document the vast system of enforced disappearances perpetrated in Argentina during the military dictatorship and "Dirty War," which led to trials of some of the most responsible perpetrators and a much clearer understanding of that dark period in the country's history. We have seen similar experiences in much of Latin America, through truth commissions, other commissions of inquiry and historical clarification, trials, and reparation programs.

Lasting Effects of the Armenian Genocide

Some countries have taken other approaches to uncovering their sordid histories. In South Africa, the history and abuses of apartheid were partly exposed through the Truth and Reconciliation Commission. Many countries in eastern and central Europe have pursued processes of lustration (or vetting) after the Cold War, exposing and penalizing those behind state-sponsored abuses. In the former Yugoslavia, denial is still strong in some places regarding crimes like the genocide in Srebrenica; yet, trials at the national and international levels have established the culpability of many of the perpetrators and helped get the truth to the public.

There are many other experiences to draw on, and they all point to the importance of acknowledgment of both genocide and other serious crimes and the state's failure to protect its citizens. In the case of Turkey, where there are no perpetrators of the genocide presently alive, criminal trials have no role left to play; that makes it all the more important that criminal processes not be turned against those who tell the truth, who expose the genocide and speak for the victims, as in the case of Pamuk.

That would be a small but significant step toward addressing Turkey's historic debt to the Armenians and one expected of a country that proclaims to be a member of the family of modern democracies.

An important first step would be for President Erdoğan to apologize to the Armenian community for the genocide. A tepid statement using euphemisms like "the events of 1915" only makes matters worse. He is in a strong position in Turkey, and politically he can afford to take this morally right action. It is his duty as president of all citizens of the country to set the record straight. Official contrition would help in healing the deep injuries and damage suffered by the Armenian community, in Armenia and in the diaspora. Such an apology ought to be accompanied by measures to establish full diplomatic relations with the Republic of Armenia, which would be a meaningful goodwill gesture.

The benefits of such an act would not only be directed at Armenians, but at Turkey itself. By acknowledging these crimes, the Turkish state would send a message to the many minorities within its borders and to all of its citizens that the state takes their rights and the rule of law seriously. It would also be a signal that when the state violates or fails to protect its citizens' rights, the Turkish authorities would provide a remedy to them, in line with international law.

More broadly, Turkey has an important role to play internationally and regionally and the recognition of the genocide would, in the long term, make the country appear stronger and more trustworthy to all.

Its current position is not only morally unsustainable but undermines its position as an honest partner and a legitimate regional power. A break with the current policy of denial would show the maturity of Turkish democracy and could help to increase regional stability. The potential impact of an apology on its neighbors, notably the Republic of Armenia, would open the possibility for dialogue and strengthen Turkey's role in the region regarding unresolved issues like Nagorno-Karabakh.

Not only would this apology send an important message inside Turkey and to its neighbors, it is a message that would resonate well beyond the borders of the country. In the Balkans, where Turkey has increasing sway, denial is alive and well, and presents a significant obstacle to re-establishing confidence between former warring parties, such as Serbia, Bosnia and Herzegovina, Croatia and Kosovo. An act of acknowledgement would substantially increase Turkey's ability to mediate and support initiatives in contexts where impunity reigns, from Israel and Palestine to Syria to Sudan and many other places.

If Turkey and President Erdoğan were serious about reversing the culture of denial, there is more to do. A crucial measure would be to establish a truthful and accurate historical record of what happened to the Armenians. This could be in the form of an official Commission of Historical Clarification, composed of impartial and respected experts, which would examine the historical record and issue a report that would accurately reflect the history of the period and establish how the crimes were committed. Such a commission would need to be composed of experts that were objective, credible and fair minded.

Using international commissioners or a mixture of international and national experts, which has occurred in a number of truth commissions and other processes, would add considerable credibility to the process. The Commission for the Truth in El Salvador and the Commission for Historical Clarification in Guatemala are good examples of mixed national-international commissions. Such a commission should build on the work of the earlier unofficial Turkish Armenian Reconciliation Commission.

Some form of reparations for the Armenian community in Turkey would have to be provided. After all, the plunder of their property enriched the modern Turkish state. While too much time may have passed for individual reparations to be awarded, projects could be undertaken to support Armenian communities inside and outside of Turkey to address their material needs and, at least symbolically, their losses. Symbolic reparations in the form of monuments and memorials can serve an important purpose in recognizing victims and helping to remind the affected communities that the state acknowledges its failures and will guard against these abuses happening again.

Perhaps most important, Turkey can demonstrate a serious commitment to reforming laws and institutions that are meant to protect the human rights of all of its citizens. In doing so, the state would find effective ways to improve its weak record on these issues in the courts in Strasbourg and beyond. It would also send a message to its citizens that the crimes like those perpetrated against Armenians would never be permitted in contemporary Turkey.

There is no doubt many other steps could and should be taken in the Turkish case, but the process would best begin with an apology and acknowledgement by President Erdoğan. He need not go on his knees like Willy Brandt, for he is his own person, but in his own way he needs to apologize on behalf of the Turkish state, to say "never again." In doing so he would personify a new Turkey, one determined to heed the warning sounded by Israel Charny: "We must fight denials because the denial of genocide is . . . a process which is intended to desensitize and make[s] possible the emergence of new forms of genocidal violence to peoples in the future."‡‡‡

Notes

* Sara Cohan, "A Brief History of the Armenian Genocide," *Social Education 69*, no. 6 (2005): 336–337.

† Samantha Power, *A Problem from Hell: America and the Age of Genocide*, c2002., 14.

‡ Ibid., 15.

§ Alayarian, Consequences of Denial, 17–18.

ǀ Cohan, "A Brief History of the Armenian Genocide," 337.

¶ Kévorkian, The Armenian Genocide, 811.

** Ibid., 807–812.

†† Roger W. Smith, Eric Markusen, and Robert Jay Lifton, "Professional Ethics and the Denial of Armenian Genocide," *Holocaust and Genocide Studies 9*, no. 1 (March 20, 1995): 11.

‡‡ See, for instance, Michael M. Gunter, Armenian History and the Question of Genocide (Palgrave Macmillan, 2011), chap. 2. It is worth noting that in a very legal narrow sense, the term genocide has its limits: the massive killings in Cambodia—some 25% - 40% of the population was exterminated, but because they were largely of same ethnic group, the killings fall into the category of crimes against humanity, rather than genocide.

§§ Smith, Markusen, and Lifton, "Professional Ethics and the Denial of Armenian Genocide," 4.

ǀǀ Iryna Marchuk, The Fundamental Concept of Crime in International Criminal Law: A Comparative Law Analysis (Springer Berlin Heidelberg, 2014), 87.

¶¶ See, for instance, the Human Rights Committee Concluding Observations on the initial report of Turkey adopted by the Committee at its 106th session (15 October–2 November 2012), UN Doc. CCPR/C/TUR/CO/1, 13 November 2010.

*** See Annual Report 2013 of the European Court of Human Rights, Council of Europe, 203. From 1959 to 2013, there are 2,639 judgments against Turkey in which at least one violation has been found by the Court.

††† Alayarian, Consequences of Denial, 129.

‡‡‡ Israel W. Charny, The psychological satisfaction of denials of the Holocaust or other genocides by non-extremists or bigots, and even by known scholars, IDEA J SOC 1 (2001).

Viewpoint 3

Alternatives for Ending Genocidal Events
Alex de Waal and Bridget Conley-Zilkic

In the following viewpoint, the authors consider alternate ways to bring genocidal events to an end. They discuss genocide scholarship and summarize several genocides during the 20th century. A crucial insight is that, while genocide is occurring, governments allow the suspension of ethical rules. Author Alex de Waal is Executive Director of the World Peace Foundation and a professor at Fletcher School at Tufts University. His scholarly work focuses on humanitarian crisis response, human rights, and governance in Africa. Author Bridget Conley-Zilkic is Research Director of the World Peace Foundation and assistant professor at the Fletcher School at Tufts University. Her scholarly writing is extensive on topics of mass atrocities and genocide.

Genocide and the Canon of Historical Tragedy

Stepping from 14th Street in Washington, DC into the U.S. Holocaust Memorial Museum, the visitor to the main exhibition is immediately placed in the shoes of the soldiers of the U.S. Army as they liberated the concentration camp at Dachau in 1944. The personal recollections of General Eisenhower as he visited the camp provide the opening tableau that allows the visitor to make the imaginative leap from U.S. citizen—until this moment unable to comprehend such horrors—to personal witness to genocide.

"Reflections on How Genocidal Killings are Brought to an End," by Alex de Waal and Bridget Conley-Zilkic, Social Science Research Council, December 22, 2016. Reprinted by Permission.

This moment of liberation has taken on meaning well beyond its immediate historical context. In popular, scholarly, and activist imaginations, international military intervention is not simply historical fact for the Holocaust, but it has taken on prescriptive value in relation to all cases of genocide. International military intervention is how genocides ought to end.

In beginning with such prescriptive assumptions, analysis of genocides past conventionally fall into a pattern of simplified representation of the complexities and uncertainties that existed at the time, in favor of a certain knowledge that had international military intervention occurred (or occurred earlier, or with more conviction), that genocide would not have resulted. Events are portrayed as inexorable tragedy, in which everything unfolds upon a familiar path. The early-warning signs of ethnic discrimination and dehumanization are catalogued (and years later, in other countries, monitored). Victims are stripped of all agency as perpetrators mark them for death. At each stage in the unfolding story we see how the final outcome could have been prevented, had the villains flinched or the heroes been more decisive or lucky. The chorus, moralizing tragic events for an audience of spectators, decries the absence of a *deus ex machina*: international military-humanitarian intervention. Throughout, we know what happens in Act Five: the horror that will unfold in the denouement.

Prevention of genocide is typically constructed using the same assumptions of predictability, but with an idealized ending. This time—a theoretical future, this time—the international (i.e. western) troops do arrive, the people are saved, and the villain is chased from the scene. This is the activists' clamor for Darfur. While underplaying the role of the international system in generating the forces that create genocide, this narrative posits salvation in the actions of the international community.

A true appreciation of tragedy means looking at the events without flinching, bearing witness to the real choices and challenges facing all the actors, perpetrators, victims, bystanders, and those with mixed roles or who changed sides. This perspective alerts us that there are other possible endings, not circumscribed by the dominant narrative of genocide and its ending. The killers may get tired of their bloody work and call a halt, deciding "we have killed enough." Or like thieves the killers may fall out among themselves. Alternatively, the victims themselves may resist and survive, or unexpected events may intrude and alter the course of events.

To those involved at the time, matters are typically confused and complex. After the fact, it is difficult for us to make the imaginative leap to a state of uncertainty that the narrative might not have unfolded as it did. Even in a case such as Darfur since 2003, where mass killing has occurred under the world's scrutiny, the most resonant narratives are those that stress the inevitability that Khartoum's alleged genocidal project will be completed unless the world acts. Now, some three years later, it is time to admit that the urgency to help does not reduce the necessity to fully consider what actions might sustain improvements in the situation.

To understand genocide and how to prevent it, we must escape three traps. We must not be seduced by teleologies that allow for only two endings: a completed genocide and a foreign military intervention. While it is important to acknowledge responsibility for violence, we must recognize the agency of all the actors, the complexities of their motives, and the difficulty of applying simple and unconditional labels such as "perpetrator" and "victim." We must also not fall prey to the desire to advocate doing something which might be satisfying to demand when lives are at risk, but which is incapable of actually improving the situation for any duration. This allows us to take a perspective that studies the genesis, escalation and de-escalation of genocidal violence without making any assumptions about the ultimate outcome, and without obscuring political complexities by using simplified labels.

A Focus on De-escalating Violence

Genocide scholarship, for years the concern of only a handful of academicians, has since the 1990s grown considerably in depth and range.[1] But it has largely neglected an empirical study of that crucial

The Armenian Genocide

part of the story: how genocide ends. A closely-related question is how mass killing, short of genocide, is halted before reaching a level that qualifies it as genocide. Commonly, the ending is rapidly covered in a few concluding paragraphs of a study focusing on the origins and unfolding of the crime. This neglect of how genocides end is a remarkable gap in the literature. This forum is a foray into the field.

Genocide and mass killing of civilians typically happen during war, but our concern here is not with how wars are ended—we are narrowing our attention to how mass killing of civilians comes to an end. Genocide scholars have already broadened the corpus of cases considered within the remit of "genocide studies" to include many more than the consensually-accepted instances of the Armenian genocide, the Nazi's Final Solution and Rwanda in 1994, plus the cases of Cambodia and Bosnia, to consider a range of cases such as Indonesia in 1965-6, Bangladesh, Biafra, and Stalin's purges, deportations and the starvation of the Ukraine. In the context of ending mass killing, or stepping back from the brink of genocide, we can broaden our remit still further, embracing the fact we can legitimately include cases that stopped short of a point readily identifiable as genocide.

Let us take a preliminary, cursory overview of episodes of mass killing during the 20th century, some of which have been treated as instances of genocide, and others which fell short, in each case asking the question: how was this brought to an end? The list below is incomplete and the summaries are exceptionally brief—intended more as a challenge to the experts in the field than a considered assessment. Six of the cases (Stalin, Biafra, Bangladesh, Guatemala, Uganda and the Nuba Mountains of Sudan) were discussed in a seminar at the U.S. Holocaust Memorial Museum in January 2004, and the summaries draw on the presentations at that meeting.

The Herero genocide, Namibia, 1904.
The main reason why the German colonialists' campaign of starvation and killing ended was that the generals in charge

considered they had completed their task. There was also an outcry at home in Germany, leading to the decision to intern the Herero survivors rather than exterminate them entirely.

The Armenian genocide.
The killings, deportation and starvation of the Armenians came to an end when the Ottoman Turkish authorities considered their aims had been accomplished. Although there was exposure and condemnation by some of the Allies, this seems to have been too modest and too late to have had a significant impact.

The Soviet Union under Stalin.
Genocidal episodes during Stalin's rule included the starvation of the Ukraine in 1932–3, deportations and terror. In each case, Stalin used extreme violence instrumentally, as a means to a specific political end. In command of an exceptionally powerful and centralized state, Stalin was able to end the violence at will, while retaining the capability for restarting it at will. These episodes were definitively halted with the death of Stalin. Dissent within the leadership was impossible. There was neither organized domestic resistance nor effective international opposition.

The Nazi Final Solution.
For Hitler, violence was more than a means to an end: it was an end in itself. The Nazis' violence escalated during the entire period of the Third Reich, without lull, constrained only by the loss of territory in the last two years of World War II. Domestic opposition played no significant role. Military defeat by the Allied armies brought the killing definitively to an end.

Mao's China.
Genocidal actions in revolutionary China include the repression of Tibet, Inner Mongolia, the Uigurs and other minorities, and also waves of terror, notably the Cultural Revolution. These were started and stopped by Mao himself, who retained the capacity to re-launch similar extreme actions at any time.

Indonesia: the massacre of the Communists in 1965–6.
The power struggle between President Sukarno and General Suharto involved widespread violence, notably the systematic murder of suspected communists. This was brought to an end when the communists were eliminated as a political force and the power struggle was decisively resolved in favor of Suharto.

The Biafran war 1967–70.
Genocidal violence during the Nigerian civil war was a product of the Federal Government's determined attempt to stop the secession of Biafra. The ruling coalition supported the war, but only some of its members—not including the head of state, General Gowon—supported genocidal actions. When the Federal forces won the war, the violence rapidly de-escalated. Although there was an international outcry against the massacres and the blockade of Biafra, this contributed little to the government's decisions.

Bangladesh 1970.
Attempting to thwart the independence of Bangladesh, Pakistani army generals sought to eliminate the Bangladeshi leadership. However, there was limited support for the massacres among Pakistan's rulers, and the army was reluctant to pursue the policy of mass killing for long. The pace of killings slowed, and the conflict became a more regular confrontation between the army and the Bengali guerrillas. The killings finally came to an end with intervention of the Indian army. While international public opinion was sympathetic to the Bangladeshi cause, Pakistan remained a valued ally of the west (especially given its pivotal role in the U.S.-China rapprochement) and there was no significant international pressure to halt the killings.

Burundi 1972.
The Tutsi-dominated government of President Micombero undertook the elimination of Hutus who were suspected of rebel sympathies and much of the Hutu educated class as well. The killings lasted three months, after which it appears that the

government and army concluded that they had accomplished their task. There was minimal international protest.

The Red Terror in Ethiopia.
In the context of an urban insurgency, the military junta headed by Colonel Mengistu Haile Mariam unleashed a wave of terror aimed at the regime's political opponents. Successive waves of killings targeted new categories of suspects, until Mengistu felt his grip on power was consolidated. International condemnation had no appreciable impact; domestic opposition was silenced or driven to armed rebellion in the hills—where the government attacked them and the civilian populations they lived among with extreme violence. The counter-insurgency campaigns in Eritrea and Tigray in the 1980s, using population control, forced relocation and famine as weapons of war, came close to genocide in both intent and effect.

Cambodia's Year Zero.
The mass killings perpetrated by the Khmer Rouge were, like the political murders of other modern totalitarian regimes, mounted in waves. The government and party machinery could order an end to mass killing just as it could order their (re-)start. There was no domestic opposition to speak of. A decisive end to the genocide was brought about by the Vietnamese invasion and military defeat of the Khmer Rouge. Protected by a peculiar twist of Cold War politics, international moral condemnation of the killings meant little.

The Guatemalan counter-insurgency.
Culminating in the mid-1980s, the counter-insurgency was genocidal in its targeting of ethnic Mayans in the countryside. The killings slowed when the government had achieved its aim of establishing firm military control of the countryside. The guerrillas' resistance was ineffective: they were unable to protect the people. Constitutional safeguards meant nothing. Abuses were reported by human rights activists and their foreign colleagues,

but to little effect. Although Congressional sanctions prevented the U.S. from directly supporting the Guatemalan military activities, the Reagan Administration was firmly behind the Guatemalan government, and did nothing that might have discouraged its vicious counterinsurgency.

The "Luwero Triangle" massacres in Uganda 1983-4.
The government of Milton Obote perpetrated genocidal massacres in the course of a vicious counter-insurgency of a type that has become all-too-common in Africa. The extremity of violence was a product of the weakness of the state and its inability to consolidate power, and the massacres were ended when the ruling coalition fell apart. Armed rebellion by the National Resistance Army was the spark for the massacres. The NRA provided limited physical protection but eventually did succeed in bringing down the government and ending the killings. The NRA did not, however, end the cycle of violence in Uganda—instead displacing it to other areas and other groups. The Luwero massacres caused hardly a blip on the radar screen of international concern.

Saddam Hussein's Anfal against the Kurds.
Having miscalculated in attacking Iran, Saddam Hussein used ever-more extreme measures both on the battlefront and in suppressing the Kurdish rebellion. The Anfal was a uniquely comprehensive and brutal counter-insurgency that consolidated Iraqi control over a rebellious region. It was halted when the military objectives were attained, and the regime retained the capability and readiness to enact similar measures again, notably against the Marsh Arabs. Domestic dissent was impossible and the Kurdish guerrillas provided little protection. International condemnation was muted by Iraq's then-favored status in the west vis-à-vis Iran. After 1991, the combination of sanctions and a no-fly zone enforced by U.S. and British warplanes curbed the prospect of new Iraqi government military offensives against both Kurds and Marsh Arabs, a possibility that was definitively removed by the invasion and overthrow of Saddam Hussein in 2003. However, the

legacy of intolerance and readiness to address political problems with extreme violence remains. Iraq is not free from the threat of genocidal massacre.

Extreme clan-targeted violence in Somalia (including the destruction of the northern Somali cities in 1988 and the brutalization and deliberate starvation of Bay Region in 1991-2).
The military regime of President Mohamed Siad Barre massacred civilians in its counter-insurgency, a means of warfare that continued after his government was overthrown and the country was riven by factional warfare. Episodes of extreme violence in Somalia have ended when political realignments changed the logic of war, local resistance became too strong, or peace agreements were negotiated. The U.S.-UN military intervention in 1992 briefly interrupted the cycle of violence before becoming party to that violence itself. The potential for continuing extreme violence continues.

Mass killings and relocations in the civil war in Sudan, especially in the South and the Nuba Mountains.
The Sudanese civil war from 1983 to the present provides multiple examples of mass killings of civilians that arguably rise to the level of genocide, including the militia massacres in Bahr el Ghazal in 1985-8, the assault on the Nuba Mountains in 1992, the killings in Juba in 1992, the clearances of the oilfields in 1997-2000, and several episodes of internecine conflict between Southern Sudanese factions. Of these, the jihad in the Nuba Mountains was the most sustained and most genocidal, insofar as there was a clear plan for the comprehensive relocation of the Nuba people and the destruction of their identity in pursuit of ideological goals. The Nuba jihad was ended because the ruling elite disagreed on strategy (those who wanted a more limited counter-insurgency won out) and because of resistance by the Nuba people themselves. International pressure played a very minor role. While the genocidal assault was ended, the war continued with ongoing killings and abuses, and the government retained the capacity for other extremely

violent campaigns. The pattern of internal disagreement and local resistance has usually brought transitory reductions in violence and ultimately brought a negotiated end to the war in the South and the Nuba Mountains. International engagement in support of the Sudanese peace process was instrumental in achieving that negotiated settlement, which now looks fragile, in the shadow of the ongoing war and killing in Darfur.

Rwanda 1994.
The genocide of the Rwandese Tutsis orchestrated by the Hutu Power regime was ended when the rebel Rwandese Patriotic Front scored a decisive military victory. Domestic opposition was eliminated and the regime showed few signs of internal dissension (possibly because its stay in power was so brief). A UN force saved thousands of people but did not stop the killing. The French Operation Turquoise did save some survivors in western Rwanda, but it also protected the genocidaires and allowed them to flee to Zaire in safety. While the prospects of a new genocide against the Tutsis in Rwanda is remote—at least as long as the current government remains in power—the genocide and its aftermath unleashed violence across the Great Lakes region, especially the Democratic Republic of Congo, that arguably includes episodes of genocidal killing.

Bosnia-Hercegovina.
Despite intensive international scrutiny and engagement on Bosnia throughout the conflict—manifest in a large humanitarian aid effort, international peacekeepers, the creation of an international criminal tribunal, and diplomatic efforts—civilians were conspicuously not protected. It was not until the maps were "cleaned up" following the fall of the Bosnian government outposts ("safe havens") in eastern Bosnia that a negotiated solution was possible. The fact that large-scale massacres, including the killing of some 8,000 men and boys at Srebrenica, attended this development prompted increased NATO support for the Bosnian government. A counter-offensive by the Croat forces in alliance with the finally well-armed Bosnian

government, coupled with disagreement between the Bosnian Serbs and their patron in Belgrade, Slobodan Milosevic, pushed the Serbian leadership to make key concessions at the negotiating table. These concessions were also possible because the core gains of ethnic cleansing were protected in the final agreement. The negotiated settlement at Dayton formalized the end to the violence.

Kosovo.
In the subsequent case of Kosovo, sustained NATO bombing ultimately caused the Milosevic regime to capitulate, but there are questions as to whether the beginning of the NATO air campaign accelerated the very atrocities it was supposed to prevent.

General Themes
These nineteen instances, cursorily presented, allow us to draw out some general themes and unanswered questions.

When do killers stop killing?
A repeated unanswered question in these instances is, why did the perpetrators decided to stop the killing? We have little insight into the point at which the commanders decided "we have killed enough," and almost as little into the internal debates among ruling elites, which may have led to a decision to de-escalate the violence. In short, we know remarkably little about the precise calculations that have helped bring these episodes to an end.

What is an "end" to the killing?
In some cases—for example on Stalin's death, Hitler's defeat, the Nigerian victory in Biafra, or Bangladeshi independence—we can in retrospect say that the killing was ended for good, although a legacy of bitterness remains. More commonly, what is the ending of mass killing is in fact the ending of an episode in mass killing, with the perpetrators (usually the state) retaining the capacity to restart at any point. Stalin while alive, Mao, Suharto in Indonesia, Mengistu in Ethiopia, the Milosevic regime after Dayton, and the Sudan government are examples. In some instances, one pattern

of killing is ended, but a cycle of killing has been set in motion that witnesses comparable levels of massacre, directed against different groups. Uganda, Rwanda and Iraq are examples. A related issue is the existence of peaks and lulls in the violence. Many cases demonstrate an escalation of violence from an already high level to a genocidal peak. The pattern is different in each case: in the USSR, purges and relocations were very discrete events, whose beginnings and endings can be dated to exact dates and decrees. In Sudan, Uganda and Guatemala, a steady background of counter-insurgency violence was the basis for a rapid explosion into genocidal killing.

Ideologies and their roles.
In all cases, the motives for genocidal violence were mixed, including control of territory and people and the pursuit of an ideological and/or political goal. Several cases were Communist totalitarian regimes, which used violence in an instrumental manner, in pursuit of power and social transformation, a noted contrast with the "essentialist" violence of Nazi Germany. Leninist-Stalinist organization proved capable of the most extraordinary feats of social engineering, including mass murder. Ethnic essentialism in Rwanda rivaled the industrial powers and bureaucratic states in its efficiency of killing, combining both an instrumentalist use of violence (to create an ethnically homogenous state) and an essentialist use, in which violence was to transform the identity of the perpetrators. Islamist jihad as exhibited in Sudan possesses an essentialist element, but in this case it is as much associated with the mujahid dying as with killing. The weak socio-political theory possessed by Islamism proved (fortunately) a hindrance to successful prosecution of genocide in the Nuba Mountains. State-building and state preservation motivated violence in Indonesia, Biafra and Bangladesh, with political leaders clothing their strategies in nationalist garb. Other cases of genocidal killing were driven by motives in which ideology was less prominent, notably cases in

which mass killing was part of a counter-insurgency strategy by a state under threat.

The army, war and counter-insurgency.
In every case looked at, an army or militarized security force was the main instrument of mass killing and relocation. An army, as a centralized, hierarchical and professionally violent institution, is the obvious instrument for a state set on genocide. But professional armies are ambiguous instruments. While soldiers are schooled in obedience and the great majority will carry out their orders, they may also demonstrate disgust and weariness after some time. Soldiers are not necessarily professional killers, especially outside combat, and the perpetrators of genocide have regularly rediscovered that they may require special forces from outside the regular army in order to instigate mass killing.

Many of the genocidal killings were perpetrated in the context of counter-insurgency campaigns that involved draconian controls on the civilian population, suspected of sympathizing with rebels. The Herero genocide and the Iraqi Anfal are paradigms of counter-insurgency taken to genocidal extreme, and the Ethiopian military campaigns in Eritrea and Tigray come close (at least). The Armenian genocide had at least as its pretext the fear of rebellion. The combination of an ethnic dimension to the conflict and a weak state, which relies on franchising paramilitaries to conduct much of its killing, creates perfect conditions for genocidal violence. Thus in Uganda, Guatemala, Somalia, Sudan and (arguably) Indonesia, ethnically-targeted violence is instigated as a mechanism for combating insurgency, and is escalated to the point of genocidal massacre. These cases have the special difficulty that once these forces have been unleashed, they are difficult to rein back in.

In secessionist wars the logic can be different. During the Biafran war of independence from Nigeria, the Federal Government's violence was aimed precisely at keeping the Biafrans within the state, though relatively powerless. The Pakistani violence in Bangladesh had a similar logic. Bosnia and Kosovo combine counter-secessionism and ethnic agendas in a particularly virulent mix. In all these cases, extreme violence was instrumental in pursuit of a state agenda.

What all these cases have in common is that the state concerned suspended ethical rules for the duration. Servants of the state were permitted or encouraged to act with impunity. The logic can be encapsulated in the command, "do what is necessary to ensure total submission, and don't report back on the details." In Sudan, the war areas have been described as "ethics-free zones."[2]

Famine as a tool.
A related question is the use of starvation and destruction of livelihoods as a weapon of both war and genocide. Man-made famine was an instrument for the elimination of groups in Namibia in 1904 and the Ukraine in 1932, but the provision in the 1948 Genocide Convention that specifies "deliberately inflicting on the group conditions of life calculated to bring about its physical destruction in whole or in part"[3] had not been used in a formal determination of genocide or a prosecution for genocide until the case of Darfur was investigated by the U.S. State Department and the Coalition for International Justice in 2004.[4] Given that counter-insurgencies typically involve the forcible displacement and the destruction of their livelihoods, this represents a potentially very significant broadening of the scope of episodes identified as "genocide" by scholars.[5] If this broadening becomes consensually adopted, then this has implications for what it means to end a genocide that has been conducted primarily through these methods. Is humanitarian assistance and socio-economic redevelopment sufficient to represent the end of such a genocide?

Civil society and constitutional rule.
When we consider the factors that give rise to a society prone to mass killing and the recovery of a society that has been riven by conflict and genocidal massacre, the role of civil society is pivotal. But during the episodes of genocidal killing themselves, civil society

is an irrelevant force. This should not surprise us: wars are almost always accompanied by states of emergency in which civil rights are repressed; those committing genocidal massacre commonly justify it through facing an external enemy (often an effective means of creating social unity); and for the intended victims of a genocide, civil society-type responses are no longer useful.

In most cases, constitutionalism had broken down or was a sham, masking dictatorial rule. But there are intriguing instances in which constitutional safeguards were in place throughout the period of genocidal violence, but signally failed to prevent it. These cases include Indonesia, Biafra and Guatemala, where governments were able to overcome constitutional restraint and disregard dissent. A constitution is only as good as those prepared to enforce it.

There is a potential exception to this rule: if local civil society can in some way generate an international response, using its contacts with foreign groups to launch a moral boomerang that hopefully comes back to strike the perpetrators of genocide.[6] In some of our cases (Biafra, Guatemala, Sudan, and notably, Bosnia) civil society groups managed to feed information to international human rights groups, and that information was sometimes used to good effect, though only very rarely did it spark international action sufficient to stop genocide. The case of Darfur may yet be the exception that proves the rule.

Negotiations.

In many cases, final political settlements have been negotiated when there is a military fait accompli. In just a few cases—notably Bosnia and the Nuba Mountains and Southern Sudan—negotiations have helped to end mass killing of civilians. These are both recent cases, reflecting the fact that until the end of the Cold War, the major powers allowed civil wars to continue until there was a military victory by one side or the other. International readiness to bring negotiated solutions to civil wars is a recent phenomenon. In parallel there has been increased concern with genocide and with accountability for human rights violations. There is a rather obvious tension between these two trends. In both the Bosnian and Sudanese instances, although humanitarian concern and the mass killing of civilians was undoubtedly a motivation for the international initiative to end the wars, the negotiations were framed primarily as peace talks to end a civil war rather than the ending of a genocide. Trying to frame negotiations as "ending genocide" has the obvious drawback that the label itself criminalizes one party.

International Pressure and Intervention

In only three cases in the compendium did foreign military intervention decisively bring the killings to an end. Those cases are the Allied victory over the Third Reich, Indian intervention in Bangladesh and the Vietnamese invasion of Cambodia. All were undertaken more for political self-interest than humanitarian concern. The NATO interventions in Bosnia and Kosovo had more debatable impacts on ending the violence. Only in two—Bosnia and Sudan's North-South peace agreement—were international actors significantly involved in mediating an end to violence.

The rarity of international pressure or intervention having a significant impact is closely associated with the fact that most cases under consideration occurred during the Cold War, when one superpower or another protected genocidal regimes. The end of the Cold War opened up the possibility of international force being used to this end. In practice, this has yet to happen, but international scrutiny of human rights has at least meant that extreme atrocities rarely unfold in the dark, as was common in earlier decades.

The role of international troops is complex in part because of the ambiguity of the term "humanitarian," which may refer either to humanitarian law in general (including the prohibition on genocide) or specifically to the provision of relief assistance to stricken populations. For most of the 1990s, it was much easier for western governments to agree on the narrower form of "humanitarian intervention," and thus troops were dispatched to Iraqi Kurdistan, Somalia, Bosnia and Rwanda with a limited mandate. The presence of UN troops signally failed to stop killings in Bosnia and Rwanda. The centerpiece of Darfur advocacy has been that this failure should not be repeated. In Bosnia, humanitarian activities even served to deter armed intervention, for fear that the UN troops would be endangered and humanitarian operations halted should international forces attack the Serb forces.

International military intervention has become the principal focus for anti-genocide activism. This reflects the shadow of the Holocaust as much as the failures of the subsequent sixty years. The paradigmatic instance of stopping genocidal killing by morally uncomplicated means is still the Allied liberation of Nazi concentration camps. The 1990s NATO bombings of the Serbs, the only other instance that comes close, suffer from too many question marks to meet the standard of an ethically-clear anti-genocide intervention. The Bosnian intervention was too late and the Kosovo air campaign had many complicated side-effects.

The relevance of international military intervention is over-determined in writings on genocide prevention, existing throughout the body of literature as the final tool in the bag or as the culmination of a national or international policy. Almost without fail military intervention is presented as a politically neutral engagement on behalf on innocently suffering civilians. Thus the Brahimi Report advocates for an early warning system tied to international capacity to militarily intervene and the report "The Responsibility to Protect" by the International Commission on Intervention and State Sovereignty (December 2001)[7] argues there is a responsibility to intervene (with military intervention as the last resort) on behalf of threatened civilians. Similarly this is the clear direction of work by prominent genocide scholars, such as Samantha Power.[8] Given the preliminary findings of this survey, current emphasis on this tool should be reconsidered.

Preliminary Conclusions

This section addresses four questions: how violence was de-escalated, why the international community played so small a role, why the cases do not appear to match the consensus of the genocide literature, and what lessons we can draw for the future.

What de-escalated the violence?

In some of the cases, de-escalation occurred when those perpetrating the violence achieved their goals. Clearly, this is a discouraging conclusion, especially when those goals include genocide. But Stalin, however cruel, did not intend to eliminate entire nationalities, even when he had labeled them as "enemy." The Nigerian and Guatemalan governments were concerned with military control. Eliminationist racism is rare, most obviously present in the Herero killings, the Final Solution and the Rwandese genocide. This is disturbing insofar as goals that fall short of eliminationist racism can also lead to very high levels of violence including genocidal massacre.

A second reason for de-escalation was successful resistance. This in turn depended on the extent to which the targeted group could call upon an armed force able to mount effective military campaigns. Several of these (the Sudanese Nuba, the Eritreans and Tigrayans, several Somali groups, the Ugandan National Resistance Army and the Rwandese Patriotic Front) resisted without external support, while the Bangladeshis had the assistance and ultimately the direct intervention of India.

The third reason was elite dissension. In several cases there is a clear lack of consensus among elites, commonly united on the need for an effective war effort, but not on methods that involve genocidal massacre. The military leadership itself can serve as a restraining force: those instructed to carry out the killing may be more reluctant than their civilian superiors.

Invasion—military intervention primarily for self-interested reasons—was a fourth means whereby genocide was ended. Invading forces brought an end to genocide in Bangladesh and

Cambodia as well as ending the Nazis' Final Solution. The impurity of both motive and method of the invaders should not detract from the reality that these were effective in bringing genocides to an end. Other instances of intervention with a humanitarian rationale, such as the Tanzanian invasion of Uganda to overthrow Idi Amin in 1979, the French Operation Turquoise in Rwanda in 1994, and the U.S.-led overthrow of Saddam Hussein in 2003, may have achieved short-term political and humanitarian objectives, but did not decisively end the violence, and indeed contributed to new cycles of killing.

Why was the international community so marginal?
The commonest explanation for international indifference to suffering is lack of knowledge. This was definitely the case for Stalin's and Mao's campaigns, but the communications revolution and the growth of human rights advocacy means that secret genocides are more and more difficult. The case of the Nuba Mountains in the early 1990s may be the last case in which a threatened population was almost completely cut off from the rest of the world (though we should be alert to the dangers of North Korea). But, as studies of the Holocaust, Bosnia and Rwanda have repeatedly shown, ignorance was never the principal reason for failure to act. This is glaringly so in the case of Darfur.

The most important reason for international non-engagement is mixed political motives of both the perpetrators and foreign governments. Perpetrators may have goals that stop short of genocide, and some of their other policies may command the backing of powerful international friends. Their internal opponents (likely to be those targeted in the genocide) may be groups that foreign governments are reluctant to support, such as left-wing insurgents. A perpetrator government's internal debates and external public relations may obscure the genocidal effects of their actions. These factors complicate how the violence is perceived and responded to by outside forces. And, invariably, foreign governments have their own competing interests in play, some of them domestic (keeping out of overseas adventures) and some of them foreign (supporting a friendly regime). The importance of sustaining Sudan's North-South peace process played a large role in lowering international interest in Darfur at the time of the peak of violence in 2003-04. Stopping mass violence has rarely been a high priority for those foreign governments that have the capacity to intervene. Arguably, one of the greatest successes of the international human rights movement has been to insist that this changes, and indeed, over the years, western governments have become more sensitive on this issue.

But greater sensitivity to human rights and humanitarian concerns has its complications too. Potential genocide may not be the sole or overriding concern of an ambassador with a conscience. In Bosnia, Sudan and Uganda, diplomats and humanitarian professionals alike fell into a "humanitarian trap": they compromised with abusive authorities in order to maintain a humanitarian presence in the country. Essentially, they traded ongoing humanitarian programs, which were providing assistance to thousands of people, against speaking out against mass killing. It is interesting to note, however, that in Biafra and Bangladesh, humanitarian assistance (by NGOs) was combined with political solidarity for the victims, a tradition that has reasserted itself with the advocacy over Darfur.

Another version of this is the "best of all worlds" trap. This is the failure to advocate a realistic response, because it is not a perfect response. This was significant in Rwanda. When the genocide was unleashed, the international community's search for simultaneous solutions to the massacres, the war, the humanitarian crisis, the protection of UN personnel, and the restoration of a broad-based government committed to democracy, stood in the way of finding a response to the most severe problem, the genocide. In the event, the Rwandese Patriotic Front halted the genocide, and could have done so earlier had it received international support. But the international community's justifiable concern that the RPF would not solve problems of democracy, human rights, humanitarian access and armed conflict, meant that it was not supported as an instrument to end the genocide. A similar analysis would fit for Bosnia, where both the government and Serb forces were treated as equal "warring parties" by international negotiators, despite the proclaimed commitment of the Serbian forces to ethnic cleansing. If genocide is indeed an absolute evil, and it is justifiable to suspend other considerations in order to stop it, then support for those groups that are actively resisting genocide, however unattractive they may be in other ways, must be a serious option.

What are the lessons for the future?

The final question concerns drawing lessons for policy. This forum is deliberately not an exercise in identifying lists of doables for western governments or the UN. On the contrary, it is an exercise in provoking reflection on how relevant are today's typical lists of policy recommendations. The final question continues in this spirit with an observation: *genocidaires learn.* Not only are advocates and policymakers concerned with preventing and punishing genocide carefully seeking how to do their task better, but aspiring criminals-against-humanity are doing so as well.

The prime example of would-be genocidaires learning their trade and sharpening their tools is the three years preceding the April 1994 Rwanda genocide. Over this period, methods of mass killing were tested, alongside methods of silencing and confusing the international community (for example by killing peacekeepers to ensure the withdrawal of the UN force, and sending bishops abroad to plead for the regime).[9] On that instance, the genocidaires learned faster than their adversaries.

Undoubtedly, it is getting more difficult for aspirant genocidal states. Totalitarian rule is almost gone (North Korea being an obvious exception), and so one particular configuration of political circumstance is much rarer than in past decades. The sophistication of the media and civil society means that it is harder to control information, both for one's own citizens and the world. Diplomats and journalists are much more attuned to the familiar signs of potential genocide. In the case of war-time genocides, humanitarians are more attuned to the trap of silence in exchange for access—not least because journalists are more ready to criticize them for it. The debate about Darfur has conspicuously avoided this danger.

But there are reasons for caution. First, governments have strategies to neutralize these pressures. These may include professional public relations and protection provided by a major power, which in turn may be associated with strategic interests such as possession of oil reserves or cooperation in counter-terrorist activities or the suppression of the narcotic trade. Second, events can move quickly. A genocide can be launched so quickly as to take the international community off guard (as was the case in Rwanda, if we overlook the warning signs). Or a country can slide from a favorite to a pariah very quickly, as happened with Iraq in 1990 and Zimbabwe in the last few years. Counter-insurgency and counter-secessionist genocides remain an ever-present danger whenever there is a serious military challenge to a state. The basic ingredients for genocide can be found in many different countries: too often, it is just the motive and political organization that is lacking.

Endnotes

1. For example, Steven Jensen (ed.), *Genocide: Cases, Comparisons and Contemporary Debates*, Copenhagen, Danish Center for Holocaust and Genocide Studies, 2003. See also: A. Jones, *Genocide, War Crimes and the West: History and Complicity*, London: Zed Books, 2004; Alexander L. Hinton, *Genocide: An Anthropological Reader*, Macmillan, 2002; Samuel Totten (ed.) *Teaching about Genocide: Issues, Approaches and Resources*, Greenwich CT, IAP, 2004.

2. Alex de Waal, "Starving out the South," in Martin Daly and Awad Alsikainga, *Civil War in the Sudan*, London, British Academic Press, 1994.

3. Article 2(c).

4. Samuel Totten and Eric Markusen (eds.) *Genocide in Darfur: Investigating the Atrocities in the Sudan*, New York, Routledge, 2006.

5. The dominant genocide scholars in the U.S. have tended to emphasize closeness to the Holocaust paradigm as a definitional prerequisite for genocide rather than conformity with the letter of the 1948 Genocide Convention. The Darfur genocide determination dramatically reverses these emphases.

6. For a wider analysis of these domestic-international linkages in human rights activism, see: Thomas Risse and Kathryn Sikkink, 'The socialization of international human rights

norms into domestic practices: introduction,' in Thomas Risse, Stephen Ropp and Kathryn Sikkink (eds.) *The Power of Human Rights: International Norms and Domestic Change*, Cambridge, Cambridge University Press, 1999.

7. http://www.dfait-maeci.gc.ca/iciss-ciise/pdf/Commission-Report.pdf.

8. Samantha Power, *'A Problem from Hell': America and the Age of Genocide*, New York: Basic Books, 2002.

9. African Rights, *Rwanda: Death, Despair and Defiance*, London, 1994, chapter 2.

Viewpoint 4

Students Are Still Fighting for Genocide Recognition

Melanie Nakashian

One hundred years after the Armenian Genocide, student activists are still demanding recognition of the brutalities that occurred. In the following viewpoint, writer Melanie Nakashian details the ongoing efforts of the Armenian Students Association at the University of California and the grassroots Armenian Youth Federation—including a hashtag campaign, #DivestTurkey, and outreach and action on-campus at UCLA. Melanie Nakashian is an international activist from New York who was living in Armenia at the time this viewpoint was published. She has been involved with various media, environmental and political organizations and also lived in Israel-Palestine for more than a year.

April 24, 2015 marks the centennial of the first genocide of the 20th century, when 1.5 million Armenians were systematically annihilated under the Ottoman Empire in what is sometimes referred to as a prototype for the Jewish holocaust. Due to a century of active denial and censorship by the Republic of Turkey, successor state of the Ottomans, much of the world remains ignorant of the existence and history of Armenia and its people.

Recently, however, the issue has been receiving unprecedented amounts of international attention. Earlier this month, television star and half-Armenian Kim Kardashian traveled to Armenia for

---

"New student movement protests 100 years of Armenian genocide denial," by Melanie Nakashian, April 23, 2015, Waging Nonviolence, https://wagingnonviolence.org/feature/100-years-of-denial-sparks-new-student-movement-pushing-for-armenian-genocide-recognition/. CC BY 4.0

the first time with her family and husband Kanye West. George and Amal Clooney also plan to travel there for the centennial. Last week, Turkey's denial was the subject of a *New York Times* cover story and editorial. Turkey also withdrew its Vatican ambassador in a fury over Pope Francis' use of the word "genocide" to describe what happened 100 years ago.

As happens every April 24, various events take place around the world to both remember and combat the lack of common knowledge surrounding this issue. Such annual events include a march in Los Angeles and a gathering in Times Square. Other activities are scheduled this year to specifically mark 100 years, including a campaign that launched in January called 100 Days of Action and a joint Armenian-Turkish effort called Project 2015, which will fly hundreds of ethnic Armenians to Istanbul for a commemoration.

Going beyond these commemorative events, however, is a campaign organized by the Armenian Students Association, or ASA, at the University of California and the grassroots community organization Armenian Youth Federation-Western Region, or AYF. Following in the footsteps of recent campus boycott and divestment campaigns—which have targeted everything from the fossil fuel industry to Israel to Sudan to the school-to-prison pipeline—comes #DivestTurkey. Since late 2014, UC students have been demanding that the university withdraw the more than $70 million it has directly invested in the Republic of Turkey.

Unlike similar campaigns targeting unjust policies, #DivestTurkey does not include a consumer boycott of Turkish-made goods. The campaign is focused on protesting the modern-day Turkish government's perpetuation of the erasure of Armenian history and identity through its denial and censorship of past crimes. It is also protesting Turkey's lack of progress in making reparations for these crimes.

The commonly referred-to launch date of the genocide is April 24, 1915, when about 250 Armenian community leaders and intellectuals living in Constantinople (today Istanbul) were

The Armenian Genocide

rounded up and executed. It is said to have lasted from then until 1923, though there had been massacres since the 1890s. The 1.5 million Armenians killed constituted three quarters of the population at that time. There were also other victimized minorities in the region such as Greeks and Assyrians.

What makes this markedly different from other major genocides is the ongoing aggressive denial by Turkey despite extensive evidence and press coverage from that time. It has been erased from their memory and replaced with the story of just another World War I conflict with deaths on both sides. In reality, the word "genocide" was coined with the actual events in mind—yet it is precisely this word that is made taboo.

Today in Turkey, which is no stranger to censorship in general, it is illegal to raise the question of the genocide. Doing so is a codified crime of "insulting the Turkish nation" under Article 301 of the Turkish Penal Code. One prominent example of this is the case of Hrant Dink, a journalist who was prosecuted and then assassinated by ultra-nationalists in the streets of Istanbul just eight years ago. In a similar and more recent act of censorship, a German photographer was denied entry to Turkey after flying there earlier this month to cover the centennial.

The stalemate and misrepresentation of history is enabled by major governments such as the United States and Israel, which have not officially recognized the genocide—although 43 U.S. states, 24 countries, the European Parliament and various regional governments have passed their own proclamations labeling the genocide as such. While often coming close, with empty campaign promises from President Obama and an Armenian Genocide Resolution waiting to be passed in the House of Representatives, the United States has routinely caved to Turkish pressure in order to protect their strategic relationships.

Today, there is a tiny, extremely poor, very Christian, landlocked Republic of Armenia in the Caucasus. Its post-Ottoman borders were drawn with the help of the United States and then re-drawn after the fall of the Soviet Union, which had annexed it during its rule. The country's modern-day territory does not include the majority of what Armenians consider to be their homeland from which they were ethnically cleansed. That land remains painfully visible on the horizon yet untouchable due to closed borders. For some, territorial reparations are even more significant than recognition of the crime, especially the holy Mount Ararat, which remains one of their most prominent cultural symbols. Most of today's ethnic Armenian population is diasporic, with one of the largest communities residing in California, where the #DivestTurkey campaign is underway and spreading.

The first student government vote for #DivestTurkey took place at UCLA in January. As UCLA-ASA president Mikael Matossian recalled, "After doing research into UC's investments, we were shocked that over $70 million was directly invested in the Republic of Turkey's government. As many of our members, including myself, have family who were affected or killed by the genocide, we took offense to the fact that our tuition dollars were going directly towards the government that actively denies and therefore perpetuates the Armenian genocide." That's when they decided to launch the campaign.

UCLA-ASA made a proactive effort to reach out to the groups they sensed might oppose their proposal: the Turkish Cultural Club and the Muslim Students Association, which includes some Turkish-Americans. In safely administered discussion groups, they went through each clause of the resolution. Many students who were hearing about the resolution for the first time came out in support of it. According to Matossian, "They realized the problematic nature of the investments." But at the next student government council meeting, some members of the Turkish Cultural Club, which was not usually very active on campus, "made a presentation in which they unfortunately denied the genocide outright, [stating] that they did not believe there was enough evidence. Others did acknowledge it, but stated that the Turkish government should not be held responsible [for the Ottoman Empire's actions], even though it actively denies it."

Following another presentation by ASA at the next student government council meeting, the resolution was approved unanimously. According to AYF Central Executive Board member Gev Iskajyan, opposition to the campaign comes from a few Turkish students, but not the majority. Perhaps more problematic, he explained, is the Turkish Vice-Consul requesting and holding a meeting with various student leaders across the UC system, encouraging them to oppose the resolution. The vice-consul reportedly reached out to both Turkish and non-Turkish student organizations, but has not yet reached out to any Armenian students. "[This] is obviously of some concern," Iskajyan said, adding, "not just to us, but to anyone who sees foreign government intervention in our universities as a problem, especially when they are pursuing an agenda of genocide denial."

Despite opposition, the students' second proposal for divestment was approved at UC Berkeley in February. The vote was again unanimous, as it had been at UCLA. Helping the cause in both cases was the decision to revise the original proposal—which in some ways was inspired by the Boycott, Divestment and Sanctions, or BDS, campaign targeting Israel's violation of Palestinian rights—to call only for divestment of the more than $70 million directly invested in the Turkish government. This decision, they believe, will keep the campaign focused on stigmatizing the policies and those who make them, rather than those who live under them.

While some may still see divestment as a divisive tactic, UCLA-ASA argues that it's the university's investments that are divisive. According to Matossian, it's "ethically incorrect" for a world-renowned academic system such as the UC system to "invest millions in a government that denies historical events that are actively taught and researched at universities like UCLA." Matossian and the rest of UCLA-ASA feel it is a campaign for all students who value human rights to get behind, not just those of Armenian descent—and this is evident by the fact that both votes have been unanimous.

So far, Matossian explained, the most significant achievement of #DivestTurkey has been raising awareness and holding university officials accountable for investments made with the tuition dollars of students who were never consulted. "At this important stage of [university students' lives], right before they enter the professional world," he said, "initiatives like these can educate people, help them realize the horrible nature of crimes against humanity like the Armenian genocide, and hopefully inspire them to fight against denial of past genocides, and ultimately prevent the start of future genocide." Ultimately, he argued, the educational impact has been and will likely remain far greater than any financial impact—an argument that could also be shared by other divestment campaigns, like BDS or Fossil Free. But ultimately, he does hope to induce financial pressure on the Republic of Turkey once #DivestTurkey has spread to enough UC schools that they can then take their cause to the UC Regents.

In the meantime, students will continue to organize, raise awareness and hold their institutions accountable with what Matossian said should be viewed "as a legitimate tactic to place nonviolent pressure on entities that offend or marginalize students, whether they be Jews, Palestinians or Armenians." Following UCLA and UC Berkeley, the third vote will take place this month at UC Davis, though they would like to keep their organizing efforts out of the public eye until after the vote. The recent explosion of mainstream attention, however, may only strengthen their cause, as #DivestTurkey spreads throughout the universities of California.

Chronology

330

May 11 The Roman emperor Constantine declares the town of Byzantium (renamed Constantinople) the Roman empire's capital.

1453

May 29 The Byzantine Empire ends. The city of Constantinople is conquered by the Ottoman sultan Memhet II.

1858–1865

In Circassia, there are systemic massacres and expulsions of Muslims to the Ottoman Empire.

1877–78

During the Russo-Turkish War, the Ottoman Empire loses territories in the Caucasus to Russia.

1878

Abdul Hamid II suspends the constitution and the Ottoman Parliament, restoring his autocratic powers as sultan.

1907

The Anglo-Russian Convention identifies British and Russian areas of control on the eastern border of the Ottoman Empire.

1908

June — Military officers among the Young Turk movement are alarmed by a meeting between England's Edward VII and Nicholas II of Russia, fearing they intend to partition Macedonia from the Empire.

July 24 — Abdul Hamid II capitulates to the Young Turk Revolution, restoring the Constitution.

1909

March 31 — An attempted monarchist counterrevolution in favour of Abdul Hamid II fails. His brother takes the throne as Mehmed V.

April 14–27 — The counter-coup spills over into pogroms against Armenians. When Ottoman troops are called in, they pillage Armenian enclaves. These are the Adana Massacres.

1914

July 28 — The first World War begins between the Central Powers of Europe and the Allied Forces.

November 2 — The Ottoman Empire enters the war on the side of the Central powers.

December 24 — Minister of War Enver Pasha loses a crucial battle and publicly blames his defeat on Armenians siding with the Russians.

1915

February 25 — Enver Pasha releases Directive 8682 to all Ottoman military units, calling for them

The Armenian Genocide

April 19	The governor of Van, Jevdet Bey, demands the city provide him with 4,000 men for armed service. Bey has already massacred Armenians in nearby villages.
April 20	The siege of Van begins and lasts until relieved by the arrival of Russian troops.
April 23–24	The Ottoman government imprisons 250 Armenian community leaders and intellectuals. Allied troops land at Gallipolli.
May 29	Tehcir Law gives the Ottoman government authority to deport threats to national security. Armenians are massacred or forcibly deported on foot.
September 13	The Ottoman parliament passes a Temporary Law of Expropriation and Confiscation to confiscate all property belonging to Armenians.

1918

November 11	End of World War I, and defeat of the Ottoman Empire by the Allied forces.
May 28	The Armenian National Council declares the Democratic Republic of Armenia an independent nation.

1920

November 29	The Communist Party of Armenia proclaims that it now has control of the Soviet Socialist Republic of Armenia.

1921

March — Armenia is occupied by the Red Army and annexed to the Soviet Union as the Armenian Soviet Socialist Republic.

October — The Treaty of Kars establishes the border between Turkey and the Armenian Soviet Socialist Republic.

1922

November 1 — The National Assembly of Turkey abolishes the Sultanate, deposing Mehmet VI and expelling him from the country.

1923

Declaration of the Republic of Turkey. The organized killing of Armenians by Turkish government forces comes to an end.

1939

August 22 — At a meeting, Hitler refers to the Turkish massacres of Armenians.

1990

August 23 — The Soviet Socialist Republic of Armenia adopts Armenia's Declaration of Independence, ending Soviet rule and becoming the Republic of Armenia

Bibliography

Books

Thomas de Waal, *Great Catastrophe: Armenians and Turks in the Shadow of Genocide*. Oxford, UK: Oxford University Press, 2017.

Adam Jones, *Genocide: A Comprehensive Introduction*, 3rd edition. Abington, UK: Routledge/Taylor & Francis, 2017.

Kayl Karadijian, (Hagob Karadijian, translator) *Remembering Avedik: The True Story of a Genocide Survivor*. Seattle, WA: Amazon Digital Services LLC, 2017.

Henry Morgenthau, Sr, *Ambassador Morgenthau's Story: A Personal Account of the Armenian Genocide*. North Charleston, SC: CreateSpace, 2017.

Elif Şafak, *The Bastard of Istanbul*. London, UK: Penguin Books, 2007.

Ronald Grigor Suny, *They Can Live in the Desert but Nowhere Else: A History of the Armenian Genocide*. Princeton, NJ: Princeton University Press, 2017.

Meline Toumani, *There Was and There Was Not: A Journey Through Hate and Possibility in Turkey, Armenia, and Beyond*. London, UK: Picador/Macmillan, 2015.

Periodicals

Jacob Glass, "Religion and Reproductive Rights," NewSecurityBeat, September 23, 2103. www.newsecuritybeat.com

Websites

Armenian National Committee of America (ANCAWR.org)

The Armenian National Committee of America-Western Region (ANCA-WR) is a Los Angeles-based grassroots public affairs organization devoted to advancing issues of concern to the Armenian American community.

The Armenian National Institute (www.armenian-genocide.org)

This research institute is dedicated to studying the Armenian genocide. ANI's website includes historical records and official documents, a FAQ section, and educational resources.

The Genocide Education Project (GenocideEducation.org)

The Genocide Education Project features detailed pages on many genocide events around the world. Intended as teaching materials, these pages are designed for educational use by students and teachers.

Facing History and Ourselves (www.facinghistory.org)

FHAO provides practical print resources on the Armenian genocide and also includes online lesson plans. The section called "Lessons and Readings on the Armenian Genocide" was developed in collaboration with *Teaching Tolerance Magazine*.

The Legacy Project (www.legacy-project.org)

The Legacy Project is a collection of visual arts and literature created by descendants of those who survived some of the most horrific atrocities of the 20th century including the Armenian genocide, the Holocaust, and the Cambodian genocide.

Peace Pledge Union (www.ppu.org.uk)

The Peace Pledge Union is the oldest secular pacifist organization in Britain. Since 1934, it has been campaigning for a warless world. It features multiple resources on pacifism, conscientious objection, and militarism.

Index

A

Abdul-Hamid II, 19, 20, 29, 37, 75, 88, 110, 135, 144
Adana
    Armenian public sphere in, 36–39
    Ottoman public sphere in, 34–36
    public sphere of, 31–34
Adana massacres, 13, 16, 20, 25–46, 144
    breaking point for, 39–40
    first waves, 40–41
    historiography of, 31
    second wave, 44–45
    transition from verbal to physical violence, 41–44
Ali, Zor, 34, 36, 40
Anfal, 184–185
Armenia, Republic of, 17, 90, 112, 155, 173, 174, 202
Armenian Genocide,
    classification as genocide, 93–104
    contemporary international knowledge of, 90–91
    continued struggle for recognition of, 200–205
    "Dead Marches" of, 112
    denial of, 23–24, 91–92, 167–176
    effect of on descendants of survivors, 142–161
    government responsibility for, 87–92
    history of, 20–23
    impact of World War I on, 13, 21–22, 27–28, 31, 81, 83, 87, 89, 97–99, 101, 102, 104, 105, 109, 111, 145–147
    influence on Hitler, 58–68, 87
    precursors to, 88–89
    story of a survivor, 135–139
Armenian Massacres in Ottoman Turkey, The, 102–104
Armenians
    diaspora of, 147–148
    early massacres of, 17–19
    history of, 17–20, 88, 143–147
    who escaped the genocide, 80–84
Armenian Students Association (ASA), 200, 201, 203, 204
Armenian Youth Federation (AYF), 200, 201, 204
Assyrian genocide, 15, 87, 168, 169, 170, 202
    denial of, 78–79

Index

as distinct from the Armenian Genocide, 72–79
persecutions of Assyrians following, 77–78
Assyrians
history of, 72–73
in Ottoman Empire, 73–74
Ataturk, Kemal, 23, 65, 169

B

Bagdadizade, Abdü lkadir, 34, 36, 46
Balkan Wars, 21, 88, 111
Bangladesh/Pakistan conflict, 182
Biafran war, 182, 189
Bosnia-Hercegovina, 186–187

C

China, under Mao, 181
Cohan, Sara, 16–24
Combat Genocide Association, The, 72–79
Committee of Union and Progress (CUP), 20, 21, 28, 31, 32, 34–36, 41, 46, 110–111, 144, 146, 168
Communists, Indonesian massacre of, 182
Conley-Zilkic, Bridget, 177–199
Constantinople, 17, 20, 23, 67, 88, 89, 112, 144, 201

D

Davis, Leslie, 90, 145–146
Der Matossian, Bedross, 25–57
de Waal, Alex, 177–199
Dimijian, Gregory G., 115–134
DivestTurkey Twitter campaign, 200, 201, 203, 205

E

Erdoğan, Recep Tayyip, 13, 92, 168, 173, 174, 175

F

Fikri, Ihsan, 34, 35–36, 41, 42, 46

G

genocide
armies/counter-insurgencies in, 189–190
defining end of, 187–188
ending events of, 177–198
famine as tool in, 190
international pressure/intervention, 192–193
negotiations and, 191–192
preventing, 129–130
role of civil society/constitutional rule in, 190–191

role of ideologies in, 188–189
why killing stops, 187
"Genocide, The," 22
genocide, term and its ambiguousness, 23, 93–96
Guatemalan counter-insurgency, 183–184
Gunter, Michael, 93–108

H

Hamidian massacres, 13, 15, 16, 19, 20, 25, 110
"Hayastan," 17
Herero genocide, 180–181, 189, 194
Hitler, Adolf, 12, 15, 22, 58, 59, 60, 61, 62, 63, 64, 65, 66, 67, 68, 87, 105, 147, 171, 181, 187
Hitler's "Armenian Quote," 59–61, 62–63
Holocaust, 24, 58, 62, 63, 68, 82, 87, 90, 94, 125–126, 141, 142, 143, 148, 149, 151, 155–156, 157–158, 160, 172, 177, 178, 180, 193, 195, 200
human nature
  and ethnic conflict, 125–127
  and genocide, 115–133
  vs individual psychopathology, 127–129
  ingroup and outgroup viewpoints of, 118–120
  inherent violence of, 120–121
  and mobs and militias, 124–125
  self-protection instinct of, 117–118
  and suicide terrorism, 121
  and torture, 122–124
  and we-they tendency, 116–117
Hutu massacre, 182–183

I

International Criminal Court (ICC), 94–95
Isfendiar, 39, 43
Istanbul, Turkey, 17, 22, 25, 27, 28, 30, 34, 38, 39, 40, 43, 46, 82, 105, 137, 144, 145, 201, 202
Itidal, 35, 36, 37, 41, 42, 43, 44

K

Kalayjian, Anie, 142–166
Kardashian, Kim, 12, 200
  effect of Armenian Genocide on, 80–84
Katchaznouni, Hovhannes, manifesto of, 99–100
Kosovo bombing, 187
Kurds, 20, 33, 40, 74, 75, 78, 93, 110, 184–185

L

League of Nations, 86, 109, 113
Lemkin, Raphael, 23, 99
Lewy, Guenter, 102–104
Lochner, Louis, 59, 60, 61, 63
"Luwero Triangle" massacres, 184

N

Nakashian, Melanie, 200–205
Nazis, 12, 23, 58, 59, 61, 62, 63, 64, 65, 66, 67, 122, 123, 127, 131, 170, 172, 180, 188, 193, 195
  Final Solution, 181
Nuremberg trials, 59–61, 62, 63, 172
Nuri, Burhan, 42, 43

O

Obama, Barack, 80–81, 82, 141, 202
Ottoman Empire, 12, 13, 15, 16–23, 26, 27–28, 43, 44, 58, 59, 60, 67, 68, 72, 75, 77, 79, 81, 82, 86, 87, 88, 89, 97, 103, 109, 111, 112, 113, 143, 144, 145, 146, 147, 168, 169, 170, 200, 203
  ancien régime of, 25–26, 32, 34, 45
  Assyrians in, 73–74
  political history of, 17–20
  public sphere of, 29–31
  Second Constitutional Period, 27
Ottoman Liberals, 20
Ottoman Turks, 12, 17, 143

P

Pan-Turkism, 20, 75
Papazian, Kapriel Serope, 100–102
Pasa, Mustafa Remzi, 44, 46
Patriotism Perverted?, 100–102

R

Red Terror, Ethiopia, 183
Russo-Turkish War, 13, 104

S

Sefa, Ismail, 42–43, 46
Seljuk Turks, 15, 17
Simele Massacre, 78
Snyder, Michael, 80–84
Somalia clan violence, 185
Soviet Union, 17, 65, 90, 202
  under Stalin, 181
Stone, Michael J., 135–139
Sudanese civil war, 185–186

T

Talaat, Mehmet, 21, 144, 145
Tolbert, David, 167–176

Tourian, Leon (archbishop), 101
Travis, Hannibal, 58–71
Turkey
   consequences of denial in, 171–176
   culture of denial in, 168–171
Tutsis genocide, 186

U

United Nations, 12, 13, 23, 109, 115, 118
   Genocide Convention, 93
United to End Genocide, 87–92
Universidad Iberoamericana, 109–114

W

Weisberg, Marian, 142–166
World War I, 13, 17, 21, 27, 28, 31, 66–67, 72, 77, 78, 81, 83, 87, 89, 97, 98, 99, 100, 101, 102, 104, 105, 109, 110, 111, 113, 117, 145, 146, 147, 148, 202
World War II, 93, 99, 121, 148, 158, 181

Y

Year Zero, Cambodia, 183
Yemenidjian, Knar, 135–139

Young Turk Revolution of 1908, 27–28
Young Turks, 20, 25, 30, 32, 34, 36, 59, 66, 67, 81, 90, 102, 113, 135–136, 144, 168
   revolutions of, 27–28, 110–111
   rise of, 75, 89